**"Right n
up again**

"I am."

Two little words shouldn't have been so powerful, but her throat filled over them. And for just a moment, she didn't feel so alone. "I suppose you're expecting me to ask you to help me now. For the girls' sakes."

The side of his mouth lifted. "Wouldn't be the worst idea you ever had. And it looks like the driver didn't see me, so I can still be that back channel."

He crossed and uncrossed his legs, signaling it still bothered him that he'd failed to be there for her.

"But how can I be sure you won't take everything I tell you and give it to the investigators trying to build a case against Riley?"

"You can't."

She squinted at him, holding her hands wide. "And how will I know that you won't be one of the people searching for evidence against my brother?"

"You won't."

Dear Reader,

I'm excited to introduce you to Station 1 and the people of Mount Isabel. These characters and this small Michigan town have lived in my head for several years, and I'm delighted to have the opportunity to bring their stories to the page. The research for this book took me to the Novi (Michigan) Fire Department—coincidentally, Station 1—where six firefighters shared stories and details with me, too many to make it inside this book or any of its sequels.

In Mick and Rachel's story, I had the chance to explore concepts of family (even the bruised kind); the debilitating impact of secrets and lies; addiction and recovery; true heroism; and most of all, hope. There are some pretty fun mysteries in there, too. I hope you enjoy reading the twists as much as I enjoyed writing them. I love hearing from readers. Please reach out to me through my Dana Nussio author page on Facebook or join my newsletter to see what's next at www.dananussio.com.

Happy reading!

Dana Nussio

INTO THE FIRE

DANA NUSSIO

ROMANTIC SUSPENSE

If you purchased this book without a cover you should be aware that this book is stolen property. It was reported as "unsold and destroyed" to the publisher, and neither the author nor the publisher has received any payment for this "stripped book."

ISBN-13: 978-1-335-47186-4

Into the Fire

Copyright © 2026 by Dana Corbit Nussio

All rights reserved. No part of this book may be used or reproduced in any manner whatsoever without written permission.

Without limiting the exclusive rights of any author, contributor or the publisher of this publication, any unauthorized use of this publication to train generative artificial intelligence (AI) technologies is expressly prohibited. Harlequin also exercises their rights under Article 4(3) of the Digital Single Market Directive 2019/790 and expressly reserves this publication from the text and data mining exception.

This is a work of fiction. Names, characters, places and incidents are either the product of the author's imagination or are used fictitiously. Any resemblance to actual persons, living or dead, businesses, companies, events or locales is entirely coincidental.

For questions and comments about the quality of this book, please contact us at CustomerService@Harlequin.com.

TM and ® are trademarks of Harlequin Enterprises ULC.

 Harlequin Enterprises ULC
22 Adelaide St. West, 41st Floor
Toronto, Ontario M5H 4E3, Canada
www.Harlequin.com

HarperCollins Publishers
Macken House, 39/40 Mayor Street Upper,
Dublin 1, D01 C9W8, Ireland
www.HarperCollins.com

Printed in Lithuania

Recycling programs for this product may not exist in your area.

Dana Nussio began telling "people stories" around the same time she started talking. She's continued both activities, nonstop, ever since. She left a career as an award-winning newspaper reporter to raise three daughters, but the stories followed her home as she discovered the joy of writing fiction. Now an award-winning author and member of Romance Writers of America's Honor Roll of bestselling authors, she loves telling emotional stories filled with honorable but flawed characters.

Books by Dana Nussio

Harlequin Romantic Suspense

Heroes of Station 1

Into the Fire

The Coltons of Mustang Valley

In Colton's Custody

The Coltons of Grave Gulch

Colton Nursery Hideout

The Coltons of Colorado

To Trust a Colton Cowboy

The Coltons of New York

Agent Colton's Secret Investigation

Visit the Author Profile page at Harlequin.com for more titles.

To our brand-new granddaughter, Emory. You've stolen my heart.

A special thanks to the firefighters of Novi (Michigan) Fire Department Station 1—Zahi Kassab, Steven Behan, Jan Rief, Noah Jackson, Todd Seog and Mark Prokes—for opening your fascinating world to me. You are true, humble heroes. And thank you to Melissa Baxter, president/CEO of the Waukesha County (Wisconsin) Community Foundation, for answering my questions about foundations; and to Breanna Thomas Polin, for sharing her journey as a family member of someone battling addiction. Though they've all helped me create a more realistic story, any creative liberties or factual mistakes are my own.

Prologue

The first visible flame would be the sweetest. The one that the grayed, splintered wood and those raised shingles could no longer contain. His pulse hammered, his palms slick as he pictured it, the same rickety, snow-covered structure across the field from him now, only with sparks shooting through the holes in its roof like the best illegal fireworks on the Fourth of July. Plastic inside melting and curling. A satisfying shattering of glass.

He couldn't wait.

Closing his eyes, he breathed in the intoxicating scent of smoke and let the bitter taste of ashes settle on his tongue. His fingers closed around the object in his pocket, firm against his palm, its energy stored and nearly vibrating in readiness. Every muscle in his body twitched and hummed, spinning wheels instead of rolling forward.

He hated these delays. The guilty needed to be punished, the truth laid bare. But he couldn't afford to be reckless now when the stakes were so high. When spotlights had sprouted near many of the best new locations and even among the old. When even the least nosy neighbors were worried enough to watch and report.

No. He shook his head until his neck ached. After all the time he'd spent planning this blaze, weighing his methods and considering every possible outcome, there was no way he would let his anxiousness to hit *Liftoff* be responsible for a failed mission. Mistakes wouldn't be tolerated.

With a sigh, he withdrew his hand from his pocket, allowing the cigarette lighter to drop to the bottom, its spark wheel never striking the stone. Like him, it would continue to bide its time.

As the unsettling sensation of being watched tripped along his spine, he flipped up the collar of his duck coat and glanced over his shoulder. Just scraggly pines that tipped their hats to the wind and their barren neighbors that sat waiting for the unfurling of spring. Though it appeared that no one had followed him, his gut told him it was time to move on. He scanned the whole scene once more to store the image and then grabbed his bag and started on the quarter-mile jog down the country road to his car.

Snow crunched under his boots as he first stomped and then smoothed the traces of his footsteps. Even if local officials were on constant watch now, they couldn't keep up that level of vigilance forever. When they let their guards down again, he would be there, ready to make them sorry, ready to strike both the location and the match.

"Burn, baby, burn."

At the music of his own laughter, he shot one more look around to ensure that only he and the deserted road shared his secret for now. Soon everyone would know. And if the too curious got in the way, he would welcome them inside the building and then watch the flames devour them.

Chapter 1

Firehouses didn't sparkle this way back on the South Side of Chicago. Not even close. And though Mick Prentiss had psyched himself up to march through the door with at least the illusion of confidence, he couldn't help but stop and stare like a dumbfounded toddler at the yawning fire palace before him. A place where no sooty turnout jackets and helmets nor the stench of smoke and human sweat belonged. As they'd all soon discover, he had no business being there, either.

Mick unwound his scarf, soaked and itchy, and unzipped his parka as he stepped deeper into the abandoned apparatus bay where the firefighting and emergency response vehicles were stored. He'd heard that some of the newer stations were like Taj Mahals, but until today, he'd never seen one like that up close.

Everything in the place had to be brand-new. Epoxy-covered concrete floors, shiny enough for firefighters to catch their reflections in them while suiting up for their charity calendar shoots. Four bright red engines and a matching fire-and-rescue truck so pristine that they all could have come right out of their boxes. Had the taxpayers agreed to pay for all of this?

Based on what he'd learned about suspicious fires and

possible corruption in this tiny southeastern Michigan town—technically a village—his new station was as much *smoke and mirrors* as his fitness to be back on the job.

"That you, Prentiss?"

Mick scanned the empty room, trying to locate that familiar voice. He found it when he tilted his head back and peered toward the massive rafters. Peter Russo waved down at him from the landing of the steel staircase, mounted to the concrete wall. Of course, the place would have a balcony, à la Juliet, but he doubted the House of Capulet also had a firefighter's pole.

"Good to see you, Russo." Well, *good* might have been an overstatement, but everything about his first week would require spin. And having a familiar face around while he settled in couldn't hurt.

"Same, buddy. I mean 'Chief.'"

Peter started down the stairs, the thuds of his black athletic shoes echoing with each step. Though it couldn't have been more than thirty degrees outside, he still wore a short-sleeve polo with his matching navy work pants. The symbol for fire service, the Maltese cross, plus the words *Mount Isabel*, covered his heart on the uniform shirt. His last name was embroidered on the opposite side.

Both men reaching the landing at the same time, Peter jutted out his hand, and Mick gripped it.

"Welcome to Station 1," Peter said. "I know you don't officially start until tomorrow, but I thought you said you'd stop by earlier. That drive on I-94 must have been a skating rink."

"Yeah, it was slow going in my truck. Happy first week of March in Michigan."

"Not to worry. Spring will be here in two more weeks, probably bringing more snow with it." Peter's shoes squeaked on the floor as he shifted his feet. "I was glad to hear you changed your mind about applying for the chief job. It was short notice. And I wasn't sure you would at all…you know…*after*."

Mick nodded at the other man's meaningful look, his throat thickening as he waited for questions about the events in Chicago last September. A rig-size weight lifted off his chest when Peter didn't ask.

"I was surprised to hear from you, too. Hasn't it been five years since you abandoned us for a job in your hometown?"

"Six. But we needed some help around here. Fast." Peter dragged his front teeth over his bottom lip. "And I'd heard you were, uh, available."

Mick wasn't surprised that the news had traveled across state lines. The firefighting community could be a small one, especially when tragedies occurred.

"It's been like fire-style whack-a-mole around here these past two months." The younger man indicated the apparatus bay with a sweep of his hand. "Sometimes as many as two intentionally set fires a week since early January. It's like somebody's trying to burn down Mount Isabel."

"That's why I'm here," Mick said. "We have to stop whoever's setting them before someone gets killed."

Though he was no longer arrogant enough to consider himself a worthy opponent of the flames, he hadn't been able to resist that call for help. Even if he could never atone for those he'd failed to save six months before, maybe, just maybe, protecting a few lives here would give him a start toward redemption.

"It's not just the fires." Peter lifted one shoulder and let it drop. "The police have also opened another investigation, looking at former Fire Chief Hoffman."

"I know it's been tough." He'd been briefed about that and the other cause for his predecessor's removal—he'd shown up drunk on the job—but Mick didn't say more. Though none of the village leaders he'd spoken with had suggested a connection between the string of arsons and the embezzlement investigation involving the former chief, Mick found the timing suspicious. He didn't believe in coincidences.

"Doesn't anyone work around here?" He gestured to the five deserted bays.

"You know what time it is, don't you?"

He peeked at his watch, only then noticing that the time had updated. "Right. Eastern Time Zone. Did the dinner bell already ring?"

Come to think of it, the aroma of something spicy and delicious had melded with the scents of wax and wheel cleaners in the room.

"Long past," Peter said.

"Pans already licked clean?"

"Since Ingram cooked tonight, that's a likely guess. Scott's the Emeril Lagasse of the firehouse."

"Glad I picked something up on the way, then." He hoped his stomach wouldn't growl and prove him a liar. "Any interesting calls on the log this week?"

"Just property-damage accidents, a couple of unintentional, false alarms from our frequent flyers and not one but *two* cats stuck in trees. We've had no structure fires in five days. And not one fatality traffic accident. We're definitely due."

At Mick's hard look, Peter shifted his sneakers on the floor. "Sorry, boss. I just—"

"I know what you meant."

Out of the public eye, first responders often referred to

life-and-death situations in crass terms, which they believed helped them keep their distance and their edge. But the way his friend kept glancing over his shoulder, his hands jammed in his pockets, made Mick wonder whether Peter had lost both. With questions swirling about the former chief's misconduct compounding the already tense situation involving the fires, the whole crew had to be wound tighter than a broken music box.

"Like I said in the email, I'm really sorry about the guys back at the old station." Peter stopped and cleared his throat. "It must have been awful—"

"Thanks," Mick rushed to say, as he dodged the slideshow of images that played on repeat in his thoughts. More so since he'd accepted the new position. "Sounds like we all could use a fresh start."

"You can say that again."

Mick took another look around the apparatus bay, not surprised that Peter had been the only crew member who'd made the effort to greet him. None of them could be happy that the village council had brought in an outsider—and expedited his hiring process—rather than promote from within. Just like thirteen years earlier, when he'd shown up at his former station as a probie hose jockey, he would have to prove himself to his crew and himself at the same time.

"I'll just get a soda and introduce myself to the guys before I pick up the keys to my apartment." He pressed his lips together, hating that he'd misspoken. "I mean the men *and* women."

"Your slip's safe with me," Peter said. "Only two females in the whole crew, Felicia Lucas and Emily Garritt. Lucas is on Rotation 3, and Garritt is paid-on-call, mostly weekends. Word to the wise, never accept if Lucas challenges you to an arm wrestling match."

"I'll try to remember that." He also needed to be more careful with his words. Crew members with connections, criminal or otherwise, to the former chief might be watching *him*. As much as he hated to consider it, that could also include Peter.

"About the job, don't thank me too soon."

"What do you mean?"

Peter gestured with a tilt of his head to a half-glass door beneath the staircase. "Some guests have been waiting for you in your office."

"Guests?"

"Rachel Hoffman." Peter nodded when Mick lifted a brow. "Yeah, one of *those* Hoffmans. Sister to the most recent chief, Riley, and daughter of former chief, Stan. I mean the *late* former—"

"I get it." Even if firefighters were statistically more likely to die by suicide than in the line of duty, they usually avoided discussing that dark truth. "Why's the sister here now?"

"Guess you'll have to ask her that. Well, them. She's here with her kids."

Mick rolled his eyes but followed his friend down the hall and around the corner. They stopped in front of a second half-glass door, this one frosted at the top.

"How long have they been in there?" He pointed to the window.

"A while. She wanted to wait. And, like I said before, we expected you a lot earlier."

"Great," Mick ground out.

"Go easy on her, okay, Chief? She's had to deal with a lot in the past year."

That made two of them. But if he hoped to earn the respect of his crew, he couldn't have disgruntled family members of former employees camping out in his office. He gestured for the younger man to step aside.

"I'll meet you in the day room. Ten minutes tops."

Peter rolled his lips inward and stared at his shoes. "See you in there."

His friend wasn't the only one who doubted he would escape this moment easily. Wasn't it challenging enough that he'd assumed a position he might not be ready for, surrounded by a crew who had to be equally skeptical? Now, before he could pick up his keys and wolf down a pizza in his empty apartment, he would have to face a woman with more reason than most to want him out of Mount Isabel.

Chapter 2

Mick's low-lit office appeared to be the antithesis to the rest of the fancy building he'd toured so far. Just the glow from a fire-hydrant-shaped lamp on the filing cabinet, a steel desk, an office chair that had probably been breaking backs since the '90s, an old sofa against the wall and two straight-back visitors' seats.

He slid out of his coat, releasing a slow breath as he recognized that the room was also unoccupied. Maybe he'd dodged a bullet, and his unwelcome visitor had given up and gone home. Though he couldn't avoid the former chief's sister altogether if she was determined to speak with him, he hoped she would at least wait until he'd officially punched the clock. But since he'd already located his new office, he decided to look around before navigating the back halls to the day room, which would include the station's kitchen, dining room and living area.

A yelp came from what had been a dark corner the moment he flipped the wall switch. He blinked the now-bright room into focus. On the far end of the sofa sat a pretty brunette with a pair of dark-haired little girls draped over her like a blanket, both sound asleep.

The woman, who had to be Rachel Hoffman, struggled to sit up under the children's dead weight. Wispy tresses that poked out every which way from her loose bun, along with a coat she'd balled up as a pillow, offered hints that the kids weren't the only ones who'd been napping in his office.

"Uh, hello." He fought a grin but lost the battle.

His guest squinted at the rude invasion of light as she scooted the girls off her lap, earning a chorus of groans. Once they were on the cracked leather cushions, their matching dark pink jackets draped over them, they spooned together and settled back into their dreams.

If only all that cuteness had been enough to keep him from noticing the girls' mother as she struggled to a seated position. She yanked down her short red V-neck that had ridden high enough to reveal a slice of pale midriff. That image, combined with those still sleepy eyes, the soft-looking mouth and the mussed hair that might as well have been fanned on a real pillow, hit him squarely below the belt.

But the ice storm in her sable-colored eyes when she caught him watching warned him to never stare at her again. At least not without wearing a cup. Why the devil had he looked in the first place when Peter had given him a heads-up over who to expect in his office? He wouldn't recommend checking out any woman he met at the firehouse, but gawking at a relative of the ejected official whose fingerprints still lingered there topped the list of lousy ideas.

He focused on the gaudy lamp over his shoulder, giving the woman time to situate herself. When he turned back, she'd righted her clothes and patted down her hair. Still not looking his way, she rubbed a finger along her lash line, removing makeup smudges that formed shadows on her light olive skin.

"I should say 'Wake up, Goldilocks,' but it looks like you're already awake."

Again, she glared at him, grading his attempt at humor—his go-to in uncomfortable situations—a fail.

"If you say, 'Who's been sleeping on my couch?' don't be surprised if you get punched in the face."

At least it was just *the face*. "I'll keep that in mind. Besides, we wouldn't want to cause a ruckus by calling in the Mount Isabel PD and awakening the two little bears."

"We wouldn't want that," she deadpanned.

When his guest sat forward and crossed her arms, causing the upper curves of delicate skin to peek from her sweater's vee, he averted his gaze. Even if only a monk—one *actively* praying—could have avoided noticing Rachel Hoffman, he didn't have a death wish.

"Why don't we start over? I'm Mick Prentiss...the new fire chief."

The tight shift of her shoulders told him he should have stopped with the name. He lowered his outstretched hand and stepped behind the desk, figuring that a barrier between them would be wise. After draping his coat over the back of the office chair and settling in it, he gestured for her to take one of the visitors' seats. Her gaze narrowed, but she surprised him by following his instruction.

"You must be Mrs. Hoffman." He cleared his throat, recognizing that she shared her brother's surname. "I mean, Ms."

"It's Rachel. And, actually, it's *Miss*."

His gaze shifted to her hands that she'd stacked on her lap. The third finger on her left one was bare, like his was these days, but she wore an emerald ring with a cluster of tiny diamonds on her right. Catching him watching, she crossed her arms, covering both.

Mick rolled the sleeves of the flannel shirt he wore open over a T-shirt. What was it to him that she'd never married?

"And who are these sleeping beauties?"

"Thought they were bears."

As the corner of her pillowy-looking lips lifted, Mick swallowed, his mouth dry. Why did everything about this woman keep reminding him of pillows? And why was he acting like a sex-starved teenager? He was thirty-seven years old. He barely remembered his *twenties*, and he hadn't been hungry for even the diddle dash that the hookup apps promised since the fire. And the divorce.

"Those are my daughters," she said. "They're six. And identical twins if you haven't guessed."

"They're *yours*?" He took in the matching sizes, complexions and even short hair styles that would have made him do a double take earlier if he hadn't been so riveted on their mother. "You don't look—"

"I know. I don't look old enough to be their mother. I am. I'm twenty-five."

Mick recognized a sensitive topic when he heard one. He gestured to the girls. "They look exhausted."

"We've been in here a while. The guys told me they expected you to arrive—" she paused to glance down at her watch "—ninety minutes ago."

"I can't believe they let you stay all this time."

"I told them I wasn't leaving unless they carried me out. Most of them have known me long enough to believe what I say."

Even acquainted with her for less than ten minutes, Mick would have put money on any announcement Rachel Hoffman made as well. That didn't mean he would have let her set up camp on the fire chief's couch for two hours no matter how alluring she was. Or how long it had been since he'd touched feminine skin or wound his fingers in long, satiny hair.

He shot a look through the blurry glass and into the hall. Had his crew *invited* Hoffman's overly hot sister to show up as a firehouse prank on the new guy? If so, they'd soon learn that paybacks were hell when coming from the boss.

"That's right. You probably grew up around the old Station 1. I bet you recognize all the furniture in this office." He managed not to ask her if she'd napped on any of it before.

Her eyes softened as she scanned the room, from the odd lamp to the chair and the desk. Then her gaze snapped back to his, icicles burying all that tenderness.

"I'm not here for a walk down memory lane, *Chief* Prentiss. But I do want to talk about recent developments here."

He was still digesting the way she'd said his title—like a profanity—when the second part registered. Her dad *and* her brother. If seeing Rachel in his office had made him forget about the reports he'd read in the past few days, he could have at least remembered the information Peter had offered not twenty minutes before.

"Please accept my condolences about your father. I'm sorry about your brother's...uh...situation as well."

Though he didn't know what she expected him to do about Riley Hoffman's job loss, he still had a soft spot for the loved ones of alcoholics. He'd taken more than his share of turns on the slip-and-slide of his dad's addiction, so he could relate.

"Thanks, but I don't need you to feel sorry for me, either."

Mick laced his fingers, resting his wrists on the edge of his desk. So much for ten minutes. The woman probably wouldn't leave before her daughters' bedtime.

"Look, Miss Hoffman, I can see that this change must be difficult for you. Your family's been a part of the MIFD for decades. But I had no part in past personnel decisions. In fact, I was hired *because* I'm an outsider since—" He stopped himself, considered and began again. "Since investigations are ongoing."

"You've got that part right. You *are* an outsider. They're not welcome here."

"I'd sensed that."

She rested her hands flat on his desk. "You should also prepare yourself for things not being what they seem."

He knew better than to respond to that, but he couldn't stop the words from coming. "It can be tempting to try to shield a loved one who's hurting, but—"

"You can stop your careful stepping around it because I'm *not* enabling my brother or dismissing his addiction."

She stared at him for so long that he shifted in his chair, its cushion as unforgiving as he'd predicted. "Then I'm not sure what we have to talk about here."

Rachel settled back in her seat and crossed both her arms and legs this time.

"You must have read the history on my family before you agreed to come here. I've done some research on you, too. Three-alarm fire last September. Three casualties. Two of them members of your crew."

Mick pressed his forearm against his rolling insides as the faces of those men appeared on the desk's surface. Suárez, of course. But even Wheeler, who didn't deserve his sympathy but still should have walked away from that fire. It didn't surprise him that Hoffman's sister had searched for ammunition against him before showing up in his office, but her words still struck him like a fresh gash, appearing alongside others that had barely crusted over.

"The council knows about what happened in Chicago. I held nothing back."

"Not even that you quit right after it happened?" She tilted her head, delicate brow lifting. "That you were ready to hang up your helmet for good?"

"Yes, they know that I took *a break*." One that he'd planned to be permanent. He didn't mention that part. "If you researched me, then you know I was cleared of any responsibility in the accident."

"Are you saying you were innocent?"

At Rachel's sharp tone, her daughters stirred on the sofa. Mick welcomed the distraction and the chance to avoid her question. No matter what the final report had shown, he was command on that scene. He would never give himself a pass over decisions he'd made that day. They still kept him awake at night.

She held her finger to her lips and watched the children as though she hoped they would go back to sleep. Instead, one little head popped up from the leather. The other lifted seconds later. The girls rubbed tiny fists over eyes as deep brown as their mother's and then climbed down and squeezed onto her lap, leaving the seat next to her empty.

"Girls, this is Mr. Prentiss."

Mick didn't miss that she avoided using his title altogether this time. "Hi, young ladies."

"These two are Carly and Carissa."

One raised her hand and then the other as though used to helping people tell them apart. They both said bashful hellos.

The child on Rachel's left leg, who'd identified herself as Carly, pressed her forehead to her mother's shoulder.

"Can we go now, Mommy? I'm sleepy."

"It's hot in here," Carissa whined. "I want to go home."

"Just a few more minutes." Rachel waited until their frowns turned to reluctant nods.

"We can take this up at another time," Mick offered though he still didn't know what she expected from him.

"I need to say this now."

Her determination shouldn't have surprised him after she'd waited in his office for so long. He twirled one hand, giving her the chance to say what was on her mind.

"My brother is innocent. Just like you." She lifted her chin, daring him to contradict her. "Yes, he has a drinking problem. But he did none of the other things he's being investigated for. He would never have embezzled funds or doctored incident reports."

She shook her head hard. "I know he didn't."

At the waver in Rachel's voice, Mick straightened. She wasn't as certain as she wanted him to believe. A lump settled at the back of his throat, her moment of vulnerability touching him in a way her tough act never could have. Even if predicting what an addict would or wouldn't do was like fortune-telling with a cracked crystal ball, he understood her need to explain what she couldn't understand.

"You know sometimes when a whole story comes out—"

"Names are cleared," she finished before he had the chance.

He didn't bother saying that the opposite was also true. She wouldn't look at him, anyway, suddenly focused on brushing back Carissa's hair and then Carly's.

"My brother's been in rehab for two weeks now," she said, when she lifted her head. "He can't defend himself. Somebody's going to have to do it for him."

"Why don't you just let the authorities—"

"Do you really believe anyone's looking out for Riley's interests here? Someone who's tarnished the fine reputation of the storied Mount Isabel FD?" She stared him down, waiting until he shrugged. "That's what I thought."

"I'm sure they're as interested in finding the truth as you are."

His words tasted like acid on his tongue. Like they'd agreed, he was a stranger in that little town. He couldn't know whether anyone there cared about determining the facts. Her skeptical look told him she knew it, too.

She watched him for several seconds longer and then tilted her head from side to side as though considering whether to say more.

"I shouldn't be telling you this, but I believe Riley might have uncovered information that certain individuals didn't want him to find."

"What do you mean? Who was hiding something? And what were they covering up?"

She pushed back her shoulders. "If I knew those answers, don't you think I'd be shouting them in the middle of Main Street to anyone who'd listen?"

"Then who do you *think*—"

"I don't know yet." She blew out an exasperated breath. "Someone in a position to keep Riley quiet. And something bad enough that they're willing to burn down half the city to hide it."

A shiver crawled up the back of his neck. It made no sense that the first person in town to suggest a tie between the series of fires and the station scandal would also be one whose family had the most to lose if she'd guessed wrong and her brother were implicated in both.

"You think there's a connection?"

She tucked her chin, looking at him from beneath her lashes. "Don't you?"

"It's too soon for me to guess. But wouldn't you say your theory on how they're linked is a little convenient?" That it was also plausible made him shift his feet under the desk.

"A guy who lucked into this job shouldn't be asking anyone about convenience."

"That's fair," he said, though he wouldn't say he'd won the lottery in accepting the position. "Do you have any proof?"

Her eyes flashed with uncertainty then froze over again. "Not yet, but I will."

A memory of a two-way radio transmission stole into his thoughts, the sound crackling in his ears. A call for a check-in that went unanswered. An interminable wait. Then those earsplitting beeps from two Personal Alert Safety System devices, indicating that the firefighters were motionless. If he'd issued a stronger order at the time, then maybe...

Sweat gathered at the back of his neck. "I know it's difficult, but I need you to stay out of the investigation."

When she started to argue, he held up a hand. "If I see signs that the investigators aren't searching for the truth, wherever it leads, I'll—"

"Do nothing. Just like everyone else."

Without looking at him, she helped the twins slide off her lap and stood. She'd already yanked open the door before he could come to his feet and find his words.

"Rachel—I mean Miss Hoffman—wait."

She ushered her daughters into the hall and then glanced over her shoulder, giving him the chance to speak.

"If you're right about someone targeting your brother,

then you have to know that it's dangerous for you to get involved. You shouldn't take that kind of risk."

"And if you'd ever cared about anyone, you'd understand that I have no choice."

She slipped through the gap and closed the door behind her.

Mick rounded the desk and yanked it open again. The hallway was already deserted. Only the light floral fragrance that lingered in his office and the dents on the sofa proved that anyone had been there at all.

You should also prepare yourself for things not being what they seem. As Rachel's words replayed in his thoughts, the hair at his nape stood. He would have gone after them, but he would have had to explain to his new crew why he'd chased local residents through the building.

What was he thinking, accepting this job in the first place? His hero complex should have sputtered and died after the events in Chicago. He'd clung to it instead only to land in this sinkhole, with questions spreading like crevices in all directions. Were those inside the MIFD, including the former fire chief, guilty of corruption, or could it have come from outside these brick walls? And how did those matters connect with the work of a possible serial arsonist?

He had no answers to those questions, but the one thing he did know was that he and the investigators wouldn't be the only ones asking them. If Rachel was right that someone had targeted her brother for nosing into private matters, what else would they be willing to do to keep their secrets buried?

Mick closed his eyes and shivered. He wouldn't have to learn that answer because he would keep Rachel far from that investigation. The flutter in his gut over the possibility of seeing her again warned him that he should steer clear of Riley Hoffman's too-sexy sister, but, like she'd said, he had no choice. He couldn't allow anyone else to be hurt—or worse—on his watch.

Chapter 3

Two baths, four books and a pair of bug-in-a-rug tuck-ins after her return from Station 1, Rachel tromped down the stairs of her duplex, arms and legs as heavy as her head. With two years of practice to guide her, she maneuvered easily around the squeaky fourth step. If only the window next to the landing, the one that always welcomed the chill with an engraved invitation, could have helped to cool the heated skin on her face.

She slumped on the lumpy sofa, adjusted her robe over her pajamas and closed her eyelids though she still had at least two hours of computer work to finish before bed. The meeting with Prentiss hadn't gone well, but what had she expected when she'd bulldozed the man the moment he'd arrived at the firehouse? It was naive to think that the new guy, who owed his position to Riley's termination, would care what happened to her brother, but she hadn't wanted his help, anyway. If she had, she should have been nicer to him.

Her shoulders lifted and her jaw flexed as she recalled his placating comments about her brother's "situation." His words were almost as infuriating as the pity in those deceptively warm brown eyes. Who did he think he was? Her therapist? If that were true, then the way he'd stared at her would have gotten his license revoked. Like a starving man drooling over a double cheeseburger and extra fries.

Rachel's eyes popped open as a sizzle like the one she'd experienced under the fire chief's inappropriate gaze swept over her from collarbones to fingertips and hips to pinkie toes. Just like then, the scrambling sensation left every bit of skin in its path not just awake but *abuzz*. What was that about?

She leaped up from the couch, rubbed her upper arms over her sweater to brush away the gooseflesh beneath the knit and stomped into the kitchen. Maybe she could blame grogginess for those ridiculous tingles when she'd caught him watching her earlier, but she had no excuse for them now. Nor for her inability to get the guy in the lumberjack getup out of her head. He must have worn his flannel shirt two sizes too small to get the sleeves to cling to his arms that way. Same for the darn near indecent T-shirt that had hugged his chest beneath it.

"He's the enemy," she hissed, then shot a look at the thin wall that separated her kitchen sink from her neighbor's faucet. The last thing she needed was to be overheard and make her fellow tenants more curious about her than they already were. Continual front-page news coverage of the fires had made the Mount Isabel gossip mill grind faster than usual these days. And there was no way to separate the Hoffman family from the MIFD.

Enemy. She considered the word again. Though it was premature to declare Prentiss a true adversary, she couldn't call him an ally, either. Whichever he was, she shouldn't have been ogling him, though the short dark hair that probably had never met a comb and the five-o'clock shadow—closer to seven thirty—made him impossible to ignore.

Not to mention the cleft in his chin that a different woman might have been tempted to dab with the tip of her tongue.

Stop it. She lunged for the bottle of merlot on her countertop, wiped off the dust and dug into the drawer for a corkscrew. What was the matter with her? Even if an internet search for "sexy, late-thirties firefighter" would have produced Mick's photo—in turnout pants, shirtless, with or without suspenders and wielding an ax—what kind of sister swooned over her brother's *replacement*? Apparently, one who was semi-famous for her lousy taste in men and had a record of bailing on her family.

She slid the bottle back to its spot on the counter, its cork unpierced. Flipping on the electric teakettle instead, she pulled a packet of chamomile from a ceramic container. It was just as well. Though she rarely drank, and never in front of Riley, tonight wasn't the time to start. She needed to keep a clear head, unlike the new fire chief. He'd been breathing in too many diesel fumes if he believed the investigators really wanted the truth. She refused to consider the possibility that those answers wouldn't clear her brother's name.

Rachel frowned at her reflection in the mug of boiling water and then shattered the image by dunking the tea bag. After two unsupervised hours in the fire chief's office, plus the nail file, paper clip and bobby pin she'd smuggled into the station, she should have produced some helpful information. She hadn't even been able to pick the filing cabinet lock. Burglars' tools probably worked only in movies. She should have brought a sledgehammer.

No matter what her excuses, she'd failed Riley. Again. Just as she had their father.

"I'm sorry," she whispered to the mustard-and-white-colored tiles of the backsplash, her throat thickening, heat building at the back of her eyes.

Riley hadn't comprehended her apology any better during their mostly silent drive to the Forward Path Rehabilitation Center than that ugly wall did now. But even if he hadn't been too defeated, too terrified and desperate to hear anything she'd said to him, her older brother still would have had no reason to forgive her. His relapse was her fault as surely as if she'd cracked a seal and handed him a bottle.

As the memory of his stifled sobs ripped through her chest and pounded in her ears, she swiped at the tears escaping down her cheeks. Why had she assumed that just because Riley had been a champion youth swimmer—while she broke into a sweat jumping into the kiddie pool—he was better equipped to handle all the tragedies they'd faced? Selfish people believed whatever necessary to help them sleep soundly while the rest of the world paced in the dark.

Rachel jerked the mug up from the counter, causing steaming liquid to slosh over her hand. She winced. Served her right for letting the new chief distract her when she needed to focus all her attention on clearing Riley's name. When she wasn't doing the medical transcription work that helped keep milk, eggs and grape jelly in her refrigerator, anyway.

After sopping up the spill, she carried the mug to the dining table that doubled as her desk. Rather than listen to her first audio recording of the night, she opened her browser and tried again to hack into her brother's email. She'd already tried out familiar possibilities like their long-buried cat, "Elliot," and also "Engine5," their dad's equally dead pickup that still hogged space in their garage, so she had to come up with something new.

"Come on, Riley," she whispered to the screen. "What did you use?"

After squinting at the blank square for several seconds, she typed, "SealsTeam," the name of his youth club swim team. When she received that same credentials-mismatch message, she banged the keyboard with her forehead. If she'd taken the time to really know her brother, she wouldn't be forced to rely on details about him like the club's name. He'd quit that group abruptly, anyway, right after—

Rachel pushed up from the keys, the top of her head prickling. It was just a guess. Still, she couldn't help but wonder if the number eleven, Riley's age when they'd lost their mother, had split his life's timeline into *before* and *after*, just as nine had severed hers. She added two ones to the end of the team's name and clicked Enter.

A list of her brother's recent emails appeared on the screen. She sat up straighter as shivers skipped up both arms. After a few seconds of scrolling, though, she was certain she'd wasted time hacking into a useless account, filled with spam emails. "Ever heard of 'Unsubscribe'?"

Instead of continuing from the top of the feed, she paged back to early December when she'd begged Riley to ask more questions about their dad's suicide. She'd been convinced it was an accident. Maybe he'd reached out to some local officials, who'd responded. At a web-based email address with only a few lines appearing in the preview panel, she paused.

"Four be the things I'd been better without: Love, CURIOSITY, freckles, and doubt."—Dorothy Parker (1893-1967)

She reread the words. Maybe she didn't know Riley that well, but she didn't picture him as the daily-quote-subscription type. She continued to scroll until another quote appeared in the panel. Only the email address didn't match the first one.

"I shall be as secret as the grave."—Miguel de Cervantes (1547-1616)

As Rachel's throat tightened, she closed her lips and forced a deep breath through her nose. She had to be reading too much into the quotes, but "curiosity" put in uppercase letters, "secret," *and* "grave"? When taken together, the message could sound threatening, even to someone who didn't need to explain away a sibling's potential wrongdoing. And maybe to a new fire chief, who hadn't offered to help her find answers.

She laid her left hand flat on the desk for the firm security of it and pressed the up arrow with her right. A dozen entries higher, a more recent quote appeared from yet another email address. Only this one was an idiom, not a quotation, and it offered a direct threat.

"Curiosity killed the cat."

Rachel slammed the laptop closed as a disconcerting sensation settled over her. Like an aquarium, only she was the one swimming in circles inside the glass. She turned in her chair to face her unit's narrow, triple-hung windows. As usual, she'd forgotten to close the blinds. A sinister night sky stared back at her, faraway streetlights and television screens straining to cast their eerie yellow glow over piles of shoveled snow.

Could someone have been out there watching her all this time? She shook her head but still rushed over to close all three sets of blinds. Even with the emails and the possible warnings addressed to her brother, no one had a reason to threaten her. No one else even knew she'd been asking questions.

But didn't they? She blinked, her chest tightening. Now the statement she'd made by her refusal to leave Station 1 earlier returned to haunt her. She'd practically announced to the whole crew that she was looking into matters connected with Riley's dismissal. Until today, she would have sworn she knew every firefighter working one of the three shifts in that building, but did she really?

You shouldn't take that kind of risk. She'd tried not to absorb Mick's words when he'd said it was dangerous for her to get involved. Now they pelted her from all directions. Was the outsider right? Had she put herself and her girls in danger?

She shot a look at the staircase, her heart racing as for the first time she noticed the child sitting on the bottom step in flannel pajamas and lion slippers. Rachel leaped up from her seat.

"Carissa, what are you doing out of bed?" As her daughter stared back at her with wide eyes over her sharp tone, she tried again in a softer voice. "Did something scare you, honey?"

Instead of answering, the child padded over, wrapped her arms around her mother's waist and buried her face in her belly.

"Is it in the closet?"

Carissa turned her head from side to side against the front of her robe.

"Under the bed," she mumbled.

"We'd better go find it." As a parent, Rachel could at

least handle imaginary nighttime monsters. She wasn't sure any more about the real ones.

After flipping off the light above the table, she hoisted Carissa on her hip, though both girls were getting too heavy for that. They passed the first twin bed where Carly slept soundly. Then she lowered Carissa to her own mattress, the covers wadded into a ball at its center.

"Mommy, can you stay with me?"

"Okay, but just until you go to sleep."

Neither mentioned the creature under the bed again, but she knew from experience that monsters vanished once Mom was there for protection. Rachel shook out the blankets and settled in next to her daughter, covering them both with the comforter. Her throat thickened as Carissa rested a tiny hand in her palm. If only all the problems the girls would face could be solved with an extra cuddle.

She stared up at the glow-in-the-dark stars on the bedroom ceiling, those she'd put there herself two years before when dreams and a normal life seemed within her little family's grasp. When her father was still with them. And Riley was happy and two years sober. Everything had changed. Now her brother needed her, and she couldn't choose between him and her children. She had to protect them all.

Just as Carissa's breathing settled in sleep, and Rachel let her own eyes close, a sound as familiar as her own heartbeat blared in the distance. A firehouse siren. Another one? Her heart thudding, she unfolded herself from the tangle of her daughter's limbs. She slid from beneath the covers and tiptoed out of the room.

The siren didn't necessarily signal a fire, she reminded herself, as she stepped past her bedroom doorway. Even if it was, that didn't automatically connect it to the string of arsons.

When the racket stopped just as she reached the top of the stairs, she sighed. Only the absence of that noise continued to vibrate in her ears, the words from Riley's emails clinging to those pulsating sounds like lyrics set to a chorus of chaos. That message, originally meant for her brother, offered a warning to her as well.

I shall be as secret as the grave.

Her shiver began before she reached the faulty window at the landing. It followed her back to the dining room table. She shot a look at the front windows, the closed blinds no longer offering a cocoon of security.

She slid the laptop to the far end of the table and settled in that seat, careful to keep both the staircase and the windows in view. Avoiding the emails, she logged into the private network for her job, slid on her earphones and clicked the arrow for the first medical recording. She might as well get some work done since there was no way she would be sleeping tonight.

The fire couldn't have been a bigger disappointment. No delicious flames that stretched toward the canopy of leafless trees, threatening to spread through narrow limbs and sprawling branches. No promise of a heap of smoldering ash before those obnoxious red engines could race from one of the stations.

This looked more like a cartoon campfire from soggy wood, the billowing smoke barely seeping out the abandoned house's chimney, let alone lapping through its walls. It made no statement at all. Certainly not the message he'd planned to deliver.

"I should have waited."

Grinding his teeth, he crouched lower in the ditch. He didn't know why he bothered trying to hide. The heavy

Chapter 4

"That was your welcome to Mount Isabel, Chief."

The words from behind Mick came with a friendly slap on the back of his turnout jacket with still an hour to go before the sun would sneak peeks through the line of trees across the field. He jerked to turn back, catching Noah Carlson in the beam of his helmet lamp and feeling a twinge in his neck at the same time. He made his wince look like a smile behind his mask.

From the ache between his shoulder blades, he could have sworn he'd bench-pressed the pumper truck instead of just helping to check for trapped victims and assisting with one of the hoses. He'd never felt so old. To rub it in, Noah, one of the youngest crew members at twenty-two, nearly bounced at his side, his mask hanging at his chest, his white-teeth grin contrasting with the sooty smears on his face.

"Just another shift around here." Noah pushed his Nomex protective hood back, his helmet under his arm and the full mask of his Self-Contained Breathing Apparatus dangling from his gloved hand. "But we wrestled this one into submission in no time. Practically ripped the matches right out of the arsonist's hands with our response. Maybe with the next one we can stop the dude before he gets the chance to light it."

container of gasoline. Those rags. The matches that had refused to light. All of it useless. No one would even notice what should have been a major blaze until morning.

Then he heard it. The sound came from far away like a squeal captured in a tunnel. Someone must have seen the smoke. Or maybe there were a few good flames, only on the opposite side of the house. His heart pounded louder as the sound filled the atmosphere, pregnant with possibility and blossoming.

While relocating to his planned position behind the row of trees, he made sure to cover his boot tracks. When the first big rig barreled over the county road, its lights flashing but its siren muted now because of the hour, he settled in for the big show.

And he smiled.

His own breaths still whooshing out like Darth Vader through his SCBA, Mick chuckled, but he turned away before the younger man could catch him rolling his eyes. Oh, to be that innocent again and still believe that good had a fighting chance against evil. Had he *ever* been as optimistic as Noah, who perfectly matched his nickname, "Sunny"? If so, someone had pounded the Pollyanna out of him that first week at the Chicago firehouse. He appreciated knowing that another crew member besides Peter wouldn't be giving him the cold shoulder, but he suspected that this probie was still too green to have declared fealty to the former chief.

He pulled off his helmet and mask and pushed back his hood over his soaked hair, coughing immediately over his first breath without protection from the acrid smoke.

"Good work out there tonight, Carlson." Despite the sweat trailing beneath his collar, Mick shivered as the near-freezing temperature cut through his turnout gear more now than when he'd first arrived, its job to keep him safe, not warm. "I mean this morning."

"You, too, boss. Heck of a way to start your first day on the job. I guess it was *before* your first day."

"Heard the firehouse siren and headed over. You know…muscle memory."

"You showed up like a paid-on-call crew member, and this fire wasn't even an all-call," Noah said, indicating the signal for every available firefighter to respond to an emergency. "Though don't those guys usually suit up at the station and ride on the truck?"

Noah gestured first to Mick's turnout gear and then to his pickup, parked on the side of the road near a pile of dirt-striped snow.

No way would Mick admit that he'd been tempted to

ignore the call altogether. To stay sprawled on the lonely air mattress on his apartment's living room floor, gnawing on pizza and trying to shut off that conversation that had repeated in his thoughts. The one with Rachel Hoffman. Even fighting a fire, the effort straining his out-of-practice muscles, the snug fit of his mask making him feel like a scuba diver under twenty feet of water, had only briefly helped to interrupt that loop.

If you'd ever cared about anyone... Her words, unfair and untrue, still stung. She knew nothing about him other than what she'd read. And if he had any sense, he wouldn't let himself crave more information about her. He already knew she was the former chief's sister. That should have been enough.

"Good thing you set up your locker before you went home last night," Noah continued with their conversation as though Mick hadn't already left it. "Don't know about you, but I could eat an elephant right now."

"Sorry. No enormous land mammals here. I ordered a pizza last night. Just finished the first slice when the fire whistle started up. Pepperoni and banana peppers." His stomach roiled at the thought of all the greasy meat and congealed cheese back in his otherwise empty refrigerator.

"Have it in the truck?" Noah pointed to it, his body positioned to run.

"Sorry again."

His shoulders slumped. "Too bad. Could've shared."

At least someone would have eaten it then. Before the younger man could bring up food again, Mick switched topics. "You mentioned the arsonist earlier. Remember, this incident is only 'suspicious' so far." He paused to add the air quotes. "Possibly intentionally set, but it's above our pay grade to declare it arson. Only the prosecutor gets to make that official charge."

"I know." Noah gave him a side-eye. "But just 'suspicious,' huh?"

The younger man stopped and stared at the pile of soggy wood, scattered roof tiles and insulation sludge that had once been a building. After hours of work, no visible curls of smoldering threat remained. When Noah turned back, he raised an eyebrow, the lines of ash creasing on his forehead. Maybe the probie wasn't so green, after all.

"For now," Mick said, anyway.

Yellow crime-scene tape flapped where firefighters had stretched it around trees and orange caution cones to mark the scene's perimeter. Investigators would continue to comb through the debris for several hours this morning, but there was no doubt that this fire had been intentionally set. Not first-degree arson since that charge was reserved for incidents where multi-unit buildings or mines were the targets or those resulting in physical injuries, but Michigan's penal code offered four more degrees. One of them surely would fit this situation.

Still, something about this scene bothered him. Reports from recent fires had shown different fuels, ignition sites and burn patterns, but this one was even more of an outlier. Comically amateurish, in fact. The suspects had left the can of gasoline, used as the accelerant, in the middle of the living room floor like a bull's-eye. Hopefully, with fingerprints all over it.

"Copycats," he breathed the word, the possibility of it pressing down on his neck and making it ache even more. Mick slid a glance to Noah, who was looking at something on the phone he should have left on the rig and didn't appear to have heard him. But the thought of imitators continued to eat at him. If the original fires had been the work of a serial arsonist, then copycats would make the crimes more difficult to unravel. And nearly impossible to stop.

After tucking his phone away, Noah paused again to stare over at what was left of the building. He spun to point to a site where two pickups had been parked earlier.

"Didn't pull much of an audience for our fine work today. Usually I get assigned to take photos of the crowd in case the suspect is there, admiring his handiwork, but Golden told me not to bother," Noah said, indicating Captain Joe Golden, who'd been command on the scene.

"Since we've already interviewed both of them, I'd say he made the right call," Mick said. One of the farmers had even called in the fire.

"I don't recall any of the other incidents as involving houses," Noah said. "Weren't they all barns or outbuildings?"

That was another thing that had bugged Mick. Though vacant at least a few years, this had been someone's *home*, maybe lost to foreclosure. A place where report cards were celebrated or feared. Where holidays and births and deaths were nailed into the frame as surely as baseboards and sheets of drywall.

Where someone like Rachel Hoffman could have lived with her two little girls.

He shivered again and tried to blink away a picture his mind had conjured, its potential melding with true images from his too recent past. Why was he thinking about her in that context? Rachel might have been taking a risk by asking too many questions, but it was a leap for him to imagine her being a victim in another fire.

"You guys want to hang out here all day, or are you going to get back on the truck?"

Mick jerked at the voice coming from off to his left and turned to identify it. Backlit by one of the LED scene lights, Joe Golden approached, swiping a sleeve over the red ring of hair that lingered on his pale, bald head. Senior firefighter Rodney Sampson caught up with them and then slowed to wipe a streak of sweat dripping down his ruddy cheek.

"I don't know about you guys, but I have a mattress and a pillow calling my name," Rodney said, before brushing off the other side of his face.

"Pizza first," Noah said and then started off again toward the brand-new rig, Engine 1.

Rodney pointed after him. "Did he say pizza? For breakfast?"

"Kids," Joe scoffed. "Can eat whatever they want 'til the doctor starts chasing them around with bottles of statins."

"You kidding? Sunny eats more salads than either of us." Rodney gestured to Mick. "Don't know about the chief yet."

"I try." Mick grinned and shook the tension from his shoulders.

Already, some of the crew were beginning to relax around him instead of watching him like a kid caught shoplifting a bag of gummy bears. Soon, they'd figure out that their former leader's job loss wasn't his fault. If he was lucky, Rachel would eventually stop blaming him as well, though he reminded himself it didn't matter what she thought.

Ahead of them, Ladder 1 pulled back up the drive, having refilled its water supply and done a crew change for those coming off their twenty-four-hour shift. The fresh firefighters, who'd arrived early to make the switch, would remain on the site with the investigator, monitoring for hot spots that could cause an embarrassing rekindling.

Outside of Engine 1, Noah helped Darnell Andrews, the driver and pump operator, store equipment and check hoses. The other three joined them in finishing the work.

"We need to get on the road." Darnell stared up into a gunmetal sky that already showed at first light. "It's begun to spit, and that thing on my phone is predicting three to six inches. Hate these storms, especially on my forty-eight off."

"You can build a snowman with your kids," Joe said and then laughed at his own joke. "Or maybe sleep first."

Once they'd stored the last hose, Rodney pointed to Mick's pickup, its windshield already dotted with snowflakes.

"You leaving that here?"

"Figured I'd ride back on the rig, get cleaned up, meet some of the Rotation 2 crew, and then come back to pick it up later." He held his hands wide to indicate the filth on his gear.

"Can't say I blame him," Noah said, as he rounded the rig's rear work platform. "I wouldn't want to muck up that sweet ride, either. None of you will be taking a step in the half-ton pickup I plan to buy. Not without showering first."

"And putting on those shoe booties like surgeons wear," Joe piped, earning a laugh.

"Catching a ride, Chief?" Darnell waved Mick into the rear-facing jump seat inside a cab so spacious that all but the tallest among the crew could stand up inside it.

Mick didn't miss looks exchanged among the men since, as the most senior officer on the site, he should have been given the officer's seat, next to the driver. Joe, whom Mick had left in command when he'd arrived, slid into that spot street clothes for his locker and convince someone to drive him to get his truck.

As the image of that destroyed house filtered through his thoughts again, his pulse rushed. The sense of doom he'd carried most days since the Chicago tragedy, no matter how well he'd fooled the psychologist at his required debriefing, gripped his chest, twisting and squeezing.

Had he let his guilt over past events push him to make a bigger deal out of this call than necessary? A suspicious fire taking place right after his arrival wasn't all that surprising when they'd happened so frequently. But what if it was more than that? A warning for the new chief? A declaration of some sort?

Whether intended as a message or not, this fire bolstered his determination to find Rachel's address and pay her a visit after work. Somehow he had to convince a woman, who'd already proven to be stubborn, to stay out of the investigation into her brother's actions. That task might prove doubly challenging since just the thought of seeing her again or being close enough to breathe in her wildflower scent set all of his nerve endings on high alert.

His exhaustion evaporating faster than the nearly three thousand gallons of water they'd used to extinguish the flames, he was suddenly wide awake. He turned his head to the side and took several deep breaths to slow his pulse.

If accepting the position at Station 1 had been a mistake, allowing himself to spend more time around Rachel Hoffman could prove to be an even bigger one. He didn't need a career in firefighting to remind him that those who played with fire got burned.

instead. Since respect would need to be earned, he wouldn't rock that boat on his first day.

Having stored their masks in the compartments for that purpose, located on the outside of the cab, Rodney settled in the spot across from Mick, and Noah took the second rear-facer.

They were already on the road when Noah spoke into his headset so he could be heard over the powerful diesel engine. "I thought it was good of the chief to respond last night since he wasn't on duty yet."

"Fire Chief *Hoffman* would have been here no matter what," Rodney said coolly. "Always came. *Always*."

As if he'd recognized that he was being too welcoming to the new boss, he sat back and crossed his arms.

"I'm sure that's true," Mick said.

Noah looked between the two men, his brows knitted. "It is."

To escape tension heavier than the snow clouds above them, Mick turned to the window as a gray blur swiped past them on the two-lane highway. Whether the men really supported the former chief or were just acting after orchestrating his dismissal, he wasn't sure. But he recognized it might take him longer to settle in with the crew than he'd expected.

No one spoke again during the ten-minute ride back into town. Mick appreciated the reprieve, but he also needed to mentally reorganize his workday. His schedule would now include making a statement to the weekly *Isabel Informer* in addition to meeting with some of the new crew at 7:00 a.m. and overseeing the morning cleaning duties for the station house and firefighting apparatus. Somewhere in there, he needed to fit in time to pick up fresh

Chapter 5

That afternoon, Rachel rubbed her hands together to warm them, determined not to start her minivan's engine again for at least ten minutes. Poor dog owners, whose pets still expected walks during snow showers, had already sent curious glances her way as they'd passed. She couldn't afford to draw more attention to herself, looking like a stalker. One without the good sense to choose better weather.

Her window of time was closing fast. School let out in eighty-four minutes, and she couldn't be late to get in line in the pickup lane. Again. That she'd been out helping Riley every time she was tardy made no difference. Even if she arrived early every afternoon through the end of the school year, she would never make it off the parent naughty list.

If she didn't need Mick's help, then what was she doing here, parked outside his new apartment on the off chance he would stop by for supplies? Mick probably hadn't even rushed in to work last night's fire. Riley would have. Her dad would have. Both had been too dedicated to leave their crew in the lurch when they could help. That didn't mean this outsider would have missed a minute of beauty sleep to start his job early.

Rachel glanced up and down the street again, past cars

that were slowly disappearing beneath a speckled blanket of snow. She wouldn't need to see an out-of-state license plate to identify his midnight-blue quad-cab since she'd taken note of it in the station's parking lot last night. Only he wasn't there and probably wouldn't be before she had to leave.

"Forget it. I don't know why I thought—"

Why had she allowed herself to believe for an instant that the new chief might be concerned about her brother or her daughters or her? More proof of her inability to judge the decency in people. She'd already allowed ideas Mick had planted in her head to make her overreact to Riley's emails. Would he have her imagining spies next as they peeked out through closed curtains and hid arsenals in their kitchens like in *Mr. & Mrs. Smith*?

In quick, angry moves, she twisted the ignition and put the van in gear. As she started to pull away from the curb, she glanced in her rearview mirror and noticed someone approaching on the sidewalk. A man, she determined from the heavy stomps and wide frame, bent against the wind. No dog in sight, and no one without one would have been caught dead walking in this weather. He wore a hooded sweatshirt beneath his coat, its strings pulled so tight that only a fist-size section of his face remained exposed. Like he wanted to avoid being identified.

The hairs on the back of her neck stood, and a chill sauntered down both arms, her body ignoring that earlier dismissal of her concerns. Her thigh shook as she continued to press down on the brake, the engine idling. Was the guy following her? On foot? In this slippery mix?

Oblivious to her questions, the man started up the walk to the brick apartment building. That coat and the broad-shouldered shape of the person inside it suddenly looked familiar. As if Rachel needed more hints to his identity, her chilled hands beneath her gloves suddenly felt clammy. She shifted into Park and shut off the engine.

The bundled walker glanced back at the sound then continued toward the building. She pushed the door wide. "Prentiss, wait!"

Mick, who'd just been waving a key fob in front of a sensor for building access, turned and stared at the open van door.

"Rachel, is that you?" His words produced a white conversation bubble in the mist.

Instead of waiting for her to answer, he hurried down the walk, forced to catch himself as he lost his footing on slick spots. She had only enough time to climb out and close the door before he crossed the street and met her outside the minivan.

"Hey, Prentiss." Her teeth chattered as the wet wind seeped through her coat and hat.

He yanked on the strings to untie his hood and shoved it back. "Since you're showing up at my home now, you should start calling me Mick."

His lips spread in the kind of sexy smile that probably made other women's knees buckle. She locked hers instead.

"I shouldn't have come."

The smile vanished. "Is everything okay? You? The girls?" He cleared his throat. "Your...brother?"

"Everyone's fine," she said and then swallowed. He was concerned about Riley? Actually, her brother hadn't called her in days, and she had no way of knowing how he was doing.

"Then why are you here?" He gestured to the number above the door on his building. "And how did you get my address?"

"Ever lived in a small town?" When he shook his head, she said, "You'll soon learn that everyone knows *everything* about everyone else."

His brows pulled together, further creasing the line already forming between them. She couldn't blame him for questioning her statement. If she knew all of her fellow residents' secrets, she wouldn't have been searching for answers.

"You still haven't—" he began and then shrugged. "Want to come in? There's no place to sit down except an air mattress with a sleeping bag spread over it, but I can't stay out here. I'm freezing. Aren't you?"

She shivered as her gaze shifted from him to the building and back. Alone with Mick Prentiss in his apartment? On an air mattress? Since a two-child buffer hadn't been enough to keep her hormones in check last night, she decided the cold would be a better choice. Aborting her plan to share what she'd discovered with him would be the best one.

"Sorry to have bothered you." She opened the car door.

"Hold on, Rachel."

Slowly, she turned to face him.

"You came here instead of the station for a reason. Maybe you found something that you didn't want my crew to know about. Or you didn't want anyone to be aware that you'd spoken to me again. Which is it?"

"Both."

"You're already here, so let's talk." He pointed to her van. "How about in there?"

At her nod, Mick rushed around the vehicle to climb in on the passenger side. As soon as she'd closed her door, she recognized that the interior of the van wasn't a great idea, either. The air inside was too thin, too intimate, with scents of snow and masculine sweat twining. She sneaked a ragged breath, hoping he wouldn't notice.

"Where're we headed?" He pointed to the windshield.

"We don't need to drive anywhere."

"Didn't you just say everyone in town knows everything?"

"But—" She scanned the streets for more dog walkers or shifting curtains.

"Then let's get out of here before someone sees us *parking* right on Maple Street."

His stress on the word and his annoying grin as she pulled away from the curb made her cheeks burn.

"Sorry. Couldn't resist."

"Try."

Without a destination in mind, she turned left on Walnut Drive and then right on Willow Lane. Rows of well-kept 1950s ranches and the occasional early 1900s Queen Anne–style home marched past them in silence and her slower than normal speed on the icy roads.

"Do teenagers even use the term 'parking' anymore?" Rachel blurted when she could no longer bear the quiet. Great. She'd turned the conversation back to *that*?

Again, his smile. The uninvited tingles were hers.

"You're asking me?" He scoffed and then chuckled. "I have no idea what teenagers say now. But stop stalling. What had you upset enough to talk to me again? You might have missed it, but our conversation last night didn't go well. And, for that matter, why did you show up when I was supposed to be at work?"

"I'll answer your questions after you tell me why you were walking home in this?"

She pointed to the mess the windshield wipers shoved aside with each swipe.

"I needed clothes since I wasn't set up at the station yet when I came in to help with last night's fire." He patted the knees of his damp jeans. "And I left my truck at the scene. I needed someone to drive me back to pick it up. Thanks for volunteering."

"You could have taken a rideshare like in the big city," she said with a smirk.

"I checked my app. No drivers within fifteen miles of the station."

"Sorry. I can't help, either. I have to pick up the girls at school in—" she paused to glance at the dash clock "—seventy-six minutes. And the roads are lousy."

"That's over an hour. Isn't Mount Isabel only two miles north to south? And this is nothing for you. I thought Michiganders took pride in their superior snow-driving abilities."

She lifted her shoulder and let it drop. "Fine."

Instead of continuing straight, she moved into the right-turn lane and headed south.

"Do you know where you're going?"

"The fire was on County Road 600 East. Photos are up on the *Informer* website."

"And you always check."

He didn't present it as a question, and she didn't deny it. Having lived with a police scanner as a lullaby since childhood, she always craved immediate emergency information.

"Okay, your turn."

"After the sirens last night, I'd guessed you'd need to stop home for a few things."

"Now, how about the other question?"

She gripped the steering wheel tighter. Saying it out loud would do one of two things: make her discovery seem sillier or realer. She worried it would be the latter.

"I broke into Riley's email account last night."

"Remind me never to underestimate your sleuthing skills," he said, but sat straighter. "Didn't the police already go over his laptop?"

"It was his web-based account that I accessed."

"What did you find?"

"I never expected my brother to be a quote-of-the-day type."

Mick turned so that his knee came up on the seat. "He was receiving quotes in his emails? What kind of quotes?"

"Strange ones. Mildly menacing when taken individually but more sinister when I looked at them together." She moved her head to push away the shiver that settled at the base of her neck. "But I can't take them as a group since they all came from different email addresses."

"Wouldn't a quote-of-the-day come from *one* source? Like one newsletter?"

Rachel blinked rapidly. She hadn't thought of that. "One was from a guy who's been dead for four hundred years. 'I shall be as secret as the grave.'"

"That's creepy, all on its own."

"It could have been a warning, but j̶̶̶̶̶̶̶̶̶̶̶̶ been just a quote." Either way, she cou̶̶̶̶̶̶̶

"But you don't think so." Like earlier, it wa̶̶̶ tion.

She shook her head. "One of the other quotes wasn't attributed to a speaker at all. 'Curiosity killed the cat.'"

Mick planted his hands on the dash. "You've got to stop asking questions. It's not safe."

At the vehemence in his words, Rachel hit the brake, causing the van to slide. Once she'd managed to correct, she frowned over at him. "What was that for? I didn't share this with you so you could tell me what to do."

"Then why did you tell me?"

The heat of his stare on the side of her face made her squirm. "Because I needed someone to acknowledge that Riley could have been set up."

He didn't answer. What had she expected him to say? That they had enough evidence to go right away to the Mount Isabel PD? She couldn't tell him that she'd come to him *because* he was a stranger rather than despite it. That among the people she'd known all her life, she suddenly didn't know whom to trust.

Neither spoke as she turned from the salted and plowed two-lane highway onto the snow-covered side road. Up ahead, his pickup was buried in snow across from a blank area of sky with piles of debris where a house used to stand. She turned around in the driveway, pulled to the side of the road about thirty feet behind his truck and parked.

Mick unbuckled his seat belt and turned to face her. "If your theory is correct—and I'm still not saying it is—don't you recognize the risk you're taking in digging around for ?"

 the same thing last night, but she shook ing it. "The email senders can't even Riley's account."

 they were in the station, they know you're hunting for answers."

She shifted in her seat as he'd confirmed her concern. "All anyone who saw me can say for certain is that I'm furious Riley was forced out of his job. Which is true. And I want him to get it back. Which I do."

"Maybe. I still wish you'd leave the investigation to the professionals, but it's clear you're not going to stop. So, I'm asking you to come to me at least if you find new informa-

"Then why did you tell me?"

The heat of his stare on the side of her face made her squirm. "Because I needed someone to acknowledge that Riley could have been set up."

He didn't answer. What had she expected him to say? That they had enough evidence to go right away to the Mount Isabel PD? She couldn't tell him that she'd come to him *because* he was a stranger rather than despite it. That among the people she'd known all her life, she suddenly didn't know whom to trust.

Neither spoke as she turned from the salted and plowed two-lane highway onto the snow-covered side road. Up ahead, his pickup was buried in snow across from a blank area of sky with piles of debris where a house used to stand. She turned around in the driveway, pulled to the side of the road about thirty feet behind his truck and parked.

Mick unbuckled his seat belt and turned to face her. "If your theory is correct—and I'm still not saying it is—don't you recognize the risk you're taking in digging around for answers?"

He'd said nearly the same thing last night, but she shook her head, still rejecting it. "The email senders can't even know that I accessed Riley's account."

"But if they were in the station, they know you're hunting for answers."

She shifted in her seat as he'd confirmed her concern. "All anyone who saw me can say for certain is that I'm furious Riley was forced out of his job. Which is true. And I want him to get it back. Which I do."

"Maybe. I still wish you'd leave the investigation to the professionals, but it's clear you're not going to stop. So, I'm asking you to come to me at least if you find new informa-

"I broke into Riley's email account last night."

"Remind me never to underestimate your sleuthing skills," he said, but sat straighter. "Didn't the police already go over his laptop?"

"It was his web-based account that I accessed."

"What did you find?"

"I never expected my brother to be a quote-of-the-day type."

Mick turned so that his knee came up on the seat. "He was receiving quotes in his emails? What kind of quotes?"

"Strange ones. Mildly menacing when taken individually but more sinister when I looked at them together." She moved her head to push away the shiver that settled at the base of her neck. "But I can't take them as a group since they all came from different email addresses."

"Wouldn't a quote-of-the-day come from *one* source? Like one newsletter?"

Rachel blinked rapidly. She hadn't thought of that. "One was from a guy who's been dead for four hundred years. 'I shall be as secret as the grave.'"

"That's creepy, all on its own."

"It could have been a warning, but it also could have been just a quote." Either way, she couldn't resist shivering.

"But you don't think so." Like earlier, it wasn't a question.

She shook her head. "One of the other quotes wasn't attributed to a speaker at all. 'Curiosity killed the cat.'"

Mick planted his hands on the dash. "You've got to stop asking questions. It's not safe."

At the vehemence in his words, Rachel hit the brake, causing the van to slide. Once she'd managed to correct, she frowned over at him. "What was that for? I didn't share this with you so you could tell me what to do."

tion." He held out his hand, palm up. "A back channel, if you will. I might even be able to help."

She stiffened. "I didn't ask for your help."

"The emails are a start. But we still need to find more information before taking your theory to the police."

"And there is no *we*." She needed to remember that. It would be dangerous for her to rely on him. Or anyone else. "As I said, I didn't ask for anything from you."

"Are you willing to bet Carly's and Carissa's safety on that belief?"

She unbuckled her seat belt and faced him, lifting her chin. That was dirty pool bringing her daughters into it. Still, a tremor started at her core and spread across her shoulders. "I would never put my daughters at risk."

"Aren't you?" He climbed out of the minivan. "You keep telling yourself that, and maybe you'll believe it."

Then he closed the door and stomped away, his boots leaving deep tracks in the snow.

Chapter 6

Rachel was still glaring at Mick's back when he reached his truck, the heavy snow pelting his coat. But no matter how infuriating his suggestion was that she would risk her daughters' safety, he had a point. That Riley needed her help didn't change the fact.

"It's none of your business," she said to him as though he could hear her through the glass and the wind bending the nearby trees.

Mick wasn't paying attention to her, anyway, as he opened the quad cab's rear passenger door and pulled out an ice scraper and snow shovel. Then he went to work, clearing the passenger side first.

After putting the van in gear, Rachel inched forward, then shifted back to Park. Her father never would have forgiven her if she'd left someone stranded on the side of the road. Even someone as frustrating as Mick Prentiss. "We're the Hoffmans. We help people," her dad had always said, though only the men in the family had ever done that. Either way, she couldn't leave Mick until she'd at least made sure that his truck started.

"You're lucky I'm driven by guilt," she said, as she pulled her hat over her ears. According to the dash clock, she had fifty-five minutes before she needed to be back at the school.

Movement farther down the road caught her attention as she reached for the door handle. Another vehicle had turned off the main roadway and was headed in their direction. Something about it felt odd. Though it wasn't unheard of to pass another car on one of the narrow county roads, she couldn't remember the last time she'd seen three vehicles on one at once. Particularly in the middle of a snowstorm.

Mick must have sensed that something was off, too. He'd been working his way around the tailgate, but now he positioned himself behind the truck to observe their visitor without being noticed. Rachel could only sit and wait.

The white SUV rolled at the same steady speed past Mick's truck. The driver didn't pause near the driveway of the demolished house, either. But when it pulled alongside her minivan, the vehicle slowed to a crawl. Rachel pressed her back against the seat. Even with just four feet separating them, she could see nothing more than shadows through the black-tinted windshield and windows. The driver would have had no trouble seeing her.

Her pulse thrashed in her ears, her hands gripping the wheel so tightly that the texture had to make indentions in her palms through her gloves. All she could do was wait for the driver to stop. To roll down the window. To do... *something*.

And then it was over. Just past her rear bumper, the driver gunned the engine and sped away, barely fishtailing with the vehicle's four-wheel drive capability.

She lowered her head and covered her mouth with her hands. Mick threw open her passenger door before the SUV had disappeared completely from her rearview mirror into a backdrop of white.

"My God, Rachel. Are you all right?"

She couldn't stop shaking, let alone find the words to

answer him as her heart tried to pound its way through her coat. Mick climbed back inside and closed the door, but when he reached over to touch her shoulder, she flinched. He withdrew his hand.

"Who...was that?" She continued to stare into her mirror though only snow remained.

"I messed up." He yanked off his hood and shoved his hands back through his hair. "I thought it might be the suspect, coming to survey the damage. Or just a curious neighbor. So, I stayed hidden to get some photos. I didn't realize they'd come there for—"

"Me?" She finished it for him, but she wasn't ready to believe it.

"I didn't know—I should have been—"

"I'm fine."

"Are you?"

He leaned forward, carefully watching her like one of his EMT patients. She folded her gloved hands at the bottom of her rib cage and lifted her gaze to his. If she could make her legs stop trembling, maybe he would even believe her.

"You don't really think he was after me, do you?"

"They didn't slow down near my truck or near the crime scene."

She crossed her arms, needing the firm pressure of that self-hug. "From the road, they probably couldn't tell you were there. And it still could have been the arsonist, just finding me there and wanting to scare me away from his work."

"Could have been."

His skeptical expression suggested that he didn't think so.

"If they had nothing to do with the fire, then how would they know to find me here?"

"Were you watching closely enough to be certain you weren't followed?"

She shook her head and took a deep breath, willing her heart rate to slow. "Well, did you get any pictures?"

Mick opened a photo on his phone and enlarged it to show that the SUV had no license plate. "I guess we could still take it to the police."

"What would I tell them? That someone with no plate and illegal window tinting drove too close to my car?"

He crossed his arms, frowning. "Whether you go to the police or not, you have to take this seriously. Just like the emails, it was a warning."

It felt like more than that, but she decided not to say so. She didn't need for him to push her harder to report the incident. "I'm taking it seriously," she said instead. "Right now I just don't know what I'm up against. Or who's even on my side."

"I am."

Two little words shouldn't have been so powerful, but her throat filled over them. And for just a moment, she didn't feel so alone. "I suppose you're expecting me to ask you to help me now. For the girls' sakes."

The side of his mouth lifted. "Wouldn't be the worst idea you ever had. And it looks like the driver didn't see me, so I can still be that back channel."

He crossed and uncrossed his legs, signaling it still bothered him that he'd failed to be there for her.

"But how can I be sure you won't take everything I tell you and give it to the investigators trying to build a case against Riley?"

"You can't."

She squinted at him, holding her hands wide. "And how

will I know that you won't be one of the people searching for evidence against my brother?"

"You won't."

Then he looked into her eyes, his gaze steady like her dad's as he asked her to trust him when her history told her she shouldn't. She swallowed and nodded.

"Now go start your truck, so I can get back to the school."

His lips lifted. "That's why you didn't drive back earlier. You couldn't bear to leave me stranded. You're a good person."

"Whatever." He was wrong, but she found his words strangely comforting.

"Thanks for the ride."

He hopped out of the van like he had earlier. Only this time he glanced over his shoulder as he returned to his pickup. Then he climbed inside and started the engine.

Rachel waved as she drove past him, her throat as tight as when the driver had been so close to her. She'd just put her trust in someone who would have access to information that could hurt her brother if she were wrong to believe in him. But like with so many other things in her life lately, she didn't have a choice.

Mick shifted in that miserable office chair at the end of his workday, wishing he could stay focused on the binder filled with printed applications in front of him. He flipped through the pages, each packet containing reference letters added at the back and photos of hopeful teen boys and girls paper-clipped to the cover letters.

This was supposed to be a fun part of his job, where he would help select candidates for the Mount Isabel Fire Cadet Program. But today he found their optimism exhausting. Most of them had used the word *hero* under the question: "Why would you like to explore firefighting as a possible career?" Good firefighters never thought of themselves as heroes, and always credited their training rather than their own skills.

These kids wanted to throw on capes and wave in parades, and what they were really looking at was a job with dirty and often grueling work, even if it came with an undeniable adrenaline rush. A calling where the tragedies rubbed some of the shine off victories. Someone needed to tell them the truth, but he wasn't the one for that job.

He shut the binder. In this mindset, he wouldn't give the candidates a fair evaluation, anyway. He returned the book to the organizer on top of the filing cabinet and went back to the stack of files he'd been studying. How was it possible that since mid-January, the Mount Isabel PD had recorded sixteen intentionally set fires of sheds, barns, garages and now a residential home? A normal rate would have been one or two total fires a month, sometimes less, with cooking incidents accounting for nearly half of them.

The fire investigator's reports showed that some of the events were sophisticated, with multiple ignition points. Others were haphazard, as if the suspect had tossed a burning, automotive-grease-covered rag behind him and hoped flames would catch. Nothing seemed to connect them other than an intent to destroy property by fire.

Mick stared down at the reports until the words blurred on the pages and then closed those files as well. He rubbed the back of his neck with both hands, shifted in his chair, then stood and paced.

How was he supposed to keep his mind on even the most recent incident when he couldn't stop thinking about what had happened to Rachel earlier when she'd driven him back to the scene? A tremor slid through him at the memory of watching that white SUV creep past her van, the driver's identity masked behind smoky glass.

"You just left her out there," he muttered, his belly knotting over his failure to recognize the driver's target earlier. He hated even thinking about what could have happened if those inside that vehicle had come with more sinister plans than a warning.

What didn't make sense was why they'd shown up at that location in the first place. They could have followed her from town, as he'd suggested, but was there more to it than that? He hadn't been able to connect the arson fires to each other yet, so why was he searching for ties between them and the situation involving Riley Hoffman and his sister? Still, if he'd learned nothing else from the tragedy at his former station, he understood the peril of failing to trust his instincts. People died when he didn't.

So why had he ignored that sixth sense, and his usually trustworthy brain, when both had warned him to be cautious when Rachel had shown up outside his apartment? He blinked away the answer that came in a snapshot of her dark hair splayed on his pillow, a fantasy he couldn't afford to indulge in over a woman intent on taking unnecessary risks. Yet even on the drive back to his truck, he'd been too caught up in her wildflower scent to notice that the SUV could have been tailing them.

Now he was left with this rib-crushing need to protect a woman from a threat he couldn't clearly define. Worse, she'd only agreed to let him help once he'd brought her kids into it, the strange face-off with the other driver forcing her decision. The manipulation part he understood. His old man might have finally been proud of him over that one. His mom…not so much.

To avoid another walk over the jagged potholes of his past, he grabbed the files off his desk and carried them to the filing cabinet. But as he inserted the key from the set he'd been given at the village offices, something on the lock drew his attention. He bent at the waist to get a closer look. Tiny scratches feathered out from the keyway slot, signaling that someone had picked the lock.

His shoulders lifted toward his ears then lowered again. Though there were more questions floating around the station than even diesel fumes from the engines, he had a good guess who would want to get a look at his files. She'd had the opportunity, too, during those two unsupervised hours the night before in his office. The sheer number of scratches suggested that her burglary attempt had been just that, though.

When a knock came at his office door, he shot a look at the blurry window. He moved back to the desk, already certain he would keep that discovery to himself.

"Come in," he called after the second knock.

Holt Howard stepped inside. "Hey, Chief. Wanted to check in before you go."

Mick waved him in and gestured to his guest chairs. He didn't care if the probie firefighter had only been pleasant to him to get in good with the new chief, who might affect his future with the department. Being an outsider could get lonely, and he appreciated the company.

"Saw your truck in the parking lot. Guess you found someone to take you to pick it up. I was going to offer…"

"Thanks. Sampson had an appointment in town and dropped me off before heading home."

Mick cringed over his choice of fictional chauffeurs.

The senior firefighter had barely spoken to him before shift change. While he hoped the probie wouldn't check out his story, he should have been more concerned with how easily he lied. This was becoming a habit.

"Anything else?"

Holt stared at his hands. "I wanted to see how *your* first day went."

Though the younger man didn't get more specific, they both knew what he meant. The crew had heard about the tragedy back in Chicago. It was the chief's job, or the captain's if he wasn't around, to debrief crew members after a call, allowing them to decompress. That someone with as little seniority as Holt had performed the task for Mick instead spoke loads about his fitness for this leadership role.

"It was a great first day." He chuckled, hoping the young man would do the same. "Nothing like getting to use our training from Day One."

The firefighter's eyes narrowed, and then he shrugged. Though Holt probably hadn't heard the whole story about what happened at his former station, Mick decided to keep it that way. He had no way of knowing where the man's true allegiances stood. Like Rachel, he couldn't differentiate friend from enemy.

"Going to get a drink to celebrate your first day?" Holt indicated the five o'clock hour on the same wall clock that Rachel had pointed to not twenty-four hours before. "We have some good watering holes around here."

"Nah. Haven't even bought groceries yet, and I need to get a few things for my apartment before stores close. Looks like a squatter has taken over."

"What about all your stuff back in Chicago?"

"In storage. For now."

He didn't have to say it louder for the other man to understand that this wasn't a long-term gig for him. After the arson suspect or suspects were apprehended and the investigation of Riley Hoffman was completed, an outsider like him would no longer be needed. He could get back to Illinois and retire from public service. This time for good.

"You might find that this place grows on you," Holt said as he headed out the door. "The people, too."

After the lukewarm welcome he'd received so far, Mick would believe that when he saw it.

Chapter 7

Rachel peeked out from between her blind slats for the third time in twenty minutes and sighed. For the past two days she'd been telling herself that keeping them closed would make her feel safer. That only kept her wondering what lurked on the other side of the glass.

She scanned the street through the narrow opening. Like in both of her prior checks, mostly darkness stared back at her, along with the same shadows from other houses' outdoor lights on piles of shoveled snow. She'd kept her own light turned off so she could see outside.

"What are you looking for, Mommy?"

Startled by the sound, Rachel released the slat, and the whole collection of them slammed against the window. Carissa stared up at her, wearing her favorite nightgown, a pre-transformation Cinderella on the front. Carly, whose two-piece pajamas announced her preference for sword-bearing Mulan, reached to lift the blind herself.

"Leave it—" Rachel stopped herself and tried again. "I mean…we should keep them closed at night, okay?"

"What's out there?" Carly asked, her brows drawn together.

If only Rachel knew.

She still wasn't sure what the strange interaction with

that driver had meant, and it felt as if she'd been holding her breath ever since. The muscles in her arms and legs ached from the constant flex of waiting. For what? Or *whom*?

"Why aren't you two watching your movie?" She indicated the television where another princess flitted through an adventure on the screen, always remaining perfectly styled and coiffed. "Unless you just want to skip it and go to bed."

The twins skittered back to the couch and snuggled together under a knitted throw. No early bed for them. Or any sleep for her. At least she still had more work to do tonight as insomnia was becoming her new thing.

To avoid making the girls more curious, she settled between them, and they found their usual spots draped over her. As the princess twirled on the screen, she even took a moment to rest her eyes.

But her lids shot open when someone rapped on the door. She leaped up from the cushions in what felt like a single, chaotic move. Giggles erupted as the twins, who'd been displaced by her leap, ran for the door.

"Girls, stop."

She gave them an apologetic look when they turned back to her with wide eyes. Even if she couldn't avoid panicking herself, she didn't want to frighten them.

"I'll get it." She forced a smile, hoping they couldn't see straight through her.

In the innocent world her children had known before, people could open doors without worrying who might be on the outside. How could she explain to them that they no longer lived in that snow globe, shielded by plexiglass? Maybe they never had. Gesturing for the girls to move behind her, she stepped to the door.

"Who is it?" She couldn't get a good look through the peephole.

"Mick," came a low grumble through the wood.

Rachel blinked several times, her chest tightening. Still, she flipped the bolt, unchained the second lock and opened the door a crack. The same hooded man from two days before stood on her porch in a mixture of light and shadows since her duplex neighbors had turned on their porch lamp.

"What are you doing here?"

She yanked him inside and closed the door before he could answer her question.

"What's wrong?" he asked instead. "Are you okay? Did you see the SUV again?"

He rested his hands on her shoulders and searched her eyes, looking worried enough for the both of them.

Rachel took a step back from his touch and from her own strange impulse to lean in and let him hold her. She'd only agreed to involve him in her unauthorized investigation for the sake of her children. It could have nothing to do with her. She couldn't let it.

Tucking her chin, she caught sight of her pastel flannel pajama pants and the loose T-shirt she'd paired with it, braless. She crossed her arms to cover her chest, her face hot. Mick's gaze darted from her left ear to her right, avoiding looking lower. He hadn't missed a thing.

"It's Mr. Prentiss," Carissa called out.

Mick blinked and glanced down at her daughters as though he'd forgotten they would be there as well.

"Hi, girls. You can call me Mick. Mr. Prentiss is my… uh…father."

The flick of his gaze to the TV screen suggested there was more to that story, but since the twins were already bouncing at their guest's feet and helping him remove his coat, Rachel tucked away the thought. "Then make that *Mr.* Mick."

"Mommy was watching for you out the window," Carly said.

Her cheeks burning, Rachel shot a look at Mick and caught him watching her. That only made it worse.

"Want to watch a movie with us?" Carissa pointed to the TV.

Both girls folded their hands and looked up to him with pleading eyes. Rachel would have to warn them to be more guarded around people they didn't know well. Especially now. And while she was at it, she needed to caution herself.

"Sure," he said. "But may I speak to your mom for a few minutes first?"

The twins nodded and hurried back to their couch.

With her arms still crossed over her chest, Rachel reached for the jacket Mick had draped over his arm and hung it on the coat rack. She wasn't encouraging him to stay, she decided. Just being polite. He pushed his hood back but kept the sweatshirt zipped.

"You didn't answer my question," she said.

"I've been meaning to check in on you since the other day."

"How did you know where I live?" She raised her hand. "Scratch that. I was listed as my brother's emergency contact in his personnel file."

"*Ding. Ding. Ding.* I didn't even need the small-town information network for that one."

"Using his records to find me wasn't exactly ethical."

"I'm seeing a few gray areas," he said with a shrug. "Including not contacting the police after the incident near the fire scene."

"Besides only having a scary vibe to report, how would

you have explained why you asked *me* to take you to pick up your truck? The sister of the person you replaced wouldn't be most new chiefs' first choice."

His lips formed an O and then closed altogether. He pointed to the front window. "But if you were watching for people through the blinds, as one of your girls mentioned, then you're really *not* okay. Did something else happen?"

"That was Carly." She pointed to the twin on the far side of the sofa. "And other than seeing white SUVs everywhere the past two days—even one regularly in the school pickup line—nothing new to report."

"I've been seeing a bunch of them, too." He unzipped his sweatshirt, revealing a navy firefighter T-shirt, this time with the word *Chicago* joining the Maltese cross. "Can't anyone buy a blue vehicle like mine?"

"Speaking of your pickup, where'd you park?" She peeked out the blinds again, trying to make out a truck from among the snow-covered SUVs and sedans lining the curb. "You were right. We shouldn't be seen together."

"Left it at the apartment. I've decided I like walking."

After placing his boots on the mat, he sidled next to her, too close, and bent to peek through the same slat. She let it fall against the window.

"I thought maybe you could show me the strange emails you found."

He pointed to the kitchen table where Rachel's laptop rested in the dark, over-the-ear headphones positioned on its closed lid. She shook her head.

"I already told you about them."

"At least let me look for myself. Especially since I didn't tell the investigators about the emails or the SUV."

"Why didn't you?"

He shrugged as though the decision hadn't sat well with him, and then his gaze lifted, trapping hers in its intensity.

"Maybe I was trying to get you to trust me."

The connection lingered until she had to look away, her mouth dry. She knew better than to trust anyone lately, so why was she so tempted to rely on the man, who remained one of the biggest obstacles for her brother ever to get his life back?

"All right. I'll show you, but I don't think you'll find anything new."

"Then let's look."

Rachel shook her head. "First things first."

"What do you mean?"

With her thumb, she gestured to the television. "I believe you promised to watch a riveting princess story with two young ladies, who have—" she paused to glance at her watch "—fifteen whole minutes until bedtime."

Rachel waited, expecting him to suddenly remember something else he needed to attend to at the station. Other than her father and brother, she was used to being disappointed by men.

"Wouldn't want to forget that date," he said.

Mick padded over to the couch and settled between the girls. He spread the throw over their three laps as though they watched animated royalty together twice weekly. "Okay, who's going to tell me what I missed?"

Rachel couldn't help but stare as the girls snuggled up to him, talking over each other to provide a play-by-play of the story. She hadn't realized she'd given Mick a test until he'd aced it, pointing out the characters on the screen and asking more questions.

During a pause, Mick glanced over at her. "Aren't you going to join us?"

"Yeah, Mom." Carly waved her over. "Come watch with us."

"I'll be just a minute."

She hurried upstairs and put on a bra under her pajama top. Then, for good measure, she zipped on her University of Michigan hoodie. When she returned and slid into the empty spot near the arm of the couch, Carissa lifted the corner of the blanket. Rachel shook her head. As if she weren't already too warm in the sweater, the image in her head of the four of them cuddled together—like a family—made her long for a breeze from the ceiling fan above them. The one the landlord still hadn't fixed.

Mick pretended to be watching the movie instead of her, but the side of his mouth lifted in one of his annoying grins.

"You almost missed the best part, Mommy," Carissa said.

"I like the part where the hero comes to the rescue, too." Mick slid a glance Rachel's way, still smiling.

"I'm sure you do." Her frown did nothing to change his expression. "But not all princesses need to be rescued. Ariel saves Prince Eric from drowning. And Rapunzel heals Flynn with her magic hair and, later, with her tears."

Rachel would have kept on listing if Mick's grin hadn't turned to a chuckle. She crossed her arms and narrowed her eyes.

"Drowning? Magic hair? What are you talking about?"

"Strong heroines. Forget it." Guys like him probably would never understand the type of competent women she was encouraging her daughters to be. She turned back to the screen in time to see Prince Phillip give Princess Aurora what must have been one doozy of a kiss to awaken her from a coma. Just her luck that her daughters had chosen *Sleeping Beauty* with the most passive heroine ever.

She peeked over to find Mick watching her again, still smiling.

"It's bedtime, girls."

After a chorus of whines, the twins trailed behind her toward the stairs. At the landing, she turned back to Mick, who sat on the sofa, the blanket still on his lap.

"How about I just call you tomorrow? We can look at the stuff on the computer then." Since she had no intention of really phoning, she didn't worry about the rest.

"I'll wait."

"Really. It's late. And I have a lot of computer work to catch up on, so…" She hoped he would take the hint this time, even if she was the one reneging on the plan.

"Still, I think I'll wait."

Her jaw flexed at his closed-lipped smile. Who did he think he was, making this so hard on her? But she was stuck. The girls would think she was a worse villain than the evil Maleficent in the movie they'd just watched if she tossed their cool new friend out the door.

"Fine. Then stay." She turned back to the twins. "Girls, tell Mr. Mick good-night."

She ushered the girls upstairs for teeth brushing and chose not to rush with bedtime reading. If he got sick of waiting, he knew where the door was and how to use it. She hated to admit that a small part of her—unfortunately more Aurora than Rapunzel—hoped he would stay.

Chapter 8

Mick flipped the wall switch to light the rickety chandelier and rested in the one chair at Rachel's table that offered a good view of the staircase. Then he folded his hands and waited. And waited.

By the time the stairs creaked, he'd already convinced himself she would stay up there until he shut off the lights and headed back to his apartment. Rachel stopped at the bottom of the stairs. She still wore those soft-looking pj's, along with the unwelcome sweatshirt and bra that obscured the enjoyable silhouette from when he'd first arrived.

With folded arms, she watched him from across the room, tapping the tip of one fuzzy slipper with the toe of the other in a muffled beat. Then she walked over and gripped the back of the chair where her closed laptop rested.

"What was that about earlier? What did you mean, 'I'll wait'?"

He glanced down at the table and back up again to state the obvious that he'd done just as he'd promised. "I was going to ask *you* about your sudden change of plans. Why were you trying to back out of showing me the emails?"

She shook her head as though even she wasn't sure.

"Let's get this over with, so you can go home, and I can get to bed."

"Thought you had so much computer work to catch up on."

She met his smirk with a scowl. "I do."

Rachel slid into the spot in front of her laptop. Just like in his office and the other day in the minivan, her floral scent settled around him. Soothing and enticing. He couldn't help but draw in that aroma in a long, deep breath. That only forced him to exhale as hard as he could without making her think he was about to pass out.

Even if there hadn't been warnings in those emails nor a possible threat from that SUV driver the other day, he had to recognize the danger of getting too close to the former fire chief's sister. To his reputation, sure. But maybe to someone in as vulnerable a place as he was as well.

While Rachel clicked on a browser and navigated to a web-based email service, Mick did his own search for a safe topic.

"Is that the site of the *hacking*?"

"Do you want to see the emails or not?" She frowned at the screen while she typed in credentials. After a few seconds, an inbox appeared. "And figuring out a password isn't the same thing as 'hacking.'"

"Isn't it, though?" When she didn't answer, he added, "You're lucky your brother didn't have two-factor authentication turned on, or he would've received the code on his cell, and it wouldn't have let you in, even with a password."

She scrolled through the long list. "He doesn't have access to his cell at all at the center. Just these patient phones that during certain hours he's allowed to use to call loved ones. If he chooses to."

Though Mick was tempted to ask her about the last

part, he decided to stay on topic. "If he knew you wanted it, would he have given you the password?"

Rachel didn't answer right away. When she did, it was with her body language, shoulders curling forward and chin dipping to her chest. She splayed her fingers over the keys, not pressing any of them.

"He hasn't called me in more than a week. But when he did call, he said I should stop asking questions about things that aren't any of my business. How can clearing my brother's name, and finding out the truth about Dad's death for that matter, *not* be my business?"

Though Mick had to agree with her brother on some of that, Rachel had a point. She might have been missing the possibility that Riley had something to hide as well. Maybe even something that could prove he'd embezzled funds from the department.

"He was probably just trying to keep you safe," he said, and then rubbed the back of his neck. If his need to reassure Rachel wasn't more proof that he should back several steps away from her, then he couldn't read a caution sign.

"Anyway, sounds like you listened to him about as much as you listened to me." As usual, when he couldn't think of anything else to say, he went for a laugh.

"I don't like to be told what to do. By *anybody*."

He expected her to pin him with her stare then to reinforce that she was talking about him, but she grabbed the external mouse and started scrolling through the packed inbox instead.

"You don't find it easy to trust anyone, either."

This time she jerked her head to look at him, her hands gripping the edge of the table on either side of the laptop. "What do you mean by that?"

He blinked, as surprised by his question as her reaction to it. "I mean...someone must have done *something*—"

"You might as well just say it. 'Some dude must've really done a number on you.'"

"I didn't say—" Mick stopped himself because he'd nearly said something close to that. But since he had a shovel, he couldn't resist digging deeper with it. "I did notice that Carly and Carissa's dad isn't around, so..."

"You're expecting me to fill in the blanks, right?" She didn't wait for his answer before ticking off on her fingers. "Let me see... My mom died in a car accident when I was nine. My dad took his life last August. I'm the reason for my brother's relapse and his stint in rehab. Is that enough?"

He squirmed with the reality that he wanted to know more. But how could he admit that he was still curious about the twins' father when she'd just shared tragic details that eclipsed anything some jerk boyfriend could have done? He held up his hands in surrender.

"Sorry. It's none of my business." Even if he couldn't help but wonder what kind of idiot could have left Rachel Hoffman. Had he forgotten that one of the messages she'd found warned about what curiosity did to cats?

"Are those wounds big enough for you?" she pressed.

"I shouldn't have asked."

"No, you shouldn't have."

"Sorry about your mom, though," Mick said, after an awkward pause. His throat filled over the lost little girl, forced to bury her mother when she wasn't much older than the twins. "I didn't know."

"Angelita Flores Hoffman. I look like her in pictures, but her face is pretty blurry in my memories."

She turned back to the email box, dismissing him and his questions. As tempting as it was to tell her that she couldn't be responsible for another person's relapse, he chose to let that one drop. She wouldn't believe him, anyway.

Finally, she stopped on a message preview and clicked to open it. "Here. This is what you came to see."

She was wrong about that. He'd come to check on her, just like he'd said. The girls, too, but mostly her. Grateful for the distraction, he scooted closer to read the email. She angled the laptop to show him the quotes she'd mentioned the other day.

"Here's another one from Miguel de Cervantes, that one who wrote about secrets and graves." She pointed to the screen. "'Let every man mind his own business.'"

"That doesn't sound scary. In fact, it's good advice."

"What about this one?" Rachel scrolled down the page and read again. "'It is not every question that deserves an answer.' That's Publilius Syrus from the first century BCE."

"Still not making me tremble. If you found just that quote, would you have mentioned the emails to me at all?"

"Well, this one might give you shivers. I didn't see it before." She slid the laptop to him.

"Seeing that death, a necessary end, will come when it will come."—William Shakespeare (1564-1616)

"Even that one's not so bad." But this time he shifted his feet under the table. Like before, the warnings were vague, their threat still unformed. "Anyway, that's just *Julius Caesar*."

She shot a look at him. "How do you know that?"

"Are you saying a firefighter can't read a book? Or a play?" He shook his finger at her but couldn't help grinning. "Before you answer, remember you're from a firefighter family."

"I only meant I'm surprised you chose that one."

He rolled his eyes, not buying it. "High school literature. Extra credit project," he explained, anyway. "I know. It was so long ago that I shouldn't be able to remember it."

She opened a spiral notebook to a page with several notes on it. Beneath the others, she wrote down the sender's email address, the date and the quote. "You talk about yourself like you're a few breaths away from old age."

"Maybe I am." He pointed to her long list of email addresses.

"Either your brother signed up for a quote club with a bunch of different word fanatics, or one person's been sending messages from multiple addresses. Look at that one." He pointed to the screen, this time unable to keep himself from shivering. "Death is definitely a theme."

"It hath been often said, that it is not death, but dying which is terrible."—Henry Fielding (1707-1754)

"They're all warnings, but Riley wasn't listening."

She appeared to have said those words to herself, ironic since she, too, had chosen to ignore the messages of caution.

"There are so many of them," she said, as she jotted down another email address. "I need to start a spreadsheet."

Somehow, Mick had to convince her to avoid following her brother's example and heed the warnings.

"I have lousy taste in men."

Mick squinted at her, the comment making no sense. But as she sat taller, her gaze locked on her notebook as though her own words had surprised her, he recognized that she'd referred to his earlier question. Details he still craved, whether he should have asked or not.

"What are you saying?" he prompted after too many seconds ticked by.

"You asked about the girls' father. There's your answer."

It was hardly a *complete* one, but she didn't appear likely to share more.

"A lot of women have that problem. Just ask my ex-wife." Mick's breath hitched. She might have been surprised by her confession, but his had downright shocked him. He hadn't talked about *her* with anyone since— Well, since...

When Rachel clicked the laptop closed, Mick pushed back from the table and stood. Even if he wasn't an expert on Miss Manners's rules, he could tell when a meeting was over.

She came to her feet as well but didn't sprint over to the coat-tree for his jacket. He headed that way himself.

"Thanks for showing me the messages. If you see anything else—"

"You're kidding, right?"

Mick stopped just as he'd pulled his coat off the hook. "What do you mean?"

"You're going to hint at all that juiciness and then *leave*?"

He opened and closed his mouth, studying her. She had to realize that he wasn't the only one who'd offered a tantalizing tidbit that warranted more discussion. "I'm not sure what you're saying here."

"You've just admitted that you were a lousy guy. At least that your ex thought so. I'm sure there's a story there."

"I was talking about the guy she was having the affair

with." His throat tightened. Why couldn't he just shut up and head back out into the snow? Did he want her to know his whole pitiful story?

Rachel gestured to the chair where he'd been seated before and headed into the kitchen. From the other room she called, "I think this conversation calls for wine."

Mick bypassed the chair and followed her but stopped in the doorway. At the counter, Rachel rustled in a drawer and produced a corkscrew. Then she reached for a bottle of red on the countertop.

His chest tightened the way it always did lately when he allowed himself to think about those subjects where innocence and guilt were anything but clear. "We don't need to talk about all of that. And, anyway, you've already said you're behind on your work."

"I'll catch up tomorrow." She used the tip of the corkscrew to slice the foil seal around the bottle. "I could use the distraction."

"Then could you make it tea instead? At least for me. I don't drink."

"Sorry. I didn't know." She pushed the bottle back against the wall. "That's why you said all those things about alcohol the night I met you."

"I'm not—"

"I usually don't— Well, anyway. Do you like Earl Grey? Or I also have herbal tea. I rarely drink that myself since I need caffeine to work at night."

"Anything's fine," he said to stop her nervous babbling.

She flitted back and forth, flipping on an electric kettle and grabbing bags of regular black tea and mugs. Eventually, she slid past him, sideways so they wouldn't brush, and set a sugar bowl, spoons and napkins on the table.

"Rachel," he said, as she scooted past him again. "Like I started to say, I'm *not* an alcoholic. It's my dad."

She stepped back to the kettle just as it started beeping. Soon she followed him to the table, carrying two steaming mugs.

"Guess there are a lot of things I don't know about you," she said, as he took his first sip.

Mick closed his eyes, his tongue burning, the too-hot liquid singeing all the way down. There were a lot of things she didn't know about him, too, but she would probably like him a whole lot less when she learned more.

Chapter 9

"Why don't we start with the affair?"

Rachel pasted on a grin but rubbed her sweaty palms on her pajama bottoms as Mick coughed into his napkin. Though his story was no funnier than hers, it was easier to make light of the heavy information he'd dumped on her dining room table than to ask herself why she'd invited him to stay longer. And why she needed to hear more.

Wasn't it bad enough that she'd agreed to involve him in her search? She had plenty of her own problems without nosing into his. Still, no matter how reluctant she was to admit she could have anything in common with the interloper working Riley's job, she couldn't deny that Mick's life had been no more of a cakewalk than hers. Unless the batter was laced with glass.

"I guess that's one way to dive into it," he said with a tight chuckle.

"I'm a rip-the-bandage-off kind of girl."

"Remind me not to let you anywhere near the hospital if I'm injured at work."

Gooseflesh surprised her by peppering her arms. As a family member of first responders, she'd hated the backpack of borrowed trouble she'd always carried, dreading the call that could come. Why was she expanding those pesky worries to include Mick?

"We can start with something else if you prefer," she said, continuing the joke that had fallen flat. "Like your parents—"

"No. The affair's fine. Well, not *fine*." He closed his eyes and shook his head before opening them again. "The truth is, I'm not exactly blameless there."

"You said she had an affair. Did you force your wife to sleep with someone else?" Her insides tightened as she waited for a possible confession that he'd been a cheater, too. "Wait. Do I *want* to hear this?"

Instead of chuckling, as she'd hoped he would, Mick sighed, his shoulders lowering.

"My story's not unique. I left Tina alone a lot when I was working. Too much."

Tina. The name tasted sour on her tongue, her resentment immediate.

"It happens. We sometimes forget what's important in life." Her need to excuse Mick surprised her, but she'd forgotten some of those things herself.

"She always said I was married to my crew instead of to her."

"Was she right?"

"I did spend more time worrying about their problems than hers. Or even ours. Can't blame her for resenting that."

"No one would." The cheating part was a whole other story.

"That's why I never understood why she slept with one of my guys."

Rachel pushed back her chair, nearly tipping it. "Wait. She was involved with one of your crew members?"

"It gets worse."

How it could, she wasn't sure, but she braced herself for it, her hands slipping beneath the table to grip the sides of her chair.

"Gavin Wheeler—we called him 'Wheels'—was one of *them*."

"Them?" She shook her head, his meaning escaping her. *Called? Was?* The skin on her hands tingled as the pieces fell into place. "Are you saying…?"

"Wheels was one of the firefighters our department lost. Him and Miguel Suárez. Both of them were good out on a call. Only one, it turned out, was also a stand-up guy."

Though Rachel was tempted to point out that the firefighter hadn't been alone in that bed, she kept that observation to herself.

"I'm so sorry," she said instead. "That had to make a terrible situation worse. You couldn't even be angry, though you had every right to be."

"And a ten-year marriage slid down the drain."

"Ten years?" She couldn't imagine that amount of time in a relationship since hers had always been calculated in months. And she hadn't bothered with dating at all in a long string of those. "Any kids?"

"Never got around to it. Timing was never right."

The image of Mick, sandwiched between Carly and Carissa, stole into her thoughts then. So sweet. It was easy to picture him holding his own child, too, but she blinked away the impossible picture that replaced it. One with two babies in his arms. *Her twins*.

"I can't imagine," she blurted and then rubbed her forearms to stop the chill.

"Not having kids?"

"No. The fire. And all the other— Wait." Rachel tilted

her head and studied him. "Did you find out about the affair before or after the fire?"

"A few days before. I never had the chance to call him on it, man-to-man."

"Never?" She waited for him to squirm.

"No, it wasn't intentional. I'd compartmentalized the information from my personal life like I was trained to do, but I *was* command on the scene, so I did send the two firefighters into that building." He stared down at his hand as he brushed his finger along the scarred wood. "Neither came out."

A lump swelled in Rachel's throat over the many layers of that tragedy. "You were also cleared of any wrongdoing. Said so yourself."

"I guess I did."

His gaze caught hers and held, making her insides do an uncomfortable flip. Though they'd shared a similar conversation in his office two days before, she hadn't defended him then. What had changed, causing her to take his side?

"I don't need your pity," he said.

"Good because I'm not offering any."

She needed to stop interrogating him, but her last question slipped out before she could stop it. "Now that the competition is…well…gone, do you think you'll get back together?"

"The divorce was final last month. It's over."

The certainty in his words provided no room for doubt. His regrets were harder to gauge. She knew his answer shouldn't have mattered to her, either, but for some reason, it did.

"I'm glad you have a chance for a new start here in town."

Aware that her words sounded as empty as the condolences mourners offered at her father's funeral, she pushed back her chair and stood. The sooner she sent him home, the sooner she could reset her thoughts about him and reclaim a more acceptable distance.

"Your turn."

"What do you mean?" Since she already knew the answer to that, she shot a look at the front door, wishing for escape.

"I showed you mine, so…you know. Fair is fair." He smiled for the first time since she'd asked him to stay for tea.

"I never agreed to spill my guts."

"But you did say you have lousy taste in men. That begs for examples. Thought you were all about tearing off bandages. Just one quick rip…"

What he didn't know was that the tear would probably come with a chunk of hair and probably some skin. He waved her back to her seat.

"Come on. It doesn't hurt."

"Speak for yourself." She settled into the chair, reopening the laptop to have something to do with her hands. "My relationship history was an even bigger cliché than your divorce."

"I wouldn't think there was anything unoriginal about you."

"I was the rebellious daughter of an overprotective dad, so I claimed my independence by trying to destroy my life."

"Wait. I might have heard this one."

She crossed her arms. "Do you want me to tell it or not?"

"Sorry." He moved his hand in a circular motion for her to continue.

"Tyler Lawton was just one photo in my slideshow of losers, but he was a standout."

"It's always good to go for the best."

As much as she wanted to be annoyed with him, her lips betrayed her by curving. He was trying to make this easier on her, and she couldn't help but be grateful.

"We took off on an adventure to Indiana, planning to build a life on fairy tales and convenience-store hot dogs. And then I got pregnant."

Instead of speaking, he crossed his arms, his jaw clenched, as though already furious over what she was about to tell him. She wasn't sure what to make of that.

"At first, Tyler was almost on board with the kid idea. But when we received the news at the women's clinic that we were having twins, it must have been too much for him. When I woke up the next morning in the crappy little motor lodge where we'd been living, he was gone."

"What an asshole," he said through clenched teeth.

"He left a note that said he had someone else. More than one, in fact."

"Do you think that was true?"

"I still don't know. Not that it mattered."

"No, *he* didn't matter."

Though he hadn't said he only cared about what happened to her and the girls, warmth spread in her chest, anyway. For one sneaky moment, she let it unfurl.

"Did you go home then?"

"You might have noticed that I'm stubborn." She waited for his nod. "But after my clothes didn't fit, and I got sick of not being able to scrounge up money for pesky things like food or shelter, I called Riley. Not Dad. Soon I was on a bus headed home to face my father's disappointment."

"And his support, right?"

That same angry expression he'd directed at her ex-boyfriend was back, but this time she felt compelled to defend the target.

"Dad came around, particularly after the girls were born. They wrapped him around their tiny fingers." She paused, smiling at the memory. "I don't know what I would've done without him and Riley for those first few years. But it was important to me to finish my degree, get my own place and support the twins on my own."

"You had something to prove."

"I guess. But why did you say it like that?"

"Because you and I have a lot in common," he said, chuckling. "I was a disappointment to my family, too."

"You mean because of the divorce?"

"Before that. I dropped out as a second-year law student at Loyola to become a firefighter. My dad will never forgive me for it. I was supposed to be a third-generation attorney at Prentiss Law."

Rachel's arms crossed. "Anyone who thinks being a first responder isn't a higher calling is just plain wrong. There's more honor in that than for some dumb lawyer, who—"

"You don't have to say it. I've heard all the jokes. Told most of them."

"Still, what you're suggesting isn't the same thing at all."

"Tell that to my dad."

He was going for a laugh this time, but she wasn't biting.

"You chose a different career. You didn't desert your family when they needed you, return with two kids and still want nothing but to get out again."

She scanned the living room she'd been so proud of, the sofa cover looking dingy, the bookshelves shouting secondhand. "What I wouldn't give now for a few more days of living with Dad and Riley, even with whiskers in the sink and Dad's two chicken recipes. Dry and drier."

Her throat thickened as she caught Mick watching her, his eyes filled with compassion. Normally, she would have been offended by a reaction like his, reading pity into it, but she sensed that he could understand at least some of her regrets.

"I refused to believe it at first, you know. That Dad died by suicide. I knew he kept a rifle to handle occasional pests. But I couldn't wrap my head around the idea that—" She shook her head over a reality that would never make sense to her. "Even after the county medical examiner put it in her report, I resisted."

She brushed her fingers over the tabletop, watching her bare nails catch the light. "I didn't even know he was sad."

"Some people are good at hiding what they're going through."

The softness in Mick's eyes showed he knew something about masking pain.

"Because I couldn't accept it, I convinced Riley to take a closer look into Dad's death, even though he was the one who found his body. I needed answers. Why did he do it? Why didn't he come to us? If I'd known that Riley was in such a vulnerable place himself, I wouldn't have asked. His setback with his addiction is on me. It's *all* my fault."

"No, Rachel. You've said that before, but it isn't."

"You don't know—"

She stopped as Mick's hand came to rest across hers, his fingers and thumb curling over her skin. Her heart pounded so hard as she stared at their point of contact that Mick had to feel it. She knew she should pull away. But his touch was warm. Comforting. She couldn't resist lingering a little longer.

"I do know." He squeezed her hand and didn't let go. "You didn't force your brother to take a drink. His own demons suggested that to him. And kept suggesting."

With her eyes closed, she shook her head, rejecting his words, refusing to be let off the hook. "But I shouldn't have asked him—"

"He could have said no. He chose to look for answers just as he was the one who lost his daily battle and took that first drink. You know in your heart you weren't responsible for your dad's death, either. He lost a different battle. You just weren't aware he was fighting it."

"But I *should* have known." Rachel yanked her hand back, immediately feeling the loss in warmth. "For both of them."

The tears surprised her by coming hot and fast, her cheeks wet before she could pivot and deflect as she usually did. Her loss was almost seven months old, and yet it felt brand-new. She turned her head away and brushed at the dampness in rapid strokes.

"Please hear me, Rachel. It's not your fault."

For several seconds, neither spoke, the silence so complete that she swore she could hear her heartbeat. Maybe even his. He seemed to be nearer to her, too. So close that his warm breath tickled the back of her ear. Unable to resist any longer, she turned her head. Mick had scooted to the edge of his chair and angled his neck so that only a few inches separated them.

"Not your fault," he said again.

Rachel's breath hitched as Mick lifted his hand toward her face. She didn't deserve the comfort or the absolution, but her heart pounded as she waited for his touch.

His fingers made the first contact, cupping her chin, while he reached with his thumb to brush the most recent tears from her cheek. She pressed into his fingertips, absorbing the warmth, certain that she'd been frozen for too long.

"Not your fault," he repeated once more, this time a whisper.

He leaned even closer. She drew in a breath, held herself still and waited. Instead of her lips that already tingled in anticipation, Mick dropped a kiss on her forehead as he might have on one of the twins if he knew them better. She tucked her chin and slowly exhaled, hoping to hide her disappointment. He didn't seem to notice as he pressed his mouth to the tip of her nose, her cheekbone and then that sensitive spot just in front of her ear.

When his lips hovered over hers, so close that his breath feathered past that area of sensitized skin without granting relief, she couldn't hold back any longer. She grabbed the sides of his stubbly face and pulled him to her, cracking that last, invisible barrier between them.

Mick's lips crushed hers as he accepted her invitation with far less finesse than he'd probably planned. She didn't care. He tasted of danger and vulnerability and experience. Not bothering with preliminaries, he slanted his mouth over hers and took the kiss deep the moment she opened for him, his plundering both artistry and instinct.

She couldn't get enough. Couldn't feel enough. Though his hands had moved no farther south than her shoulders, she could feel his touch everywhere as warmth tightened, lifted and pooled in her most feminine places. It had been so long since she'd allowed herself to be anything other than a daughter, sister and mother, and now she closed her eyes, reveling in a moment of being simply a woman.

At some point, he must have drawn her to her feet and

unzipped her sweatshirt—or maybe she'd yanked him to her and pulled the tab herself—but suddenly she found herself clinging to him, his hands low on her back and sinking fast. She couldn't resist lifting on her tiptoes in her slippers and wiggling until she could fit herself to him, her pajama pants yielding easily and disguising little. She craved more pressure. More heat. More of everything.

And then it stopped.

She blinked open her eyes, the loss of sensation as startling as the red and blue dots that combined with the facets of light the chandelier cast on the walls and ceiling. What was she doing? What were they—

Mick's hands were on her upper arms now as he set her back from him as though redirecting a child. Then he let go completely, crossing his arms over the front of his jeans as though that would hide a statement already made. His eyes were dazed, his lids hooded, as he looked at everything in the room *except* her.

"I'm sorry," he said. "I don't know what I was thinking. I mean… I shouldn't have—"

Finally, he gave up trying to explain, lifted his shoulders and let them drop. He wasn't the only one who shouldn't have. She had even more to regret. He'd offered her a Get-Out-of-Blame-Free card, and she'd practically thrown him down on the table for gratitude sex. Worse, she'd nearly done it right in her living room without thinking of her daughters, who could have come downstairs at any moment, needing another drink or a parent to slay monsters in the dark.

"It's fine. Really." For something to do with her nervous hands, she reached down and pulled the tab on her zipper to her throat.

"No, it's not," he said after several seconds. "It's just… well…it's just not a great idea."

"Can we dispense with your bad rendition of 'It's not you, it's me'? It was a mistake. Not to be repeated. Ever."

Rachel forced a smile, trying to push away the sting of his rejection. She wasn't supposed to want him, either. Wasn't supposed to feel a heaviness and a void in places that hadn't seen any action for a long, long time.

She pointed to the two empty mugs on the table. "We'll blame it on the…tea. The high-octane stuff will get you every time."

Mick's tongue darted out to wet lips she'd recently tasted for herself, flavors and sensations she needed to forget right away if she had any sense.

"Maybe I should stick with herbal next time," he said, his smile tight.

Next time? She took a shallow breath. "This collaboration was a mistake, too. I don't need anybody—"

"Let's not go through that again. We'll work together as planned so we can ensure that the girls are safe. Only we'll have some strict ground rules. No being seen together in public, of course. But also no risky excursions without giving the other a heads-up."

He coughed into his elbow. "And no more *tea* sessions after the twins have gone to bed."

Rachel had meant to argue, but she found herself nodding at his reasonable suggestions, even if she'd never be able to think of "tea sessions" as opportunities for gossip again.

"Since we're setting rules, then no more showing up unannounced. Either of us," she added, when he pointed her way. "We text first. And no more using my front door, you know, just to be safe."

She held out her hand to shake on their agreement, but when he stared down at her fingers instead of gripping them, she lowered her arm.

"And you'll call if you see any white SUVs? At least any that seem out of place?"

"Of course, I will."

Mick tilted his head and studied her as though he wasn't sure whether he could believe her. After all the secrets she'd shared with him earlier, his doubt stung more than his rejection.

"I will," she repeated, lifting her chin.

She crossed to the coat-tree, collected his jacket and then pressed it into his arms.

"Thanks for showing me the emails." He pulled up his sweatshirt hood and zipped his coat.

She led him through the kitchen and opened the back door though she couldn't turn on the light for him. "Be careful on the steps," she said in a low voice. "They're steep."

As soon as she'd bolted the door, she sagged against it. What had she done? It didn't matter how many painful stories they'd shared, how much they had in common or even that Mick was beginning to believe that her brother had been targeted. What would Riley think about her nearly falling into bed with the man who was sitting in his desk and leading his crew?

She was the selfish person she'd always been, putting her needs before everyone else's, including her own family. If she relied on Mick for backup, it could only be while following the ground rules they'd set. Before she could do that, she needed to take charge of her out-of-control hormones and convince herself that she didn't want what she couldn't have.

Chapter 10

As the downstairs lights in the house across the street went dark, the driver twisted the key in the sedan's ignition for the umpteenth time, shut off the headlights and let the wipers brush away the worst of the new snow. He gritted his teeth, at least in part, so they would stop chattering while he waited for the car to warm. Nothing could prevent him from shivering.

He rubbed at the base of his neck and then wiggled aching fingers inside his gloves. After three hours of surveillance, which included a possible case of frostbite, he had at least one discovery to show for it. The single mom had a boyfriend. Apparently, one who spent the night, given that the bundled figure, who'd entered her front door a few hours earlier, remained locked inside at lights out.

"You always were a wild one, weren't you, sweetheart?" His chuckles formed puffs of condensation inside the car as he shut off the engine again.

How had he not been aware that someone was getting a thigh squeeze from Stan's defiant daughter when they'd been watching her for weeks? It didn't surprise him that the Hoffman girl had been throwing back the sheets while her little daughters were right down the hall, but he was shocked that she'd been able to keep the existence of the guy to herself.

No one in Mount Isabel could keep a secret. Well, *almost* no one. His lips lifted and immediately pressed flat again as he considered the effort required of those who still understood the covenant of silence.

Since he made a point of knowing everyone else's juicy little tidbits, the fact that he'd missed this one irked him even more. So far, he wasn't even sure how her boy toy had appeared on her doorstep since not a single car had parked on either side of Elm Street in the past three hours. Only four had tooled by on their way to somewhere else.

As for the girl playing house with her guest inside, someone should have taken her down a notch or two, long before she took off with that loser boyfriend. If he'd been a few years younger, he would have taken that assignment himself. He'd always had a taste for sweet young things, after all. Sometimes even a touch. And this young lady still resembled her captivating mother, who would never grow old. Though he often avoided digging his own fingernails in the dirt when he could find "volunteers" for unsavory tasks, he might have enjoyed a smooth dip in the mud with this one.

He smiled again until he caught sight of his phone in the passenger seat, the spider web of its crushed screen visible in the dashboard's illumination. His fingers flexed and unflexed on the steering wheel.

Maybe chucking the cell at the windshield over that update on the *Informer* website hadn't been a great idea, after all. The car's glass didn't appear to be cracked, but he wouldn't know for sure until morning. After everything else that had happened the past few days, who knew what other discoveries he would make then.

He grabbed the phone and tapped the screen to awaken it. When it didn't work, he tried again without his glove, a splinter in the glass rough under his fingertip. Damn thing. Nothing—and no one—could be trusted to do a job. He returned to the newspaper website and to the headline that nearly made him throw his phone again.

Mount Isabel PD Closing in on Arsonists

Even recognizing that the local weekly wasn't exactly *The New York Times* in its track record for accuracy, he bristled at the claim. It was too close for comfort. He scanned down the article. No one at the police department had gone on record to say they had a suspect. Just more of the same with the Public Safety Office putting out a press release that was devoid of any facts and the local media printing it word for word.

He paused on a quote that was nothing like the ones attributed only to "police investigators" or "fire inspectors."

"Significant evidence discovered at the scene gives us confidence that we'll locate a suspect quickly," said Mount Isabel Fire Chief Mick Prentiss.

"What did they do now?" He shoved his hand back through hair that grew grayer every day he was surrounded by these incompetents. The newcomer at the fire department had to be bluffing so the suspect would get jumpy. Even with years of experience in avoiding taking bait like that, a tickle edged up his spine. He squeezed his shoulder blades together, refusing to let his misgivings dig in deeper.

Clearly, Prentiss didn't know how things were done around Mount Isabel. He'd better learn quickly. In fact, a few people needed to get their acts together.

He closed the browser and clicked on his contacts, tapping one to dial.

"What the hell happened today?" he barked into the phone the moment someone answered.

"I don't know. I'm sorry. I don't—"

"Have this under control at all," he finished for the other person.

"That wasn't supposed to happen. Somebody messed up."

"What's with all this outsourcing, anyway? That got us in trouble in the first place."

"Outsourcing?" The other person's voice came out as a squeak. "Um, that was your—"

At least the idiot gathered enough sense to stop there and not say it was his idea. He wouldn't be taking the blame for any of this. "All I know is I had to clean it up."

For a few seconds, the line was quiet.

"Really, I'm—"

"I don't want your apologies. There were supposed to be no connections. No one was supposed to get *caught*."

"And no one will. Everything will be fine. Don't worry."

"Oh, I'm beyond worried. Fix it. Now. Before it's too late." After clicking off the phone, he threw it back on the seat.

He hated working with amateurs. Already today he'd been forced to help unload an SUV for someone who couldn't get through his pea-sized brain that intimidation didn't have to be up close and personal. They'd be lucky if the Hoffman girl didn't go right to the police if she thought she could trust them. This time the wrong few might believe her.

He still held out hope that she could be sidelined without any less palatable measures. Like her brother. Riley had a weakness. People with those were easier to manipulate. Rachel had two tiny, dark-headed liabilities herself.

They could leverage those, and if the new guy turned out to be married, they would have more. She needed to learn the hard way that people living in glass houses shouldn't throw stones.

Just as the dashboard lights went dark, he turned the ignition again, this time his chapped lip splitting with his smile. He dabbed at the blood with his glove, not even minding the sting.

Though he'd never been one prone to sentimentalities, he'd seen proof that fear of losing a loved one could be a great motivator to encourage silence. If the Hoffman girl didn't fall in line, then he would do what had to be done. It wouldn't be the first time. Or the last.

As for working with the imbeciles surrounding him, he just might have to adjust his plans, no matter how much he preferred an administrative role. What had he been thinking, leaving the details to someone else, anyway? That old proverb remained relevant for a reason.

If you want something done right, do it yourself.

Mick took a deep breath as he entered the building housing Mount Isabel's downtown offices on Friday morning. He'd been called on the carpet for his behavior before, mostly in high school, but he might have set a record for it this time. He stepped to the door with the nameplate that said, "Kenny Davison, Village Manager," and knocked.

"Come in," a familiar-sounding voice said from the other side.

A middle-aged man with a bad comb-over sat behind the desk. Though the manager looked up at him, he didn't stand.

"Nice to see you again, Mr. Davison." He stepped forward and extended his hand. "In person this time."

After an awkward delay, Davison stood, dispensed with the formalities and sat again. He gestured for Mick to take the seat across from him. Apparently, he still had a few minutes before getting fired from the position he'd held for four days.

Davison looked older than he had during their too-brief video interview. Thinner, too. But the past few months must have been difficult for all the town's leaders. They'd also been busy. At least that was what Mick told himself when he'd stopped by the office earlier in the week to complete the last of his employment paperwork and met only with the manager's administrative assistant, Shirley. Now he knew that Davison had time for what he thought was important.

"I suppose you know why you're here." He planted his hands on the edge of his desk as though he intended to stand again but didn't.

"I'm guessing it was about the incident that took place Monday."

"Not the incident. Your *response* to it."

"My response? I wasn't at Station 1 when we received the call. I didn't start until—"

"You know what I mean."

Mick suspected, anyway, having guessed the moment he'd been called to the principal's office. A few crew members had prepared him to expect that summons from by-the-book Kenny Davison as well.

"Do you mean my statement on the newspaper's website?"

"Of course, that's what I'm talking about. I recognize that we brought you in with little preparation and a less than rigorous background check, but you need to know that the Mount Isabel Village Council, to which you report, won't tolerate anyone causing hysteria among our residents."

As the man spoke, color climbed his pale neck, his volume increasing with each word. Mick might have mentioned that sixteen suspicious fires in two months probably had caused more panic in the community than a quote that hadn't made it to the newspaper's weekly print issue yet, but he didn't want to cause the manager's head to explode.

"It was a simple statement, sir," he said, hoping they could both be reasonable.

"What I'm saying is you weren't supposed to be making a statement at all. Mount BelFest, our community's main festival, is less than four months from now, and the new director doesn't need you adding to the negative publicity." He stopped and swallowed visibly. "More than that, you didn't have the authority."

Mick lifted his chin and squinted at him, questions whirling through his thoughts. Shouldn't the community's top priority have been bringing the suspects to justice? "I was under the impression that I was hired as Mount Isabel fire chief," he said instead of asking that.

Davison sat straighter in his seat. "That is correct, but because of lingering questions at Station 1 and the rash of recent arson fires, the council has determined that all official statements will come from the Public Safety Office. That plan has been in place since the former chief…"

Though the man's words trailed away, Mick got the idea. The gag order made sense now. No one wanted information to be free-flowing, with so much suspicion hanging over Station 1. And as the new guy, he would be bound by these tighter constraints.

"In addition to being a model for public and private partnerships in southeast Michigan, Mount Isabel is a village based on order. Our leaders follow chains of commands and specific protocols." Davison leaned forward and looked down his nose at Mick. "I don't know what type of rules you adhered to at your former station, but—"

"Same," he interjected before the local leader could defame some honest and hardworking men and women with his assumptions. He could have reminded Davison that they'd broken Mount Isabel's protocols with the council's superseding gag order but chose not to mention it. Yet. He needed to get a better read on the village manager first.

"Since I wasn't informed about the council's change, I hope you can overlook my mistake." He folded his hands in his lap like a student trying to pull one over on the principal. "I'll be more careful to seek guidance in the future."

"I'm glad to hear that," Davison said, though Mick had made no commitment to avoid speaking to the press.

He found it too entertaining watching the village manager sweat. The council could easily determine who'd dropped the ball in informing the new fire chief about the change. All arrows would point to the man sitting across from him.

"This explains a lot about the recent articles I've read." He'd seen official quotes before, but these unattributed statements managed to be both drier than the newsprint they were printed on and missing most facts.

Davison tilted his head. "What do you mean?"

"Oh, nothing. I've just been trying to catch up on the media response to the fires as I read all the official reports."

"So glad you're updating yourself on the recent incidents, but remember that the fire investigator, the police department and the county prosecutor will be the ones in charge should any of the cases move to arrest."

The other man crossed his arms and settled back in his fancy executive chair. Though he'd encouraged Mick to get up to speed on the events over the past few months, he'd been careful to remind him to stay in his lane.

"I'd hoped my statement would assist those investigators. Still do," he said evenly. "Pyromaniacs love to keep tabs on their work, so I'm sure he or she has read the article."

"We don't know that."

"Maybe not, but if I'm right, it could help draw out the suspects, which would *reassure* the community rather than cause hysteria.'" He smiled as he repeated the man's own words.

"Of course." Davison shifted in his chair. "But the statement's impact will be dependent on whether it was an accurate reflection of the crime scene evidence or whether the details were exaggerated to make headlines. That's why—"

"All official statements must come from the Public Safety Office," Mick finished for him. "I see now."

He saw, all right. Probably more than the manager had intended to reveal. First, Davison cared more about covering his own ass than stopping the arsonists. And since when were officials required to tell the truth in statements? He'd worked alongside enough law enforcement officers to know that they regularly distributed incomplete information to the press to shake up suspects.

His most interesting discovery, though, was that Davison hadn't been told about the gas can investigators had recovered at the scene. At least part of this meeting was his attempt to get Mick to spill the details. Good luck with that. If the manager wanted the information, he could request an official report once the fire investigator completed it. Just like anyone else.

Why was Davison so interested in this fire, anyway? Did he know something more about it, or was someone else relying on *him* for information?

Gooseflesh peppered Mick's arms beneath his coat sleeves as he recalled that first conversation with Rachel. She'd practically laughed at his face when he'd suggested that the authorities wanted to uncover the truth. He still didn't have enough information to say that her brother had been set up as well, but he suspected that on her first point, Rachel had guessed right.

"Don't worry. It's quality evidence." Mick knew he shouldn't say more, but he couldn't resist. "The situation will be clearer after the Public Safety Office releases its next statement."

Davison blinked his wide-set eyes as Mick stood and stepped closer to the door.

"I need to get back to the station. My crew has to be ready for the next fire, and if recent history serves as a predictor, that should be happening in the next seventy-two hours."

"Mr. Prentiss," Davison called as he opened the door.

Mick turned back to him.

"Remember that you serve at the pleasure of the village council, where my recommendation is highly valued. According to your contract, you are in a probationary period where termination does not have to be for cause."

"I appreciate the reminder," he said as he stepped through the opening. "I really have to get back. I have more fires to put out."

Only after he'd closed the door behind him did he allow his shoulders to sag. He'd played that situation all wrong, and now he needed to help Rachel find answers while he still had a job.

Chapter 11

When her phone rang late Friday morning, Rachel shut off the water, shampoo lather still covering her head and hands. With the girls at school and her brother at the center, she didn't have the luxury of letting a call go to voice mail. She threw open the curtain, stepped on the towel outside the tub and lunged for her cell on the counter.

An unfamiliar number appeared on the screen. Since every time Riley had reached out, it came from a different number, she couldn't ignore solicitation calls, either. She might have to fend off a replacement windows representative or convince a determined caller that she didn't need an extended car warranty, but if it was Riley, and she missed him, who knew when he would try to call her again.

"Come on. Come on." Her heart pounding, she tapped the screen three times with her wet finger before the call connected. "Hello?"

"Hey, little sister."

"Oh, Riley. I'm so glad you called." After wiping a circle on the foggy mirror with her towel, she used it to swipe the drips already stinging her eyes as she switched the phone to speaker. If only she could see his face through her phone. His amazing smile, though she hadn't seen much of that in a long time. The wavy dark-blond hair. And those intense sky-blue eyes that reflected their father's side of the family while she was all her mother's.

"If I'd known I'd get this kind of reception, I might have called more often."

Rachel would have mentioned that he'd also resented her for taking him to rehab, but his chuckle through the line made her feel so hopeful that she kept the comment to herself. She couldn't remember the last time she'd heard him laugh. He sounded like the old Riley. The jokester he'd been before breaking off his engagement to Jillian Lowe. He'd never been the same, but they never talked about that. Or *her*.

"How's my favorite sister?" he said, returning to the regular script of their phone conversations, lines cemented over the more than two decades of their relationship.

Despite that nothing about their lives was close to familiar, she responded with her usual line. "Your *only* sister is just fine." That might have been a stretch, but it was all she had.

"Did I catch you at a bad time?"

She wiped at the drips on her forehead again. The back of her neck was starting to itch. "Other than that shampoo is turning into glue in my hair, no."

"Get back in the shower and rinse it out."

"That can wait." She shivered, unable to wrap her body or hair with the towel when she still needed it to wipe chemicals from her eyes. "How are *you* doing? Are they treating you well? Is the food okay? How was the...uh... detox? Do you know when—"

She forced herself to stop before asking the last question. He probably didn't know when he would be released, anyway, and she shouldn't put pressure on him to come home. He would only face more scrutiny when he did.

"The sooner you rinse off, the sooner I can answer some of your questions."

She didn't miss that he hadn't offered to answer all of them and had a guess which one he might skip. As always, he would try to shield her from the tough stuff.

"Fine." She turned on the sink faucet and doused her head under the tap instead. In a minute flat, she wrapped herself with the towel, her reflection showing a red-faced woman with a mess of dripping hair.

"I'm back," she called into the speaker.

"Bet you're glad we weren't on a video chat."

He snickered, but this time his voiced sounded tight. She wished again that she could see his face. But this was about his recovery, not about her concerns. Even if he was probably thinner now. Paler. Different.

"I suppose you've met the new chief."

At his casual question, she shifted her feet and re-tucked the towel under her arms. Had one of the crew spoken to him? Told him about the scene she'd made at the station? Or, God forbid, had someone seen her and Mick together? Though she doubted any of that had happened since Riley would have had to call them for that information, instead of the other way around, her legs turned to mush beneath her. She gripped the counter for stability as guilt seeped into her recently scrubbed pores.

"I've met him."

They'd been introduced, all right. And if one of them hadn't come to his senses last night, they would have been acquainted in the most complete way possible. She let the towel drop and yanked her robe from the hook on the back of the door. Then sliding her damp arms inside it, she cinched the belt.

"Seems like an all-right guy," she said. "He'll take care of your crew. Uh, for now."

Rachel winced. If she didn't get control of her words, pretty soon she would volunteer that she'd been making out with her brother's replacement. Even as she stood there in front of the foggy mirror, several parts of her damp skin under the robe still warmed with the memory of the night she'd been trying to forget. That had to stop. Not only did she need to steer clear of any wayward thoughts about Mick Prentiss, but she also had to ensure that her brother would never know she'd had them. Or acted on them.

"Good to hear, I guess."

His voice sounded strange. She pursed her lips as she pictured him, his light-brown brows drawn together, worry in his eyes.

"I thought you were supposed to be answering *my* questions," she said, and then coughed as she wrapped her hair in the towel. So much for acting as if everything was normal. That ship had sailed a few oceans ago, and the boat was taking on water.

"Right." He paused for too long before finally continuing. "Let me see. I'm doing okay now, but sometimes I get antsy since the pace in this place is really slow. I miss the adrenaline rush at the station."

A knot formed in her throat over all that had been taken from him. Because of her. "Your crew misses you. Us, too."

"Yeah" was all he said to that. "Now, what else did you ask? Let me see. They're treating me fine."

"What about the food?" She was getting closer to the question he wouldn't want to answer, but she couldn't help herself.

"Could be worse."

"And the…"

"The *detox*? Now, that could have been better." He laughed at his own joke and then cleared his throat. "It really sucked. Worse this time than the last. My body really protested."

Her nose burned at the reminder that he'd had a few years of steady sobriety prior to this relapse. "You don't know how sorry I am."

"Sis, can we not start that again? You didn't pour the booze down my throat. I'm back following my program now. I'm attending meetings right here in the center in addition to individual and group counseling. And I'm getting back on track. That's all that matters."

It wasn't, but she wouldn't argue with him now.

"Oh. Your last question," he said. "You asked about when I get out. I'm already on borrowed time. Most Michigan inpatient substance abuse programs are only fourteen days. My counselor went to bat with the insurance company for me. Said I wasn't ready. But at twenty-eight days, they toss me. That's it."

She squinted, trying to count the days, so she and the twins could help celebrate his discharge.

"What about you?" he asked. "Are the girls okay? And are you really all right?"

"I already said—"

"Wait. You haven't been asking around about Dad, have you? Or more questions about that stuff at the station?"

"Not really."

"Rachel," he said in a warning tone. "I told you to stay out of it. You don't know how dangerous it is."

She'd had a few clues lately, but she didn't mention them. "I have to find answers. You would never do the stuff you're accused of. I have to find proof."

"Rachel, listen to me. Asking questions is what got me into this mess. Well, that and several gallons of tequila."

"Don't joke about it." She couldn't when she was the one who'd convinced him to dig for information.

"Please let me handle the situation at the station after I get out. As for the other stuff, I've learned that there are some things we just don't need to know."

"What 'things'?" She took the phone off speaker and pressed it against her ear. Only a rustling sound, maybe his breathing, filled the line. "Riley? Are you still there?"

"Did Dad ever mention anything about—" He stopped and muffled a cough. "Forget it."

"Mention what? You can't stop now." She gripped the phone tighter.

"The Bilton Foundation."

"Why are you asking that? We all know about Mount Isabel's main benefactor."

"Do we? Really?"

"Of course, we do." But even as she spoke them, her own words unsettled her. Other than its name, she knew nothing about the foundation that had funded so many local improvements.

"Is that what all of this is about? Bilton Holdings? The fires? The embezzlement questions?"

"Never mind. I shouldn't have brought it up."

"But you did." Her chest tightened. What wasn't he telling her? She considered for a few seconds and then asked, "Does this have to do with 'It is not death, but dying which is terrible'?"

"How do you—" He coughed a few more times before starting again. "What are you talking about?"

"Clearly, you're not surprised by those words." She

sighed and added, "It's one of those quotes from your emails."

"How do you even know about—"

"I figured out your email password."

"You *broke* into my email account?" His voice cracked on "broke" like it might have when he was twelve.

"It wasn't exactly breaking in when you were so uncreative with your password."

"You had no right to dig into my stuff."

She shifted against the counter, tying the belt on her robe again. "Like I said, I was looking for information that might help you. And you wouldn't have given it to me if I asked. All I found were a bunch of strange, threatening quotes."

"Those were *warnings*. Don't you get that? Those and the fires."

His voice had become a deep growl that made her shiver. He didn't sound like her mild-mannered brother. Riley was angry. And defiant. And scared.

"I need you to hear me. Stop digging for answers. About anything. Not my stuff at work. Not Dad's death. It was all a long time ago. Some things are better off buried."

"I don't understand," she squeezed in when her brother paused. What he was saying didn't make sense. This wasn't some event far in the past. Their father hadn't even been buried a year.

"You don't know who you're messing with," he continued. "I should've listened to the warnings. Now my career is destroyed. My reputation. My *life*. Firefighting is the only job I've ever wanted."

Riley gasped into the phone as though finally taking a breath.

"What worse things will they do to *you* to make you mind your own business?"

At her brother's ominous words, Rachel's heart pounded, and the white SUV appeared in her thoughts. That driver had offered a warning of his own from behind tinted glass. No way she could tell Riley about that now.

"But I have to do *something*. You'd do the same for me."

"There you go, justifying everything you do. But sometimes it isn't about you. I have enough to deal with in here without having to worry if you and the girls are safe. You don't know—" He stopped himself and didn't say more. "Just stay out of it. Please? For me?"

"Okay," she said with a sigh.

Riley let the pause between them stretch too long. He'd always been able to tell when she was lying.

"Hey, I've got to go," he said. "I have to get to group now."

"Wait." She didn't want him to end the call. Not like this. "What about visitors' day? I know you have to put me on a list so that I'm allowed to come, and you didn't do it before, but could you this week?"

"Sure. I'll add you."

"Hey, Riley, we're okay, right?"

"Of course. Always."

"Okay," she said again, her heart squeezing like it had a band tied around it, tightening by tiny increments.

She could tell when her brother was lying, too.

Chapter 12

When the knock came at her half-glass back door that night, Rachel jumped even after the five-minute-warning text had told her to expect it. Her throat tightened, and her palms were so damp that she'd never be able to turn the doorknob. Near the stove, she wiped her hands on a paper towel and tossed it into the garbage can.

"Coming," she said too softly for him to hear outside.

She couldn't allow herself to think about events from less than twenty-four hours before, when this particular guest had visited. Things that could never happen again, no matter how many locations in her body warmed at the memory of it. She conjured her brother's face to tamp down her hormones and brushed her fingers down the front of her baggy sweatpants. If her whole outfit, including a top that was closer to a dress and an oversize zipper sweatshirt, didn't help him to forget about the night before, she didn't know what would.

The tap came a second time, this one on the glass, just as she reached the entry. She slid the curtain aside though she already knew who to expect and twisted the lock. Mick pushed the door open, slid inside and closed it behind him.

"Hey," he said, stomping his boots on the mat.

Rachel took an automatic step back. Though Mick

looked away as he shoved off his hood and shook snowflakes from his messy hair, his upper lip twitched. He clearly recognized that he made her uncomfortable. After that kiss last night, that had blown her socks off—and nearly everything else—she almost resented that she didn't do the same thing for him. Not that she should care. Especially if she planned to follow the rules they'd set. And she did.

"It smells great in here, but we really have to stop meeting like this."

His chuckle sent a pleasant, though unwelcome, tremor through her, but the irony of his words settled like a rock in her gut. "You know that in the dark is the only way we *can* meet. At least, if we don't want anyone to know about it."

"That'll be even tougher after daylight savings time starts Sunday." He bent to remove his boots.

"You think there'll be more reasons for us to compare notes?" She was surprised by both his suggestion and by the flip in her tummy at the prospect of his continued visits. If she wasn't careful, she could get used to him being around.

"There might be," he said. "And if that's the case, it'll probably be the girls' bedtime before it even gets dark."

Rachel had turned away to stir the spaghetti sauce, but at his mention of her daughters' evening schedule, she whirled back to face him. Sauce from the wooden spoon still in her hand landed with a splat on the floor. They both stared at the red sunburst on the yellowed tile before Rachel lunged for a paper towel and started wiping up the mess.

"Sorry about that."

"No big deal." She waved off his apology with the messy cloth as she stood.

Mick appeared to be holding back a smile. He was joking with her, probably because she'd invited him to join the *girls and her* for dinner when he'd suggested they should meet that night.

"Guess the time change will make that tougher for any 'tea sessions.'"

"I'm sure we'll figure it out," she said.

They would have to. She didn't know what Mick thought about it, but she appreciated having those two pint-sized chaperones around them to remind her to keep her hands to herself.

"Uh, anyway, you texted me about meeting, so…"

Mick slid out of his coat and draped it over his arm. He wore jeans that fit his strong legs better than they should have and that same soft-looking flannel shirt he'd worn the night they'd met. Hadn't he gotten the memo about trying not to look good?

"You want to know what I found? Besides an excuse to get invited to dinner?"

"Yeah. Besides that."

She rolled her eyes at his joke, but her chest still tightened. Had he found something that could confirm her suspicions that someone had set up Riley? After the things her own brother had said—and didn't say—earlier, she doubted anything Mick had learned would surprise her.

"Well? Are you going to tell me?" She tried to appear nonchalant, stirring the sauce again at first. After a few seconds, she set her utensil in the spoon rest and turned back to him, leaning against the counter and crossing her arms.

"Who are you talking to, Mommy?"

Rachel jumped and then glanced at the kitchen doorway. Carissa stood there, wearing a long top and socks, her pale shins and knees peeking out where her leggings should have been. The outline under her shirt showed she'd at least left her underwear on instead of greeting company commando-style.

"Honey, what are you doing down here without any pants on?" Rachel asked instead of answering her question. "You're supposed to be taking a bath right now. I already ran the water, and I said I'd be up to help you out in a few minutes."

Her daughter wasn't paying attention as she'd figured out for herself who'd been on the other end of the conversation she'd overheard. She scrambled past Rachel to greet their guest.

"Hi, Mr. Mick."

"Hello, Carissa."

Rachel slid a glance to Mick, who grinned back at her. She hadn't identified which twin had entered the room, and yet he'd called the child by name. Unlike even some of their teachers after a few weeks in school, Mick could already tell them apart. He probably had no idea how important that was to identical twins. Or their mother.

"How did you…?" she mouthed the question to him.

He touched his cheekbone just beneath his right eye, the same spot where Carissa had a tiny freckle. Something Carly didn't have. Rachel was still digesting that he'd taken the time to notice that little detail as Mick glanced down to speak to her child.

"Are you going to eat dinner with us?" Carissa asked. "We're having spaghetti."

"It smells really good, too." He pointed to the saucepan and then the pasta pot. "Wasn't it nice of your mom to invite me?"

She'd had to do something when Mick sent her the most information-deprived text she'd ever read.

Guess what I figured out today?

After her troubling conversation with Riley that morning, she wasn't in the mood for any guessing games. She just wanted answers.

Carissa crossed her arms and tapped her stocking-clad foot on the floor. "We're starving, but Mom said we had to wait to eat dinner until *after* we took our baths."

"Oh, she did, did she?" Mick grinned when he looked over at her again.

"We get to wash each other's hair," Carissa added, lifting her chin.

Rachel turned back to the stove, though the sauce didn't need another stir, and the water in the pasta pot had yet to boil. She made a point of checking the oven that was warming for the frozen garlic bread she'd arranged on a tray.

When she turned back, Mick was bent at the waist, addressing her daughter.

"I'm pretty hungry, too. If you hurry and get cleaned up, I bet we can eat sooner. Anyway, aren't you cold?" He pointed to her bare legs.

"We're out of shampoo."

Carissa shook the bottle that had been dangling from her hand since she'd entered the room. How Rachel had missed that, she wasn't sure, though she'd probably glossed over many things while hunting for information that could help Riley. A search that no one, including her brother, wanted her to continue.

"I need to take care of this. Could you..." She gestured to the pots on the stove. "It'll just take me a minute."

"I'll make sure everything doesn't boil over," Mick said.

She followed Carissa up the stairs and to the linen closet where she stored extra supplies in tubs on the top shelf. When she returned ten minutes later, she was surprised to find Mick in the dining area, setting the table.

"I thought you were going to—"

Having just arranged the final place setting, he lifted both hands. "Don't worry. It's all under control."

She followed him into the kitchen, where she found the garlic bread in the oven and the spaghetti noodles already drained and back in the pan. Mick stepped to the stove and lowered the heat on the sauce to simmer.

"Looks like you've done this before."

He lifted a brow as he looked back at her. "That shouldn't surprise you. All firefighters can cook. It comes with the job."

"Not all of them. Like I told you, my dad was a lousy cook, but he insisted on trying." Rachel braced herself, waiting for the rush of emotions that sometimes made her want to curl in a ball when she spoke about her father. The chuckle that bubbled up through her chest surprised her.

"I bet he was a good man. Even if he couldn't cook."

"You're a good man, too."

The words were out of her mouth before she could process let alone edit them. That didn't make them any less true. The more she got to know Mick, the more she liked him. Sure, she'd responded to the hot firefighter vibe first, but now she found his qualities of both integrity and tenderness, particularly around her children, just as appealing. A twist on the dangerous bad boys who'd always drawn her like an oversize magnet, Mick was a good guy who battled danger. She felt a little safer just having him around.

Mick glanced back at her over his shoulder and dampened his lips as though trying to find his words. The rumbling on the stairs saved him from having to try and gave her a reprieve from having to explain why she'd said it.

The floor vibrated beneath their feet as both girls raced into the kitchen, pajamas sticking to their damp skin and towels on their heads.

"Is it time to eat?" Carly pointed to the stove.

"It's ready. Now get in your seats, and we'll bring out the food." She could have sent Mick out of the kitchen, too, but he'd already helped with dinner, so she doubted he would mind assisting her in serving.

She ladled some sauce into a bowl and then poured the pasta into a second one, noting that he'd added a little olive oil so it didn't stick. He put the bread on a plate and grabbed the plastic-wrap-covered salad bowl from the refrigerator and started into the dining room.

When he reached the table, he glanced back at her, his gaze so warm that it felt like a caress. Yes, it was for the best that the two of them wouldn't be eating dinner alone together tonight.

Chapter 13

"They really were hungry."

Mick grinned as he surveyed the empty serving bowls and bread platter. Rachel's twins sat behind empty plates, sated looks on their faces and more than a little of their dinners decorating their matching pink, polka dot pajama tops. Their short hair that had dried without the benefit of a comb stuck out every which way.

Rachel rolled her eyes at her daughters but smiled. "I guess showers before spaghetti wasn't my best idea."

Visiting her home tonight had not been one of his smartest plans, either. On his stealthy walk over, he'd been worried about spending time in the same room with the girls' mother while constantly looking for excuses to touch her. Now he realized that a cozy dinner with Rachel and those two sweet little girls was just as dangerous for him. Possibly more so.

Good thing the blinds were closed up tight because anyone passing by on the sidewalk and seeing the four of them through the front window would think they were a family. He was having a hard time trying to avoid imagining that picture himself. And longing for things he should have known better than to want.

"I do have a stain stick," Rachel said, still speaking about her messy daughters. "I'll need a lot of it."

"You didn't seem to be hungry." He pointed to her plate where she'd scooted around spaghetti noodles but appeared to have taken only a few bites.

"I'm a little distracted since someone still hasn't told me why it was so important that we meet tonight."

Mick blew out a breath. "Fine. Anyone ever mentioned that patience isn't your virtue? I had to meet with Kenny Davison today."

"That's it?" Then she tilted her head, her eyes narrowing. "Had to?"

Carly, who'd been too focused on the last piece of garlic bread that she'd split with her sister to pay attention to the adults before, suddenly moved her chair closer to his.

"Mr. Mick, did you know that I had gym at school today?" Carly sat higher in her chair and crossed her arms with authority. "We practiced jump rope tricks."

"I bet you're great at skipping rope," he said. "I miss nearly every time when I try."

"I could teach you."

Carissa leaned so far forward that her chin nearly touched the tabletop. "I could teach you stuff, too. I had art today. We're making bowls with clay that we roll out like snakes."

Mick pushed back from the table and glanced over at Rachel, who was watching him. He couldn't blame her for being cautious with anyone around her daughters. They already had an absentee father. She probably wanted to protect their tender feelings.

"Sounds like I'm going to be busy." He set his fork aside.

"On Monday, I'll tell my art teacher, Miss Summers, that Mr. Mick—"

"Wait," he said to interrupt Carissa and then swallowed hard.

Rachel's eyes were as wide as his must have been. He took a breath to slow his pulse.

"I mean would it be okay if we keep my visits and the lessons you girls teach me to ourselves? Like secrets?" He glanced from one twin to the other and then focused on their mother, hoping she would get the message. If he and Rachel wanted to keep their collaboration quiet, they couldn't have the girls making announcements at school.

"Right. Secrets," Rachel said. "That'll be fun, won't it, girls?"

Though both of her daughters nodded, Carly squished up her face as though she wasn't sure why keeping quiet about their repeat guest would be such a riot.

"Mommy, can we watch a show instead of books tonight?" Carly asked.

"It's Friday night," her twin added.

Rachel's expression became the pinched one as she looked from the girls to the staircase.

"Just this one night, Mom," Mick said in a low voice, grinning.

She pushed away from the table and stood. "Okay. But first I want you both to march upstairs, wash your faces, and get some clean pj's. Bring the stained ones to me."

The girls hurried from the room to follow her instructions. Rachel scooted around the table, scraping and piling plates with efficient movements. When she carried her stack through the doorway and to the sink, Mick grabbed glasses and followed her.

"They've probably already told at least their teachers

that you came to our house," she said as she turned on the faucet. "You're the new fire chief. You're a big deal. At least to them."

There it was. The reminder that even if her daughters thought of him as a celebrity, Rachel would only see a usurper who stole her brother's position. A job that had been technically available for the taking.

"Maybe they both forgot about yesterday?"

"Wouldn't count on it." She pointed to a place on the counter where he could set the glasses. "One of the girls' preschool teachers told all the parents if we would believe just half of the stories our kids brought home about her, then she would buy into only that much of those they told her about us."

"That doesn't sound promising."

"You didn't answer my question before. You *had* to meet with Davison?" She watched him in her side vision. "Was it about the quote in the *Informer*?"

He rested his hands on his hips, but he couldn't keep a straight face. "Was I the only one who didn't recognize that talking to the press could get me in trouble around here?"

"You were just poking the powers that be. Maybe a few of them. With all the chaos at Station 1, you had to know that your superiors were watching you."

"Too closely, if you ask me."

As he lifted the plates she'd stacked, he stepped back and scanned the lower row of cabinets, finding only well-worn drawer pulls and door handles. "No dishwasher?"

"I see two." She pointed to the counter for him to return the plates and then tossed him a towel. "So that's it? You went to the trouble of coming here to tell me you got called to the principal's office?"

She scrubbed a plate in the sudsy water, rinsed it and placed it in his towel-covered hand.

"Really, I just wanted to tell you something, and I thought I should do it in person."

"What's that?"

Mick chewed his lip but decided to stop stalling. "I think your theory might be right."

The plate she'd been washing slipped from her fingers and under the suds. It clinked on the metal at the bottom of the sink. When Rachel slowly turned to him, Mick gave her the towel to dry her hands.

"What changed your mind? What did Kenny say?"

"Something about how more negative publicity could hurt the village's Mount Bel Fest and that I wasn't authorized to give statements, but it felt like there was more to it."

Two lines formed between her brows. "Like what?"

"I would have thought that he'd be more—I don't know—*anxious* maybe for police to make an arrest. He seemed to be more concerned with ensuring that I understood it wasn't my investigation."

"As though Kenny had a secret that he didn't want you to find out?"

Rachel gave him a knowing smile. She'd said something similar that first night in his office, though at the time, her premise had seemed too convenient in her brother's case and too far-fetched in everyone else's.

"I might be blowing it out of proportion when he could have just been flexing his muscles as village manager. Letting me know who's boss. But what you'd said about someone covering a secret..." He paused, tilting his head back and forth. "Possibly?"

"Did you find anything else?"

"Wasn't that enough?"

She didn't get the chance to answer as the twins rushed into the kitchen, their faces fairly well scrubbed, their matching pj's this time a light yellow with daisies. Each carried a wad of pink laundry in her arms. With an apologetic look, Rachel ran the dirty clothes to the basement. Then she led the girls into the living room to set them up with their promised show.

When she returned, she hurried to the sink and went back to work. "I might have found something, too," she said, focusing on the faucet where she rinsed.

Mick took an automatic step closer, his throat tight. "What is it? You said, 'might have.' Not that you found something concrete. Which is it?"

Her shoulders shifted, but she kept washing and rinsing. Without looking at him, she held out a plate and waited for him to take it. "Riley called today. He said some things."

His fingers suddenly cold, Mick lowered the dish on the counter so he wouldn't drop it.

"Why didn't you say that before?" He faced her, but she still wouldn't look over from the water. "If I hadn't come tonight, you wouldn't have mentioned it at all, would you?"

He already knew the answer, but he waited for her to say it, anyway. When would she ever trust him?

She lifted her chin and finally turned his way. "I'm telling you now."

"Well, what 'things' did he say?"

"Like before, he said I should stop asking questions. About Dad's death. About everything. He told me to stay out of it. Even said he'd deal with the questions at the station when he got out of rehab."

"I like your brother already."

They exchanged a look that stated the obvious. No matter what happened in the investigation, he and her brother were unlikely to ever be friends.

"I'll be sure to tell him that...when I see him. *If* I see him."

She chewed the corner of her lip and stepped to the kitchen doorway to check on the girls. Mick stared at her back, searching for clues. There had to be something she wasn't telling him.

"Did you at least admit to him that you aren't going to stop looking?"

"Not exactly. But he didn't seem to believe me when I said I would."

"Then he's a smart guy, too."

She gave him a mean look before crossing into the dining room and slumping into a chair. Whether wise or not, she believed she had to keep searching.

He followed her to the table and sat on the side that faced the living room where the girls were on the couch, cuddling under the same throw from the night before.

"That's *all* he said? That you should stop looking? I mentioned that a few times myself."

Her gaze flicked to his and then back to her hands, gripped in front of her. "He asked if Dad had ever mentioned anything about Bilton Foundation to me."

"I don't know what that is."

"You're not from Mount Isabel. But everyone from around here knows a little about Bilton. At least those who care about major improvement projects in town. That foundation has funded every project I can think of for as long as I can remember."

"Like which ones?"

"Station 1 is the most recent example. Including equipment like the new Engine 1. Then there's the playground at Mill Race Park, the Isa Wildflower Garden and all the community walking paths." She ticked them off on her fingers as she provided names. "Not to mention the Mount Isabel Community Recreation Center. Have you seen that place?"

"I drove by it the other day. It's huge. I was thinking about joining."

"It beats the workout room at Station 1, and that's tough to do," she said.

"So what you're saying is Bilton's like Santa Claus for your little town." Mick stared down at his folded hands as pieces of the puzzle about his new community clicked into place.

"I'd wondered how a village of this size could afford so many improvements." He grinned at the recent memory. "Walking into Station 1, I thought I'd taken a wrong turn and ended up in a palace like Versailles."

"It's not quite like that, but we're lucky to have those kinds of facilities and improvements here. With such a small number of homes, there's no way we could have had a big enough property tax increase to cover all those planning and construction costs, let alone maintenance."

"But who is this Bilton guy? Or maybe gal? Was it some industrialist-slash-philanthropist like Carnegie or Rockefeller? And why choose this village over all the other ordinary little towns in southeast Michigan?"

She smiled at that. "The story I've heard is that Bilton Holdings owned this huge piece of property outside of town, where something like a lake of oil was discovered. The company wanted to share its good fortune, so it set up the foundation to give back."

"There had to be a whole lot of fortune to donate that

much, though some do give it all away. Andrew Carnegie did that. You still haven't told me, who is this selfless person?"

"I don't know." She lifted a shoulder and lowered it. "Until Riley brought it up, I didn't realize how little I know about Bilton. And when I asked Riley if the foundation could have something to do with the fires, or the investigation against him, he seemed to regret mentioning it at all. He gave me the hint and then tried to take it back. That's not like him."

"So now you're going to try to find everything you can about Bilton."

She crossed her arms and pressed her lips into a line. He hadn't posed it as a question.

"I have to," she said, with a firm nod. "He wouldn't have brought it up if it wasn't bugging him. I'll start with some internet sleuthing. I should be able to find something about Bilton, even if whoever runs it keeps a low profile. Someone has to know who's giving all that money away."

"You would think."

She nodded several times as though an idea were coming together in her thoughts. "Then if that doesn't work, I'll talk to some locals from my father's generation. They were around when the first projects were moving forward with help from this benefactor. Someone has to know something."

Her words weren't that scary, so he couldn't explain the shiver that coursed through him. Someone knew, all right. Only it felt as if they were racing down a dark, deserted road with no headlights or even brakes as they tried to determine *who*. He sighed then yanked that breath back in as the other part of what Rachel had said repeated in his thoughts.

"Your brother might have given you another clue."

"What do you mean?"

"He didn't just ask if you'd ever heard of Bilton. He asked you if your dad had ever mentioned anything about the foundation. That's not the same thing."

She rubbed her hands over her face and then shoved her fingers back through her hair. "What are you saying? That *my dad* could have known something about Bilton? Or maybe even some secret?"

"I didn't say that. Neither did your brother. But he did put your dad and that foundation in the same question, and you might want to find out what that means."

Still, Rachel kept shaking her head. Then she stopped. The color drained from her face. "You don't think he took his life because—"

He rested his hand on top of the pair she'd clasped together. "We don't know anything. But you said you wanted answers. Maybe that's an important clue. Maybe not. You just need to check it out."

His gut told him there was more to it, though he'd never met her father or brother. Heck, he barely knew her, other than a heart-to-heart the other night and an ill-advised kiss that got out of hand. Still, he would have to suggest that they take a closer look at her dad's past.

"You're right."

Mick blinked since she seemed to be answering his thoughts, but she shook her head and squeezed her eyes shut as though to push away the threat of tears. Then she pulled her hands from beneath his. Though a knot swelled in his throat, he tried not to be offended since their tender moment from the night before had nearly inspired them to christen the sofa.

"I'll just see what I can find on the internet over the weekend," she said.

He rubbed his suddenly cold hands together. "And when I'm back in the office on Monday, I'll check my files for the construction plans for the new Station 1. There should also be permits and such with the village and the state, but I can start there."

With a nod, Rachel stood and took a few steps toward the living room.

"I know you didn't get too far with your research on *my* files the other night." When she stopped and glanced back at him with wide eyes, he added, "You know, using a baked-in-a-cake file or whatever else it was to break into my cabinet."

"I didn't—"

He kept grinning at her until she shrugged.

"You thought I missed that? It wasn't exactly a professional break-in."

"That thing should have been easier to pop," she said with a frown.

"I'll be sure to order a more accommodating filing cabinet next time."

The credits were rolling on the TV show when she crossed the room to the twins. Both were already rubbing their eyes.

"Can Mr. Mick read us a story tonight?" Carissa pointed to Mick in the dining area doorway.

"No, honey. Remember, we agreed that the show was *instead* of books."

"But," Carly started to argue, then slumped her shoulders, too tired to make the effort.

"Maybe we can do that next time," he said.

When Rachel guided the girls to the stairs, Mick started toward the back door. Though leaving her was the last thing he wanted to do, it would probably be best for the both of them. At least for her. He needed to be a better man than he wanted to be right then, especially since they'd both agreed to their rules.

"I'll see you three soon," he called to them as they reached the landing.

Only Rachel glanced back at him and held up a finger, asking him to wait. He nodded, swallowing, his better angels floating off on feathered wings.

Minutes later, she met him in the kitchen doorway.

"I'm sorry I tried to break into your filing cabinet."

"Tell that to the Mount Isabel PD."

"Wouldn't I already be wearing silver bracelets if you were planning to turn me in?"

"Guess we're making a habit of not reporting things to the police." It was supposed to be a joke, but his words landed heavily, bringing back the memory of the white SUV and dousing any embers that threatened to reignite tonight.

"We still don't know who to trust," she said.

Except each other. He willed her to say those last words, but she let it go at that.

"I might need to check Dad's place, too," she said after a few seconds. "I told you that Riley still lives at the house."

He nodded, glad that she'd come to that conclusion herself. "But you aren't going there alone, are you? That's not safe, if someone is watching you. You said it's out in the country, right? I can go with you."

"You don't need to do that. I won't even look there unless I don't find anything about Bilton online."

As he started to argue, she held out a hand.

"And I definitely won't do it until next week while the girls are at school. If you're so worried, you can come out there with me then, if you can figure out how to get time away from the station."

"Fine," he began and then frowned. "That's going to be tough, isn't it? I'm under a microscope there, both from the crew and from the village leadership. Davison made sure to tell me that my employment was probationary."

"Skipping work during your second week on the job might not be in your best interest."

"Probably not."

Mick sensed there was something off about her relenting so easily to his suggestion that she shouldn't visit her father's house alone. In the short time he'd known her, she'd never given up a single point without an argument. Then it hit him. She'd agreed to let him join her at a time when she knew he couldn't get away because she wouldn't be waiting until then to go snoop there.

"Okay, let me know when—I mean if—you decide to look around at your dad's place. I'll see if I can make the time work."

"Sounds like a plan."

It was a plan, all right. He'd determined since his arrival in Mount Isabel that no one else would be hurt on his watch. Rachel wouldn't make it easy for him to keep that commitment.

Whether she liked it or not, ensuring her safety had become critically important to him. He suspected that she'd be taking a field trip over the weekend. What she didn't know was that Mick planned to be there as backup when she did.

Chapter 14

The whole apparatus bay was hopping with activity and noise when Mick pushed through the door of Station 1 on Saturday morning, already breaking his promise to himself not to work on weekends. This time he had an excuse. They'd had another call for a suspicious fire the night before, just as he'd predicted to Davison. Captain Al Park had kept him in the loop, assuring him that his services weren't required, but he still wanted to know more.

The parking lot hadn't been as full as he'd hoped since he'd arrived at shift change, but a few stragglers from Rotation 2 were still emerging from the locker room in their civvies. Maybe they could offer some details, possibly some that Park wouldn't include in the report.

With the fresh crew busy cleaning Engine 1 and Ladder Tower 1 and inspecting for damage, along with the sound system blasting out alternative rock, Mick hoped to make it through the side door without being noticed. But Felicia Lucas rounded Engine 1's rear step, a thermal imaging camera dangling from one hand and a flathead ax in the other.

"Good morning, Chief. Didn't you already get enough of us this week?"

"Morning, Lucas." Though most of the Rotation 3 crew

members had watched him with caution all week, the thirty-something firefighter with dark hair barely long enough to pull into a ponytail had been friendly right from the day he'd met her. As the only full-time female firefighter in a station filled with men, she had to be an expert at getting along.

"I don't know about you, Chief, but if it were my day off, I'd be at home, cuddling with my pups, and nowhere close to here." She continued past him to the side of the truck but glanced back over her shoulder. "But I guess that's why you're chief, and I'm cleaning the truck."

He chuckled since it was easier than admitting that he had nothing to do all day other than buy some furniture or linens or even a single saucepan and a bowl. Those things he would put off as long as he could after Davison's reminder that his job was contingent.

"If you ever want to switch places..."

She'd rested the camera on a tarp and was opening a compartment on the side of the truck to stow the ax, but she glanced back at him, grinning.

"With all that's gone on around here lately? I'll have to decline your kind offer." She tucked the equipment inside the storage area and closed the door.

"Who's throwing around promises now?"

Mick startled at the sound of a second female voice coming from behind him. He turned to find a sturdy-looking woman with short blonde hair, a bucket of cleaners and a deep frown. Her eyes widened when she recognized him. Since there were only two women on the crew, he didn't need the embroidered name, *Garritt*, on her shirt to place her, but he hadn't expected to see both of them on the same shift.

"Sorry, Chief. I didn't know you were here today."

"Just stopped by."

"I'm Emily Garritt." She extended the arm that didn't have a bucket hanging from it. Then noticing the rubber glove she still wore, she lowered it. "We can shake hands later."

"Nice to meet you, Garritt. I still haven't met most of the paid-on-call firefighters yet." He glanced around the room, noting several familiar faces from earlier in the week. "Are you covering for someone today?"

"McMillan had a death in the family."

"Right. I knew that."

As distracted as he'd been on the job all week, he was surprised he remembered any of the information he'd been given that didn't relate to Rachel Hoffman or her family.

"Well, they aren't going to scrub themselves, so…" Emily reached in the bucket and waved a toilet brush before disappearing through the door that led to the day room and the locker rooms.

Mick watched her through the glass as she disappeared down the hall.

"Don't mind her, Chief. She didn't know until she got here that it was McMillan's assignment to clean the locker rooms," Felicia said, with a chuckle. "Seems she draws that short straw on nearly every shift she covers."

"Probably thinks he planned that funeral so he could skip his turn."

Felicia's grin faded. "Um, also, she's been trying to get on full-time for a while."

He glanced through the window to the now empty hallway. "How long's that?"

"A while," she repeated.

Mick mentally added Garritt's record to the list of files he would need to examine on Monday. Beyond those in the Riley Hoffman camp, who didn't want Mick anywhere near Station 1, he kept finding situations where some of his crew had their own axes to grind, legitimately or not. How could he figure out who inside the station might have had a reason to target Rachel's brother when several could have had a motive?

Movement nearby startled him, and he shifted, finding Felicia still watching him, a suspicious grin on her face.

"She's involved with someone if that's what you're wondering. Me, too." She pointed to her wedding band. "Though this is marriage No. 2 for me."

Mick's face heated as he stuck his hands in his coat pockets.

Felicia threw back her head and laughed. "Lighten up, boss. We all got the memos about this being a romance-free zone."

"Good." He coughed into his jacket sleeve, wishing she would stop watching him. Even if the former chief's sister didn't count in any bans on same-shift dating—Rachel and he weren't involved, either—he had to plant his boots on the floor to keep from shifting his feet. "Glad I won't have to write up another memo on Monday."

His chuckle probably sounded strained, but it was the best he could do.

"We all know you're just trying to figure us out, Chief. We're doing the same thing with you." Felicia grinned, then shrugged. "Outsiders. You get it."

Mick nodded, trying to ignore the shiver that slithered through him.

Just as Felicia retrieved the thermal imaging camera and rounded the end of the truck to store it in a different compartment, David List exited the same door through which Emily had disappeared only moments before. The firefighter wore street clothes and carried a gym bag along with his coat. His neatly combed hair was still wet.

"Hey, Chief." David tilted his head. "Isn't this your—"

"I know. It's my day off. Just checking in."

"About the fire last night, huh?"

They both knew the answer to that, so Mick didn't bother making up something. "You the last one going off shift?"

"Yeah, Garritt told me to get out so she could clean the locker room." He widened his eyes. "That girl is intense."

At Mick's hard look, the younger man stared at the floor. "Sorry, boss. I mean woman. And…hardworking?"

Since the firefighter offered the last as a question, Mick shook his head. Emily probably had reasons to be resentful about her situation in the department that had nothing to do with Mick's arrival or Riley's firing. And some of her fellow crew had to be some of them. But that would have to be a discussion for another day.

"You headed home?" he asked David instead.

His shoulders visibly relaxed. "Drive-through breakfast and then bed."

"I'll walk you out."

"Sure, boss." His gaze remained cautious as he slid on his coat.

Once outside, Mick had to force himself not to pounce as they walked together toward the other man's mini SUV. "So, last night's call…?"

"Really, it wasn't much different than any of the other ones lately." David pursed his lips and moved his head back and forth as though considering. "Except that it was another abandoned house. Though, of course, we didn't know that going in. As Chief Hoffman always said, 'There's no such thing as an abandoned building—'"

"Until you search it," Mick finished for him. "We all say that."

"Yeah. Sorry for bringing him up."

"Park gave me most of the details last night." Mick lied smoothly while changing the subject. In truth, the captain had provided only basic details. "Anything else interesting about the call?"

He shook his head. "Burn patterns that suggest the fire was intentionally set. That's about it. We took photos of the crowd. Just the neighbors. It's kind of becoming routine."

"We can't ever think like that, List," Mick said. "If we do, we'll get sloppy, and someone will get hurt."

"You're right. We've been lucky so far." David pulled out his key fob and hit the button. With a wave, the firefighter climbed in his vehicle and drove from the parking lot.

As Mick watched him until his taillights disappeared, a question repeated in his head: Was it luck? Or was whoever had been setting these fires just playing with them until they became complacent? Would they then escalate to something bigger and more tragic than the loss of garages full of possessions or vacant property? The hard lump in his gut and the sour taste in his mouth told him he knew that answer.

All that planning for nothing. He picked through the rubble in broad daylight now that the fire investigators had finished digging around at the scene and had packed up their tools and gone home.

They wouldn't be able to track him, anyway. He was too good at this. His methods too methodical. That new fire chief wouldn't have some smug quote to say about his work like he had on the newspaper's website. Though he was dying to know what mistake had been made at that scene, he knew better than to ask too many questions. He couldn't risk looking curious, not after the little mishap with his car.

What that Prentiss guy had said was probably bullshit, anyway. The police had nothing. Just like with all the other fires.

This time was supposed to be different, though. Perfection. Like the ones on the big screen. Sure, the flames had been sweet. Eventually. After a slow start though linseed oil played a part in that. It was supposed to delay the burn. Not make it *that* slow.

Only when it took off like Independence Day, there was no crowd for the oohs and aahs. And, damn it, he deserved some of those. Instead, it had been like a cherry bomb soaked in the bathtub. A fricking dud. Hell, if the neighbors hadn't worried that the fire would eventually reach their properties, they probably wouldn't have called it in at all.

He kicked at the pile of muck with his boot, but there was nothing solid enough for even a good thunk or a stubbed toe. Just messy, smelly sludge. At this moment, he would have appreciated the pain.

Now he would have to start over again. Thinking. Planning. For something bigger, he hoped. Better. Closer to town. Maybe with casualties. Yes, that sounded better. That would teach certain people for not giving him or his work its proper due. It took an awful lot to make a headline these days in Mount Isabel. But he would show them that he still could, and he had a good idea where to do it.

Chapter 15

Early Sunday afternoon, Rachel pulled up the long driveway to the two-story house. She parked beneath the netless basketball hoop, which had become just a turnaround for cars in recent years. Then she took a long look at the house. Its beige aluminum siding above the brick had a yellow cast now. The shingles at the edge of the roof had begun to curl.

Like she had a dozen times during her drive over, she glanced in the rearview mirror. Not a single white SUV in sight. But if she didn't stop looking over her shoulder, she'd never make it through this information-finding mission. She shouldn't have lied to Mick about waiting until Monday to look for answers in her dad's home, but some things a gal had to do alone. Visiting all the ghosts inside her parents' place was one of them.

She could count on one hand the number of times she'd been inside the house in the past seven months. Okay, she needed a few extra fingers, but most of the stops had involved helping an inebriated Riley to his room after she'd rolled him out of Lou's Corner Pub. On those occasions, she'd been too busy to think about how different the place was without their father there. Now his absence would swallow her whole.

After taking a few deep breaths for courage, she climbed out of the minivan and stomped through the mixture of snow and slush to the steps. From the zipper pocket of her purse, she pulled out the spare key. Her hand trembled as she slid it into the dead bolt.

Yes, they'd built some happy memories there with the twins, but there were still rooms she couldn't enter without thinking about her mom. Now her dad's presence would fill all of them as well.

As she started to turn the key, her phone buzzed. She dug around in her purse's main compartment and pulled out her cell. Mick's name appeared on the screen. She considered letting it go to voice mail, but from what she'd already learned about him, she knew he'd only call again. With a sigh, she tapped the screen to answer.

"Hi, Mick." She coughed into her sleeve and then tried again. "Have you enjoyed your day off? Sorry you lost an hour of it with the whole 'spring forward' thing."

He chuckled into the line. "Doing great. Just driving around and trying to get to know my new community better. How about you? You're not coming down with anything, are you?"

"I'm fine." But she couldn't resist clearing her throat. "All that dry air must be getting to me."

"Why? Are you outside?"

Rachel shuffled her feet on the step and pulled her arms closer to her body before looking again over her shoulder. Still, no one was there. "Um, I'm—"

"Standing on the back step at your dad's house?"

"What?" She jerked her head back and forth, looking for him. "How do you—"

"Know that you're there? I'm good at guessing. Even better at reading people."

Just then, something squeaked near her dad's massive, detached garage, causing the thuds of her heartbeat to trample over each other. The side door popped open with another creak, and Mick stepped outside, his coat unzipped over his regular zipper hoodie. He pulled his cell away from his ear, tapped the screen to end the call and strode toward her.

"What are you doing here?" she asked as she pulled out the key. "Are you stalking me? Because I don't appreciate—"

He shook his head when she reached the bottom of the steps, but she could tell from his pinched expression that her words had hit their mark. Good enough for him. He'd scared the crap out of her.

Mick must have remembered he was angry as his jaw flexed, his eyes narrowing.

"I knew you wouldn't wait until Monday to search here. And that you'd come here without me even after we'd agreed to collaborate. You might be willing to put yourself—and your girls—at risk by being here, but I'm not. I'm going to keep my end of the bargain."

"There's only one problem with your premise. Do you see Carly and Carissa anywhere?"

He pointed to the minivan in the drive.

"They're not in there, either."

"But where…?"

"They're kids," she said with a sigh. "They do occasionally have playdates. I scheduled one for them today at my friend Stacy Kellman's. They're staying there for dinner. Stacy's even a nurse, so she can fix them right up if they get any cuts or scrapes."

Mick nodded, but he didn't apologize or even step away from her.

"Now aren't you sorry you wasted your Sunday afternoon, racing over here to protect...my girls?" Uneasiness filled her as she'd nearly said *me*. "How did you know I didn't already come yesterday?"

"From the snow still on the roof of your minivan, I figured you hadn't left the house all day. I know. Stalker."

Rachel rolled her eyes. "Now that you can see that the girls aren't here, you can go watch football or nap on your sofa or whatever else you had planned for your day off."

"You might remember that I don't currently have a sofa or a TV. Besides, you're here."

Rachel swallowed as he lifted his gaze to hers. It was so warm that she couldn't help shivering. He didn't have to say that he'd shown up at her father's house as much to protect her as her daughters. Relief she shouldn't have been feeling flooded her insides. She couldn't let it take hold. There was a difference between letting him help her search for answers and allowing herself to really need him. Though that line was blurring, she couldn't let it disappear.

"I don't need you to watch over me. I'm perfectly safe here."

Even under the threat of torture, she wouldn't confess how many times she'd checked to ensure she hadn't been followed.

"But since I'm already here, and there's not much to do at my apartment, mind if I stay? It would be a favor to me really. Something for the new guy to do on a lonely afternoon."

"Fine. Anyone ever told you that you can be over-the-top?"

"My ex-wife, but she wasn't my biggest fan," he said with a grin.

"I won't make you relive those days."

"I appreciate that."

"And I appreciate your help."

His wide-eyed response to her comment told her she should have said that before now. He'd been under no obligation to support her or her brother. But he'd shown up, anyway. And he'd kept showing up, until she'd recognized that his assistance wasn't such a bad thing.

To dodge the temptation to say more, she pointed to the garage. "What were you doing in there, anyway?"

She shot a look back at the driveway. "And where's your truck?"

"I parked it not far from here."

Mick gestured to the garage and then started back to it. Rachel stomped after him through snow that hadn't been plowed since Riley checked in at the rehab center. Some of it had already melted into patches of ice.

"But why the garage?" she asked again from behind him.

"It was the only unlocked door I could find. And it's cold out here."

"It was *unlocked*?"

Without waiting for his answer, she marched past him. He caught up to her again just as she reached the entrance. She bent and checked the doorknob, the bolt and even the strike plate.

"I didn't see any tampering, but then you're the expert," he said.

She frowned back at him. "Do you think Riley could've just forgotten to lock it?"

"People forget things all the time. Even those who aren't possibly hitting rock bottom."

Rachel blinked several times. She hadn't thought about that.

"Have you been back here since he went inpatient?"

"Once. Just long enough to turn down the heat and put the water heater on vacation mode." She didn't mention that she'd left the van running with the girls in the back, making it in and out in five minutes. "I never thought to check the garage."

"Your brother probably didn't, either. Besides, I've had the chance to look around. I didn't see anything of value. Except maybe tools."

"You're wrong. Engine 5's in there."

Rachel pushed the door open and stepped into the space that should have easily fit three cars with room to spare. Instead, overflowing shelves of boxes and containers lined the walls from floor to ceiling. She stepped past the first stall where Riley had managed to squeeze in his car.

"Dad was a bit of a hoarder. He never threw away anything."

She moved past some of the chaos and gestured game show-host-style to the tarp-covered vehicle in the far corner.

"That's what I was talking about. I give you Engine 5."

"You mean that trash heap of a truck under there?"

"How can you say that about Dad's pride and joy?" Then she shot a look back at him. "If you've already seen it, just how long have you been in here snooping?"

"An hour or so. I've peeked into several boxes but only found things like dishes and clothes. Not even books, let alone any sort of old newspapers or documents."

"He kept all his books in the house. There are a lot of those, too."

"I still don't get the point of the truck." He stepped closer to it and lifted the tarp to uncover the 1970s pickup with rust patterns decorating the front-quarter panel and widening the wheel wells. "Does this thing even run?"

"As a matter of fact, it doesn't, but that doesn't mean it's not—"

"Has it run anytime in the twenty-first century?" He glanced back, grinning.

She pursed her lips but couldn't hold that hard expression. "Maybe the first few years."

He continued to pull the tarp until the truck bed was fully uncovered.

"But it's not garbage. To our family, Engine 5 symbolizes the hard work and dedication of firefighters. It was priceless to my...*dad*."

Her voice broke as she said it, a wave of emotion washing over her, that familiar undertow of grief and regret tugging her downward. As startling as that rush had been, Mick's reaction surprised her even more. He stepped forward and tucked his hands under her elbows before her shoulders had time to slump. She didn't want his support. Shouldn't need it. But just this once it was such a relief to allow someone to catch her before she fell.

"Whoa there. Guess there's some slick spots in here, too." He lied smoothly, still holding on to her arms.

After taking several long breaths, she stepped back from him. "Thank you."

"Does that happen often? The slick spots?"

Rachel unzipped her coat as sweat gathered at the back of her neck. "Not as much as before. Sometimes it just shows up from nowhere and hits me when I thought I was over my grief."

"I'm not sure that's something you magically get over. Even if it were, this isn't *nowhere*." He gestured around the room, filled with her father's things. "Had you spent any time in your dad's house since his death? I mean before Riley was hospitalized?"

It was disconcerting how easily Mick read her. Though their experiences were different, he still seemed to understand.

"As little as possible," she admitted.

"And isn't this where your brother, uh, found…?"

She shivered as the image appeared, clear in her mind though she hadn't been present at the scene. Riley had shielded her from that, too.

"It was out in the woods back there." She gestured with a tilt of her head though they were inside, the walls saving her from having to see it. "I can't imagine how hard it must have been for Riley to come home at night with everything in the place reminding him of Dad."

"He was dealing with a lot."

Rachel brushed her hand along the pinstripe that started at the front fender and continued all the way to the bed with bubbles of rust under the paint interrupting the flow of her fingertips. "Then I asked him to do more by looking into Dad's suicide. I should have known he was spiraling, just like he did after he and Jillian broke up."

"Who?"

"He was engaged once," she said with a shrug. "Long story."

She braced herself for Mick to ask for details when she'd never been clear about some of them herself, but he watched her instead. "At some point you're going to have to stop blaming yourself."

"Interesting advice coming from you."

He smiled, but his eyes still looked sad. She could relate to that.

Mick rounded the side of the truck and opened the passenger door. "This thing might be rusty on the outside, but look how clean it is in here. No old drink cups or wrinkled maps. There's even repair tape over the cracks in the leather."

"Sometimes I'd come out here and find Dad sitting in the driver's seat. He'd tell me that he was working on something in it, but I never saw any tools."

"A man cave within a man cave," he said with a grin.

After Mick closed the door and moved to the back of the truck, Rachel wiggled out of her coat.

"Am I the only one who's getting warm in here?"

"I wouldn't say I'm overly warm, but those things do a good job." He pointed to the ceiling-mounted propane heaters. "I turned up the heat when I arrived. I didn't know how long I'd be waiting for you."

He rested his coat on a box but left on the sweatshirt over his shirt. "Since you turned down the temperature in the house, and it's already warm in here, you might want to look through these boxes first."

She grabbed one of the containers from the center of the room and unfolded the flaps.

"Sorry I didn't tell you I'd be coming to Dad's place today," she said after several minutes of digging through old T-shirts and towels. "I just had some ghosts to face. Memories in every room. That's why I wanted to do it alone."

"Well, if you still want me to, I can…"

He gestured to the door, but when she shook her head, he drew his brows together, waiting for her to explain.

"It took me all day yesterday to work up the courage to come this afternoon. I pretend I'm brave with Riley and the twins. And you." Her gaze shot to his. "But I'm not. I'm a coward."

"You're here, aren't you? Yes, there are things you'll have to work through regarding your dad, but your brother needs help, and you crave answers, so you're facing your fears." He rolled his eyes, chuckling. "Wish I could say the same. I left a whole state to avoid dealing with my own stuff. Now who's the coward?"

She shook her head, letting her ponytail flip from one shoulder to the other. "I'm not buying that. You walked away from your career after the accident, and you could have stayed away. But people needed you. So, here you are, trying to save Mount Isabel from itself."

"You make me sound like I flew in under my own power. And please don't call me—"

"A hero? I know." She shrugged. "Still, if the cape fits…"

"That isn't close to the truth. But today isn't about me. This is about you. And you wanted to spend time here alone to work through some things." He pulled his coat on again and started for the door. "So I'm going to go. I'll even drive by a few times to make sure everything's okay."

"Wait."

He opened the door and started through, but then he paused and looked back. "If you need me…" He tapped his phone in his pocket.

"But what if I do…need you?"

He tilted his head and studied her. "What are you saying?"

"I thought I wanted to do this alone. To *be* alone. But I don't want that anymore." She cleared her throat, the truth right there in her heart and still so difficult to say out loud. "I need you…and I want you to stay."

Chapter 16

Whether it was her words or the pleading look in her eyes that brought him back inside, Mick wasn't sure, but he'd passed the threshold and closed the door before he had time to process any of it. He reached her in several long strides, his arms opening and Rachel sliding into the space in what felt like a predestined move. She needed him, and God help him, he longed to be there for her—with her—more than he'd wanted anything in his life.

His mouth covered hers in a kiss that didn't come close to gentle, but his attempt to pull back, to moderate or even ask permission fell away as she met his lips with something that came closer to desperation than desire. He wasn't certain whether her request for him to stay had been a plea for support or a sensual invitation, but his mind tangled those two premises into an impossible knot.

Just like the other night, she tasted of heaven and all the other things he didn't deserve. Yet there she was, needing him and, yes, wanting him, too. He didn't have to dab his tongue to the seam of her lips to request admittance as she opened for him and deepened the kiss herself.

He knew he should think, maybe for the both of them since she seemed to be neglecting to do that for herself. Her urgency was out of character. And too difficult to resist.

As she lifted on her toes to press herself to him in every perfect place, he conceded that thinking was overrated. Whatever she craved, however much and for no matter how long she wanted it, he would oblige.

As he dragged his mouth from hers in a mad search for a place for them to land, Rachel made a frustrated sound in her throat. She moved to his neck instead. Tasting. Nipping. And finally tracing with her tongue a line above the sweatshirt's zipper and then dabbing deep in the notch between his collarbones. His eyes drifted closed, but after a few more seconds of her determined ministrations, they flew open again.

"It's been a...uh...real long time, so..."

"The truck," she whispered in a tight voice.

"You're sure?" Matching her in volume and strain, he tucked many questions into so few words. Should they be doing this in her father's truck? Or at all? Did she remember who he was? Who *she* was? Rachel answered at least a few of those questions with a nod against his neck, confirming her choice with another round of kisses on his heated skin.

Mick walked her backward, each step increasing in both friction and risk. Rachel's hands burrowed beneath his sweatshirt and shirt, smoothing up his back before dipping beneath the waistband of his jeans in mesmerizing sweeps. At the pickup's door, she reached back to release the handle while he slid out of his jacket and tossed it on the hood.

But as Rachel scooted across the bench seat, a flash of uncertainty appeared in her eyes. With his hands already on the edge of the seat as he prepared to climb in and settle himself on top of her, Mick stopped. Even if his whole body vibrated with need, the decision was hers.

"Just checking in," he said as evenly as he could. "Still sure you want to do this?"

She reached out a hand to him and smiled before lying back on the upholstery. He couldn't take his eyes off the sliver of skin, exposed between the hem of her sweater and the waistband of her jeans. The same sexy spot he'd been dreaming about since that first day in his office. He stepped up on the running board, rested one knee on the edge of the seat and bent over her, dropping a single kiss on her belly. Then another. And another. She squirmed beneath him, lifting up to him, wanting more.

"You're beautiful," he breathed the words though he'd yet to see all of her. "Perfect."

"Hardly."

Her chuckle rumbled through his chest as he stretched out over her, their feet dangling out the open door. Even with the steering wheel as a constant menace, he took her mouth again in an imitation of his plans for their bodies. All in due time. For now, though, he just wanted to taste and nibble and move against her in a tantalizing caress until they both lost their minds.

Rachel apparently had other plans. No slow seduction for her, she seemed to want all he had to give right then. She tugged his shirt up his back to his shoulder blades. He scooted back out of the cab and yanked it over his head the moment his feet touched the floor.

As he tossed it on the hood next to his sweatshirt, Rachel watched him with an appreciative grin. If any part of him wasn't already smoldering—and he doubted he could find one—heat would have covered that space, too.

By the time he'd climbed back on the running board, she'd already pushed up her sweater so that the red lace of her bra peeked out the bottom.

"Mind if I do that?" he asked before she could finish the unveiling.

"Well, since you asked so politely..." She rested back on her elbows.

Mick didn't make her wait for long. He traced a line of kisses from her navel to her sternum while his hands slid her sweater up, grazing delicate skin in their paths.

"Touch me. Please."

Though the next word might have been *now*, it started on a consonant and ended with a sigh as he slid both hands beneath her top, working what he hoped would be magic with his thumbs. Her sweet sounds suggested he was on to something.

They broke contact long enough for him to push the garment over her head. She released her bra's front clasp, allowing all that loveliness to spill out, and then wiggled out of it and tossed it aside.

"So beautiful," he murmured again.

This time she didn't argue and even arched her back, welcoming his exploration with lips and fingertips. As she pulled him to her, and he melded into all that softness, he had to remind himself to relish each sensation while his body clamored for more.

Clothes quickly became a hindrance to their shared goal. They unzipped and shimmied and wiggled, occasionally bumping their heads on the long gearshift, until they lay naked, still stacked together out of necessity, but giggling too hard to take that next step.

"I don't remember the car thing being this tough in high school." He reached up to shove back his hair.

"You did a lot of this in *high school*? You mean... I'm not the first?"

Her chuckle rumbled against his chest like it had before. Only this time with no barrier between them.

"First since the divorce, anyway." He focused on the dashboard instead of looking down at her. "The rest is so long ago that I barely remember."

"Good. Even if it was a while back, I suspect you can recall every embarrassing, fumbling minute."

Mick whacked his head on the steering wheel again and then rubbed his aching temple. "There's a whole house up the drive, probably with real beds and pillows. We could—"

He stopped as her body tightened beneath him, making him regret the suggestion he hadn't fully made. It was her father's house. To him, it might have seemed no different than her dad's favorite pickup that they were currently defiling in the best possible way, but to her, it must have been a whole other matter.

"I'm sorry," he said automatically. "I wasn't thinking."

"It's fine. Really. But as I said, I turned the heat way down in the house."

"And it's at least a little warmer out here," he said, accepting her excuse though they both knew it was more than that. He climbed off her carefully to avoid injuring either of them and then stepped around the door to grab his sweatshirt.

A heaviness settled in his chest, while the cold he hadn't noticed before prickled his skin. Though he was dying to make love with Rachel, nothing about this felt right. Not the timing. Not the location. He wanted more for them. Yet if she asked him to, he would climb right back in that truck and finish what they'd started. He'd fought the temptation to get too close to her, but it couldn't have been clearer that he'd lost the battle before the first shot was fired.

"You're not backing out, are you?"

He glanced up to find her watching him from the open doorway.

"No, but—" He gestured to the messy space all around them. If they couldn't go inside, they were out of options.

"Good. Because I have an idea." Rachel scooted out of the truck, shivered and lunged for her coat. Once she had it on, she race-tiptoed barefoot across the cold concrete.

"What's that?"

When she didn't answer, he followed after her, slipping his arms into his sweatshirt sleeves as he went. His feet stung every time they touched the floor. She moved from box to box, peeking inside a few, and then moving on to the labeled tubs.

"See if you can find anything that says 'Quilts.'"

Soon, they'd located four plastic containers, all labeled the same way, and dragged them to the room's one open space, next to the truck. Once Rachel started pulling out the heavy, colorful blankets and dumping them on the floor, he realized what she had in mind. Together, they spread out at least seven quilts until they'd created a pallet. She rolled an eighth quilt into a long pillow of sorts and held a folded one in her arms.

"Now that's better." She shook out the last blanket, settled crisscross on top of the pile and covered her lap, still wearing her coat. Then she held out a hand to him. "It's not the Ritz, but it'll do. Kind of like camping."

Mick lowered to his knees and brushed his fingers over the soft pallet but didn't take her hand. "Have you done a lot of 'camping' out here?"

Without looking up, Rachel rubbed her hand over the fancy connected-circle pattern on the cloth. "You didn't ask me that about the truck."

"I guess I didn't. I shouldn't have asked you this, either. You don't have to answer. It's none of my business." He wasn't prone to jealousy, but the burning sensation in his gut was hard to deny.

"I told you I have a past. Just like you do." Her hand stopped moving, and she looked up at him. "But if you're asking if I ever shared my mom's handmade quilts, the ones we had on every bed in the house until she died, with anyone...*ever*...then no."

Without stopping to think or talk himself out of what he wanted, Mick bent and touched his lips to hers. Though sweet and brief, it felt like the most intimate kiss they'd shared so far. His heart was entangled in this one, he realized, too late to take it back.

Rachel grabbed the hood strings of his sweatshirt and pulled him to her, drawing him in, giving him no chance to hold back anything.

They dispensed with the jackets, and then he joined her beneath the covers. Touching. Sampling. Readying. Her hands slid over him everywhere, each of the nerve endings in his skin seeming to reach out to her, craving her touch. Then just as he was certain he would explode if they didn't move forward, she flopped back in the pile of covers.

"I don't, uh, have anything. I can't take a risk like that. Again." She blew a stream of breath into her hair. "Why didn't I think—"

"Don't worry. I'm a firefighter. We try to be prepared for anything."

He grabbed his coat from the box where he'd left it, unzipped the inside pocket and pulled three linked packets from it.

She grabbed them from his hand and sat up. "You had this in mind when—"

"No. I didn't."

She held up her pinkie, ring finger and middle finger to signify the *three* condoms.

"One of my friends back in Chicago warned me that a new divorcé should be prepared in case he does something rash."

Her shoulders appearing to relax, she rolled over and straddled his lap. Then she tore off the first packet at the perforation and ripped it open with her teeth. "Is this irrational?"

Yes. No. He cleared his throat. "Maybe."

Still, when she held out the open packet to him, he took it and started to unroll. Wise or not, he wanted her. Not for just today, either, if he were honest with himself. He couldn't think about that now. Even if it was too soon for him to consider a relationship when the ink putting a legal end to his last one could still smudge on the paper. Even if they were the wrong people who met at the wrong time, players in a situation that neither of them chose.

"I guess we're not breaking one of our rules," she said. "We're not in public. It's not a risky excursion *alone*. And it's not tea after the girls' bedtime."

"We should have been more specific." And if they believed that the journey they were taking now wasn't filled to the brim with risk, they were just fooling themselves.

"Maybe."

She crouched over him and gave him a long, deep kiss as she brought them fully together. For a few seconds, they lay silently, neither moving nor breathing. No, that was just him.

"Will I regret this?" Rachel spoke the words softly near his ear. "Probably. But right now, I don't care."

Mick froze. She was joking, just like they often had

these past few days. If only that could have prevented the knot from forming in his throat. Rachel must not have noticed as she began to move above him, and he let himself be carried away in the sensation. She wanted him, and she needed him, he reminded himself. And everything between them was about to be amazing. But a question swirled at the back of his mind, blurring the edge of his bliss. Would he be able to settle for only today?

Was a crazy moment that she'd admitted she would regret enough for him?

He'd misunderstood. Rachel could see it in his eyes. The confusion eclipsing passion. The hurt entwined with need. Only she hadn't meant it the way he'd heard it. Not entirely. Sure, tomorrow she would regret this. They probably both would once the tingles stopped, their pulses slowed and the hum of desires stopped playing in their ears. But as for today, she was exactly where she wanted to be.

"You know, maybe we should—"

He cut off his own words as he eased his body back, and thumbs that had caressed her skin in mesmerizing brushes stilled.

Emotion squeezed inside her throat. Her fingers gripped his arms tighter. She had to make him understand.

"I want you. I want…this."

He didn't speak. Didn't move.

After waiting a dozen excruciating seconds, she stretched far enough so that she could touch the sides of his face. "Don't you want—" Though *me* sat like a rock on her vocal cords, she held it inside, the desperation of it shaming her.

A chuckle rumbled through his body into hers. "I'm

pretty sure I can't deny that part." He dampened his lips. "But I think we—"

"Don't think. Please. Just love me."

He strained to lift up far enough to touch his lips to hers. Then he slid his hands to her hips and jerked his shoulder to roll her onto her back. His elbow hit the floor with a thud, the pile of blankets offering little padding.

"Oof." He winced. "That was supposed to be my smooth move."

"We'll pretend it was." She reached up to rub his sore elbow.

"Gracious of you."

Mick lowered his mouth again, but there was no rush like before. He rubbed his lips over hers as though he had an overflowing account of time and no way he would rather spend it. Rachel couldn't help it. She squirmed beneath him, but he only smiled against her lips.

After a long, deep kiss that left them both gasping, he lifted his head and stared straight into her eyes, his lids hooded.

"I've been in a bed or two, and even the occasional car, but as for a pile of blankets on a garage floor, well, this is my first time," he said.

"I'll be gentle."

Rachel didn't get the chance to try. Mick brought them together again and moved with her in earnest. He reached to lace their hands near her shoulders, his mouth leaving hers only long enough to trace kisses down her throat before returning. Release washed over her, and he joined her while she floated on the waves.

For a few minutes longer, they lay together in silence, his chin resting near her collarbone.

He lifted his upper body and looked down at her. "I

don't know about you, but I'm freezing, and my knees are killing me because I'm not a—"

She held up an index finger him to stop him. "If you make another old guy joke, I'm going to take every single one of these blankets."

"Fine. You win." He rolled off her and pulled the top quilt up to his chin.

"We can't stay out here forever, you know. We'll either freeze or starve to death."

"Probably both in the next hour."

She cuddled close to his shoulder anyway, and he moved his arm so she could settle against his side. With his chest rising and falling next to hers, she closed her eyes and settled in, more content than she'd felt in months. Maybe years.

Then a thought that skimmed through her mind opened her eyes and made her whole body flinch. It was more than that she'd made a bed for Mick and herself with her mother's precious quilts. The ones that her dad couldn't bear to keep in the house following her death. Rachel had also asked Mick to love her. Not have sex. Not have a fun diversion on a Sunday afternoon. To *love her*. And whether Mick, as a new divorcé, was prepared for that—whether *she* was ready to admit she wanted something where emotions and not just bodies were involved—she knew in her heart he'd done just that.

Chapter 17

The cold won out eventually. With the quilt they'd rolled as a pillow open over his shoulders, Mick hopped around the room to give his feet minimal contact with the freezing cement while trying not to trip over the blanket. Rachel was on her own hazardous journey with a quilt wrapped around her like a tortilla. He couldn't help grinning at her hair, poking out in all directions from her ponytail, but she was clearly avoiding looking at him.

Mick knew morning-after regret when he saw it. Only it wasn't even dinnertime yet. He let his shoulders drop as he looked away and had to grasp the corners of the quilt to avoid streaking across the garage. She might no longer appreciate seeing him that way, even if he couldn't close his eyes without picturing all of her perfection. Or inhale without breathing in the touch of her perfume that lingered on his skin.

He'd messed up, all right. And he was in over his head.

His chest squeezing, he moved to the truck, its door still hanging open. He grabbed his shirt and boxers that he'd left near the right front tire. A gray sock lay beneath them.

"This is yours." He held it out to her.

"Do you see the other one?" Rachel asked but didn't approach.

"Not yet, but here's one of mine." His heavy black sock dangled from the top of his boot, but the other one wasn't anywhere near it. Under the tread of his other boot, he located a second gray sock. "Here's your other one."

She must have worked fast, he discovered, as he turned back to find her wearing her zipped coat over the quilt. Her jeans were draped over her arm, and though she'd tightly fisted her hand, satiny black panties that he knew intimately peeked out from the circle of her pinkie.

"I'll turn away so you can get dressed."

He did as he said he would until she cleared her throat. Slowly, he looked back to her. She hadn't moved.

"Um, I still don't have everything."

"Right." Leaning inside the truck door, he found her sweater rolled into a ball on the passenger-side floor mat. He shook it out and added it to the socks he was holding.

"Still not everything."

She didn't have to tell him which item she'd lost. He'd never be able to see a red bra again without picturing how amazing she'd looked in hers. But it wasn't with her sweater.

Her expression pinched, she rounded the truck to the driver's side and dressed behind that screen. The door they hadn't opened earlier squeaked when she pulled it wide. She climbed inside, still wearing her coat for a shirt.

"I'll look under the truck," he said. "I'm still missing a sock."

He bent to move outside her line of vision and put on his boxers and jeans. Then folding a blanket for extra padding for his sore knees, he lowered to the floor and peered under the truck. His second sock appeared behind the front tire. Without his phone to use as a flashlight, he smoothed his hand around on the cement, hoping to catch on something lacy.

"Not under here. Found my sock, though. Hey, think there's any food in the house? Maybe before we start digging through boxes, we could grab a bite—"

He backed out and stood but cut off his words as he found Rachel on her knees on the bench seat, her head bent as she looked behind it. After a few seconds, she reached down and pulled her lacy garment out by a strap.

"Oh, good. You found it."

Rachel didn't turn back to him or respond. Instead, she continued examining something behind the seat.

"What else did you find? Tell me it's not a mouse's nest."

He appreciated that she didn't glance over to see him openly shiver at the thought of that. Without responding, she reached down again and pulled out a messenger bag with a thick shoulder strap. The bag didn't look particularly special, its light brown leather scarred, but Rachel cradled it as though it were precious.

"Was that your dad's? Your mom's?"

Still not answering, she set it on the seat next to her, turned the clasp and threw back the flap. Three file folders had been placed inside.

"What is it? Why would your dad keep papers in the cab of his old pickup truck?"

She pulled the first file out of the bag, opened it and stared down at the paper.

"He didn't," she said finally. "The bag wasn't his. It's Riley's. A prize possession."

"So what's it doing out here? What's in it?"

Once again, she didn't answer, but she turned the paper

so that Mick could see it, too. The letterhead at the top said "Bilton Holdings."

"Well, you were looking for answers, so—"

She lifted her hand, signaling for him to stop, then pointed to words just below that letterhead and a date from nearly twenty years in the past.

To the Mount Isabel Police Department:

I wish to confess to a long list of crimes associated with Bilton Holdings Corporation and the Bilton Foundation...

Her hand moved too quickly for him to see what else the letter said as she traced two fingers down the page to a signature at the bottom and a name printed below it.

That part, he read aloud. "Stanley F. Hoffman, Chairman of the Board."

Rachel backed out of the truck and reached for the zipper pull on her coat, her hand trembling so much that she missed twice before clasping it between her thumb and forefinger. Once she'd unzipped it, she couldn't shake out of her jacket fast enough. She dumped it on the floor. What did she care if Mick saw her topless again? Nothing else mattered since she'd learned that everything she believed about her father—and her whole family—had been a lie.

There was no honor. No decency. Only lies. How could she wrap her head around the idea that her father was...*a criminal*? She didn't want to believe it, but the words were right there in black and white. Shaking her head, she tried to brush aside the questions as she slid her arms into the straps of her bra and fixed the clasp.

"Riley told me not to look," she said, not caring if Mick could hear her. "Why didn't I listen? Why couldn't I just forget about it?"

A shiver overtook her from so much more than the

cold just as Mick rounded the truck to the driver's side. Like her, he'd pulled his jeans on, but he was still shirtless and barefoot. While rocking from his heels to his toes, he held out her sweater and socks. He'd draped his own shirt over his arm.

With a nod of thanks, she accepted her clothes. She yanked the top over her head.

Mick pulled on his shirt and then coughed into his sleeve. "I know what you've found is upsetting, but—"

"Upsetting? You think that's all it is?"

He held up his hands. "No, I realize it's bad, but we haven't even read it."

"Isn't it enough already? The man just confessed to God-knows-what involving Bilton. We didn't even know he was part of that company, and he was *chairman of the board*?"

"You still don't know everything. You still have to read the rest of the file."

As gooseflesh skimmed up her arms over what she still might find, she lunged for the file folder. Then she dropped it back on the seat. "I can't read that *here*."

She jerked her hand to indicate their surroundings, which still included a pile of blankets on the floor. "I should never have come. What was I even doing here?"

The look they exchanged made her cheeks burn at the memory of Mick's touch. What they'd both been doing in the garage seemed like an even bigger mistake now. Rather than looking for information that could have helped Riley, they'd been christening her father's truck and her mother's quilts.

"You weren't the only one in that…bed." He gave her another look and stepped to the pallet to clear away the blankets.

"Let's not talk about that now. I can't—" She shook her head, trying to clear her muddled thoughts. "It was a blip in judgment. That's all."

But she couldn't look at him as she said it. Otherwise, those kind, gentle eyes would see the uncertainty in hers.

Desperate for something to do with her hands, she crossed back to the blankets on the floor. She picked one up, folded it and stowed it in one of the open tubs.

"I wasn't talking about the garage." Mick tucked a quilt in a different container. "I meant we could read it in the house. We'll turn up the heat and make some coffee and—"

"I've got to pick up the girls from Stacy's. It's getting late." Rachel let her shoulders drop as she recognized that there was probably still time to peek...if she wanted to do that. "Don't you get it? I can't be here. Anywhere."

In a place that she'd already suspected would be filled with ghosts, those records had turned the spirits sinister.

"Clearly, I didn't know the man at all," she said to fill the silence as she reached for another quilt.

Her breath caught as she recognized the double-wedding-ring design that once had been stretched over her parents' bed. Before she could stop herself, she buried her face in the cloth. When she lifted her head, she caught Mick watching her, his gaze so compassionate that her chest squeezed. She wasn't sure how to explain to him that on a day when her father had become a stranger to her, she still clung to that little-girl memory of her mother.

"How about we take the whole bag back to your house and go through them after you pick up the twins?" he asked.

"Maybe we should just—"

Mick crossed his arms and lifted both brows. He could

be as stubborn as she could, and he would never agree to leave her to deal with this discovery alone. Since she was too tired to argue about it, she nodded.

"Remember you don't know the whole story yet," he said. "Even the stuff in the bag might not tell you all of it. Like why your father wrote a confession nearly twenty years ago and then never bothered to deliver it to police."

"Maybe he had second thoughts?"

"Then why keep it where someone, like your brother or you, could find it?"

He stacked the first two tubs together and rested them against the wall. "It could be a fake. Or your dad could have been coerced into writing it. All we know for sure is your dad isn't around to tell his side of the story."

Her chest ached with the need to buy into Mick's theories, to believe that her father was innocent and that this had all been some big mistake. But as her gaze shifted to Riley's messenger bag, her throat tightened, her hope straining.

"The stuff in there will give me a good overview of my father's side. If not that, his suicide made a pretty strong statement all by itself."

Mick blinked as though he'd forgotten that part. The irony that she'd once tried to convince herself, and anyone else who'd listen, that her father's death had been an accident, niggled at her as well. She couldn't have been more wrong, but right now she was too angry and hurt to care if guilt had pushed him to that awful limit.

She returned to the truck to collect the messenger bag. Resisting the temptation to open the folder and read every word in this place that served as a reminder of her father's betrayal, she tucked it inside and closed the flap. When Rachel returned, Mick pointed to the bag.

"You don't have to look at it. You could just put it back behind the seat and pretend you never saw it. Just like your brother must have done. No one would have to know."

She tilted her head and studied him. "You'd be able to forget what you saw?"

He nodded, then shrugged. "I'd try. If whatever your father didn't involve the Mount Isabel FD, anyway. It has nothing to do with me."

"Wouldn't it bother you not to report crimes you'd become aware of?"

"Like I said, not my business."

"I don't believe that for a minute." In her gut, she already knew Mick was an honorable man, just like Riley. And, like her brother, it would kill him to keep a secret that wasn't even his.

But could *she*? For a second, she allowed herself to consider it, though nausea already rolled in waves inside her.

"Riley did ask me to forget about it. But we all know that's not who I am. He only looked into our father's suicide because I couldn't let it lie. Then he was forced to hide our dad's secrets. No wonder he—"

"You're not going to blame his relapse on yourself again, are you?"

Lifting her chin, she crossed her arms. "Like you said about being cleared of responsibility in that fire last year, I can't claim total innocence. I put him in that situation. He might have kept secrets to protect our family's reputation, but he did it mostly to shield me."

"He's a good brother."

"Wish he could say that I'm a good sister, too."

"He can. And, no matter what stories you've told me, I bet he always could."

Rachel shrugged, not ready to believe what he'd said but desperately wanting to.

"There's just one thing I don't understand," Mick said. "If he didn't want you to ask questions, then why did he mention the Bilton Foundation at all?"

She shook her head over the question that had been bugging her since Friday. But the answer was suddenly clear. "Because he knew I would look, no matter what he said. So he gave me something I could research on the internet. He probably figured that was safer than going out and asking the wrong people questions."

"And you did that, right?"

Rachel ticked off facts on her fingers. "I found a corporate address in South Carolina. And on the ChariGuide database, I found the foundation's annual Internal Revenue Service Form 990 for nonprofits and the board of directors list. No names I recognized on that."

"Riley never expected you to track down the information that *he* found."

"But I did. So, if I'm going to help him now, I need to know all of it." She patted the bag. "Want me to drop you off at your truck?"

"It would definitely shorten the walk."

When she glanced over, he grinned. "Maybe I parked a little farther than I said earlier."

Rachel rolled her eyes but then stepped to the controls for the propane heaters. They moved about the room, closing boxes and stacking tubs the best they could. Sure, it was a little awkward between them, but not as much as she would have expected. It felt like they were on the same team. One that just might be able to help Riley. Maybe they could forget that they'd made love while working together to uncover the truth. Or at least pretend to.

She had no doubt that the situation was about to get darker once they studied all the information they'd found. But for just that moment, she let herself breathe and appreciate that she wasn't alone.

Chapter 18

Even with the arrival of daylight savings time, the sun was already dipping by the time they stepped outside the garage. Rachel shivered as the wind seemed to blow right through her coat and her clothes, the temperature having dropped at least ten degrees.

"I can't believe I let it get so late," she said, taking a peek at the time on her phone. Stacy had offered to keep the girls through dinner, but she hadn't invited them for a school-night sleepover.

She rushed to lock the dead bolt but only ended up dropping her keys. Mick bent to grab them and handed them to her.

"Nobody forgot to lock up this time," he said as she inserted the key.

Then his attention shifted toward something farther down the drive. He froze.

"What is it?" Her heart thudded in her chest.

Instead of answering, Mick wrapped an arm around her and pressed them both flat against the exterior of the garage as though to shield them from being seen.

"Try to get back inside," he whispered, his voice tight.

But with the bolt set, it was too late.

A dark-colored sedan that had been right behind her

minivan spun out, its daytime running lights flashing against the cell in her hand. Then it raced down and out of the driveway. As it turned onto the two-lane road, it fishtailed and raced away.

"What was that? What were they doing here?" Her whole body trembled, so she crossed her arms to hold herself still. "Did you get a look at the driver?"

Mick shook his head. "The windows didn't appear to be tinted, but I still couldn't see inside. We've got to get out of here."

When he took hold of her arm, she jerked free and stepped back.

"But we don't know—" Only she did. No one appeared to have been at her dad's house since she'd taken Riley to rehab. No tire tracks or plowed snow. Even the unlocked door didn't seem as suspicious as it had earlier since nothing, other than a few boxes the Mick had looked in, appeared to have been touched.

And now, on her first time back visiting the house, someone had shown up there.

"Do you think they followed me?" A fresh wave of shivers took her as she suspected she already knew the answer to that. "I watched to make sure that no one did."

His quizzical look reminded her that she'd pretended not to have been concerned earlier.

"Whoever it was just saw us together," he said.

When he reached for her again, she didn't pull back but hurried with him toward the minivan.

"They could have been following you instead," she said once she'd reached the driver's side door. "You did have the quote in the *Informer*. But you don't think so, do you?"

"Neither do you."

Rachel nodded, her knees wobbly.

When they reached the minivan, instead of immediately hitting the unlock button on her key fob, she tested the door handle first. Still locked. She leaned close to the windows to check behind the seat anyway before climbing inside.

"How long do you think they were out here?" She climbed inside and inserted the key into the ignition.

"Could have been a while."

They exchanged worried looks over how they'd spent the afternoon. Rachel glanced back at the house first, then the garage. She'd checked her van lock, but they hadn't looked around for boot prints that didn't belong to either of them.

She blasted the heat inside the van, and frigid air shot to her face and feet, but the shivers that overtook her again had nothing to do with the cold. Could someone have been lurking just outside of one of the garage's three automatic doors, listening?

"I hope it wasn't long." Her stomach felt rock-hard as she added, "That was also *not* a white SUV."

Next to her, Mick dragged his teeth over his bottom lip. "And this time, we're nowhere near a fire scene."

Mick knocked on Rachel's back door ninety minutes after she dropped him off at his truck. He'd waited until the evening's stranglehold on daylight finally eased, but he no longer knew why he bothered trying to visit her in secret now. Whoever had been trying to frighten her already knew about him, and it would be more difficult than ever to keep her safe.

He adjusted the strap of the backpack he carried this time, his civvies folded inside for work in the morning. She would argue about his plan, but he would be spending the night on her couch whether she thought it was a good idea or not. He couldn't leave her and the girls there, exposed.

She pulled open the door, wearing a knee-length robe, flannel pajama pants peeking out at the bottom, fuzzy slippers on her feet. The towel wrapping her head announced that she, too, had showered. He doubted that hers had been for the same reason—that he couldn't concentrate with her scent still on him, threatening his senses every time he took a breath—but she'd washed him off all the same. She waved him inside and shut the door.

"Are the girls in bed?" he asked in a low voice.

"Just. It won't take them long to go to sleep. They played hard today."

Her gaze flicked to his, hinting that she knew of two others who'd played with some enthusiasm of their own, but she looked away and padded into the dining area. He needed to forget about those things if he hoped to help her at all.

She'd tucked the messenger bag into one of the chairs at the table, but her laptop was open at her regular spot, a notebook and pen resting next to it. He set his backpack on the floor before removing his coat and hanging it on the same chair he'd claimed lately.

"What's that?" She pointed to the backpack.

"Clothes. I should stay over." At her wide eyes, he added, "On the couch. Just to make sure everyone's safe."

"We'll talk about it later."

And later, he would convince her to let him stay, but he decided not to start an argument just yet. They still didn't know what they would find inside those folders, including what he suspected whoever had been in the driveway earlier didn't want them to see.

He pointed to the messenger bag. "Did you already...?"

She shook her head and then pulled the whole thing on top of the table. "I haven't had the chance yet."

Either that, or she wanted him to be there while she examined it. Since he suspected there would be something even more awful in those files, he was glad she'd waited. He wanted the chance to support her no matter what she found.

She pulled the first file out and tipped back the corner, hesitating.

"Last chance to put the whole thing away and pretend you don't know anything while you still mostly don't," he said.

"I think we're beyond that." She stared down at her fingers for several seconds and then looked up at him. "Whoever that was in the car, they really didn't want me to know what's in these files."

Her jaw tightened as the determination he'd come to love about her flashed in her eyes. She opened the file flat, angling the stack of papers so they both could read.

Mick heard the catch in her breath just as one word halfway down the page leaped out at him. They'd missed it earlier when they'd been so focused on her father's name and title at the bottom.

"Murder?" She gasped and poked her forefinger on the paper while she tried to catch her breath.

He repeated the name in his head but was certain he'd never heard it. "Did you ever know any 'Ben Morrison'? It doesn't say there who he was or even when...he died."

Her eyes were wild as her hands braced on the edge of the table.

"Were there any members of your dad's crew who died while he was chief?"

"The department hasn't lost a firefighter in seventy-five years. That was always a point of pride for D—" She cleared her throat. "I mean Stan."

Though Rachel didn't look at him, her pain coursed through him. She'd lost her father twice now, both times in violence. She couldn't allow herself to mourn him now. Refused to call him "dad." As for the part about no firefighter casualties, Mick ruthlessly pushed that aside. If he allowed himself to think about the crew members he'd lost, he wouldn't be in the here and now for her. And she needed him.

"Then who was he?" he asked.

She shook her head and continued to read. The confession was short and to the point. It listed bribes, falsifying documents and not one but *two* murders, all for which Stan Hoffman took full responsibility. Whether Rachel's father had truly been involved in any of it, he couldn't say. But if he had, Mick would have bet his pickup and all his furniture in storage back in Chicago that he'd had help.

"That seems a little convenient, don't you think?" Mick pointed to that part of the letter. He hated that he'd said something similar when Rachel had first come to him, claiming secrets and cover-ups. Even if they didn't have all the details, he knew now that she was right.

"What does?" She looked up from the document.

"That your dad confessed to a one-man crime spree. Seems like even if he did all these things, he would have needed help with the heavy lifting. Particularly covering up a murder." He tapped his finger on the words. "It even makes a point of stating that he 'acted alone.' That's at least a small red flag."

That she shook her head, refusing to consider the possibility, made him more determined to convince her.

"And look at it." He lifted the letter to examine it more

closely. "This isn't even an ink signature. It's a copy. Why would your dad have kept a *copy* of a confession he never turned in? And who has the original?"

She held it up, studying the handwriting. "None of this is making sense, but that's my father's signature, all right. I tried a few times to forge it when I skipped school, but I could never quite get it right."

"Do you think this could be a forgery?"

Rachel studied the signature a little longer. "It looks real."

Her sigh made his chest ache. He'd given her hope for a second only to squash it, so he tried again, like grasping for something solid in a downpour.

"It still could be possible that someone else wrote the letter and forced him to sign it, maybe as a threat to expose him for lesser crimes." He slid it closer to her again. "Look at the words. Does it read like something your father could have written?"

She frowned down at the page. "It doesn't. He couldn't spell to save his life, and grammar definitely wasn't his thing.'"

"He wouldn't have had AI available to him then, either."

Rachel pushed the paper back at him. "Okay, so maybe he didn't write it, but he still could be guilty."

Her pained expression told him how much she wished that something in all those papers could have proven that Stan was innocent. He wished he could produce those documents for her as well.

Mick planted his elbows on the table and rested his head in his splayed hands, closing his eyes. But as the memory of the car from earlier burrowed beneath his closed lids, he opened them again, his chest tight, his pulse pounding as hard as it had when he'd noticed it in the drive. Waiting for her.

"But if your dad had acted alone in all of this, why would anyone care if you and your brother found out the awful truth about him? It wouldn't have hurt anyone else."

Rachel straightened in her seat and pulled the file closer to her. "Why didn't I think of that? If they had nothing to hide, or believed that whatever we found would implicate *only* him, then why the threats? Why set Riley up at work? Why any of it?"

"It's de Cervantes's quote, 'I shall be as secret as the grave,'" he said.

She nodded several times, now on board. "They knew that even after his death, Stan had information that could still hurt them. So they wanted to ensure that my brother and I would be too scared to try to uncover it."

"Or if you did find anything, they wanted to let you know what would happen to you if you told anyone."

Rachel chewed her bottom lip. "Like that Fielding quote. Something like 'not death, but dying which is terrible.' They made that part pretty clear."

"And, like you said from the beginning, the intentionally set fires around town are just a smokescreen to ensure that secrets stay buried."

She tilted her head, studying him. "Did I say that?"

Mick lifted and lowered his shoulders. She hadn't. He'd added that part all by himself. "Something like it. That someone was willing to burn down half the city to keep it quiet."

"And now you believe me?"

He rubbed the back of his neck as he considered her question. Had he gone from skeptic to lukewarm supporter to radical believer, all in a matter of days? And had he let a leisurely exploration of her body inspire him to take that final leap? But then he pushed back his shoulders and told her the truth.

"I believe you."

Rachel blinked several times. Her eyes were damp, but she turned her head away so he couldn't see.

An ache settled in his chest that she'd had no one on her side, and he hadn't helped. "I'm sorry I didn't from the beginning."

She surprised him by chuckling. "Why would you have? We were strangers. And I was this angry woman in your office offering, like you said, 'convenient' excuses to protect my brother."

"I should have at least not dismissed it so easily. I, of anyone, should know that stories aren't as simple as they seem from the outside."

"At least you believe me now." She squinted down at the pile of papers. Then her gaze snapped up to his. "But if the fires are connected crimes involving Stan...and whoever else, then why didn't someone just burn down *his* house? If he had any incriminating evidence against them there, it would have gone up in flames, too."

"I don't know," he said, the same question still bothering him. "But maybe someone was smart enough to recognize that a suicide of one family member, possible criminal charges against another, and then a fire in their home might raise suspicions. Even from investigators who aren't looking all that hard."

"So you can finally admit that—" She stopped when he offered a close-lipped smile.

"You were right about that, too. There might be a few who are searching hard for answers, but I'd say they're in the minority. Some don't want to know the truth."

"But I do. No matter where it leads."

He met her gaze and held it for a dozen heartbeats. "And so do I."

She pulled the confession off the top of the pile and again angled the papers so they both could read.

As much as his heart ached for her in losing the parent she'd believed was an honorable man, he couldn't help but admire her determination. Whatever his other faults, the former fire chief had raised an amazing daughter and likely a fine son as well, almost entirely on his own.

And, if he could admit it to himself, he was in grave danger of falling in love with Stan Hoffman's daughter.

Chapter 19

At somewhere close to three o'clock in the morning, Rachel braced an elbow on the table and rested her jaw in the curve of her hand, eyelids heavy. Her gaze shifted to the sofa, where she and Mick had already made up a bed for him two hours earlier with a pair of twin sheets, a pink, heart-shaped pillow from the twins' room and one of her mother's quilts that she'd kept in the closet.

She'd been too exhausted to argue when he'd brought up staying over again. Now she couldn't imagine corralling the energy to climb the stairs herself.

In the chair next to her, Mick sipped from a mug of coffee that was four hours cold. She winced on his behalf.

"Did you find something else?"

She almost prayed that he hadn't. Already, they'd located several documents connecting her father to Bilton Holdings and the Bilton Foundation. Like the confession, they were copies, but if there'd ever been other signatures at the bottom, they were whited out in these versions. Though she had to agree with Mick that her father, whom she could only think of as "Stan" now, couldn't have committed all the crimes alone, so far, all of the evidence pointed to him. Only him.

As she reached for one of the most damning pieces

they'd found, nausea built in her stomach. The soil study showed the possibility of an oil reserve on the property owned by Bilton Holdings. Only it was dated two years before oil was discovered. And two months before the Bilton group even purchased the land the Mount Isabel council had looked into buying for an assisted-living facility to serve low-income seniors. Worst of all, the same Ben Morrison, who Stan had claimed as his murder victim, was the geotechnical engineer who'd written the report. A quick obituary search had confirmed that he was, indeed, dead.

"Do you think this report was ever filed with the state of Michigan?"

"What do you think?" His skeptical expression gave away his opinion.

"Yeah. Probably not. Paying off the author of that report might have been the first crime." She pointed to the confession that she'd placed in the middle of the table.

"But it was more than twenty years between the soil study and his death." He reached for the report and checked the date. "Could he have come back for more money?"

"Maybe. A lot of it doesn't make sense to me." As frustration and shame melded with exhaustion, she lowered her head. "I still can't believe that it was all just a land scheme for oil."

"Not oil. *Money*. Isn't that what everything comes down to?"

"Apparently, it did for Stan," she groused, then rubbed her eyes.

"And all his friends, who were probably listed on the originals of those documents before some clever copying." He indicated the large amount of white space at the bottom of one.

"So it's clear why Riley's emails never included the biblical quote about love of money being the root of all evil," she said with a smirk.

"That would've been off-brand." He brushed his chin, with a full weekend of stubble between his thumb and forefinger. "Mount Isabel is nice and all, but can you imagine how great it would have been if the village had owned the property, instead of Bilton, when oil was discovered?"

Rachel's neck warmed. Mick hadn't mentioned Stan's name, but that didn't change the truth that her father and his likely co-conspirators had stolen all those possibilities from every village citizen and even those from neighboring cities who could have benefited from those buildings or services.

"All those grants from the Bilton Foundation that everyone drooled over for nearly forty years were really just consolation prizes," she said. "The people in that assisted-living center could have enjoyed their senior years with dignity for free."

"But if the village purchased the land and built on it instead of choosing an alternate site for that center, oil wouldn't have been discovered at all, and there would have been no gifts."

Rachel rolled her eyes at him. "It's a little late for finding silver linings. Ben Morrison also wouldn't have been dead."

"There is that."

"I remember Stan saying he used to serve on the village council before my parents were married. Wonder who convinced them to seek an alternate location." She lifted a hand to stop him from offering an obvious guess. "And even if land outside the city was dirt cheap in the '80s, how did he come up with the money to buy it in the first place?"

"With a little help from his friends, I suspect. The same

ones who have ensured that only your dad's name is on everything."

"Good friends." She sat straighter as she realized that, like Mick, she still wanted to defend Stan. Even with all the documents showing that she shouldn't cling to her belief in him.

"Speaking of money, what do you think your dad did with it? His place is nice, at least what I've seen of it, but it isn't a palace."

"That's what I've been trying to figure out" She pointed to the soil study that they'd moved to a stack all on its own. "We weren't rich. Riley would tell you the same thing."

"At least you didn't live like it."

Her jaw tightened, and she crossed her arms, but then she dropped her hands to her lap and lowered her chin to her chest. "I guess that's what I meant. We always had everything we needed, but not necessarily everything we wanted."

"Did you have a few special things? Nice but not too nice? Paid for with cash?"

She closed her eyes, mining her memories for images. When she opened them again, her gaze landed on the emerald ring on her right hand.

"Oh no." Her stomach roiling, she covered her mouth with both hands and ran for the kitchen sink. No way would she make it to the half bath past the back door.

Though she managed to avoid decorating the sink with secondhand coffee and bile, she was still leaning over it, her face covered with sweat, when Mick approached and rested a comforting hand on her shoulder. Her throat filled, and her eyes burned. He probably thought she would shake off his touch when what she wanted to do was throw herself into his arms and sob.

Without asking where to locate anything, he moved to her cabinet and pulled out a glass. He'd been in her kitchen before, though suddenly it seemed like a lifetime ago. After twisting the faucet to the side of the sink, away from her, and filling the glass with water, he held it out to her.

"Here. Drink this if you think you can keep it down."

She lifted her head and waited for another wave of nausea to pour over her. Once she believed she could trust her stomach, she straightened and took it from him, touching it first to her warm cheek before taking a sip. After a few more seconds, she took another.

"Thanks."

"You okay?" he asked though they both knew she wasn't.

He reached for her hand and guided her back to the table. Only after he'd pushed her chair in did he return to his.

With her fingers splayed, she stared down at the ring, letting her memory of joy swell first and then burst like a popped balloon. Another lie. She ripped it off her finger and whipped it across the table. Mick caught it before it could roll to the floor.

"Stan told me it was my mother's ring when he gave it to me on my sixteenth birthday. It was supposed to be… precious." Her voice broke on the last word, but she shook her head, pressing her lips together. She refused to cry. "I thought it was old. And…hers. Not some piece of gold he'd picked up at a jewelry store. Using cash."

"You still don't know that," he said.

She stared at him until he waved a hand, conceding.

"Okay, you suspect. But it still might have been hers. Even if he lied about some things, he might have been telling the truth about the ring."

Mick offered a hopeful smile. He wanted it to have belonged to her mother as much as she did, and she loved—no *appreciated*—him so much for that.

He studied the ring in his palm and then pointed to it with his opposite hand. "Mind if I put this somewhere for safekeeping."

"Do whatever you want with it." She waved it away, sure she would never be able to wear it again. It might not have been hot, but she suspected he'd purchased it with dirty money. That felt like the same thing. If Mick left the ring with her, she would probably chuck it in the garbage.

He stowed it in the inside zipper pocket of his coat before turning back to her. "Is there anything else you remember? Besides the ring."

"Not that I can think—" She stopped herself, recalling a big item in both size and price tag. "Well, the garage."

"That did look newer than the rest of the house. And the heaters are nice."

Their gazes flicked to each other's and then away.

"Riley's basketball court, too. Those were built at about the same time. I remember the cement contractor saying how unusual it was for someone to pay with that much cash."

"How long ago was that?"

She thought about it for a few seconds. "Well, Riley was about fourteen. And he's twenty-seven now. You do the math."

"Man, you two are young to have survived so much."

"We were on the accelerated program, I guess. But we'd be happy to quit. Anyway, I don't feel young."

"I can imagine."

"Your life hasn't been exactly pain-free, either, you know," she said.

Mick tapped his finger on each pile of papers. "That's true, but this isn't my turn. We'll worry about my messed-up life another day."

"Since it's *my day*—in bonus hours since my phone says it's Monday—I just thought of something else. Stan paid my college tuition after I had the girls. That I can't give back."

They exchanged a look that told her he understood just how hard that was for her.

"How did he even manage it? Walk into the bursar's office with a briefcase full of cash?"

Even as awful as the situation seemed, she couldn't help but smile at that image. "Nothing quite that drug-deal-like. He took out a loan against his retirement account. I tried to talk him out of it. Told him I knew he couldn't afford it and was grateful for the help he and Riley were already giving me with the twins. But he insisted."

"So, at least that money was legitimate. He worked for it and saved."

"Unless you consider that if he'd figured out a way to pay back that loan to his account, it would have been with money that he'd effectively stolen from the village. Or that if he didn't pay it back, he didn't really need his retirement fund."

"That brings us back to the earlier question. Where's the money?" He thought about it for a few seconds and then continued. "What about when he died? If you received a big windfall from his will, that would have been obvious. So, what did you two inherit?"

"Just what was left in his retirement account and the house and property, which he owned outright. Apparently, Mom received a small inheritance after our grandparents died, so—" She sighed and covered her face with a hand so that her fingertips touched one cheekbone and her thumb stretched to the other. "What do you want to bet that my mother's parents never left our family any money?"

"Like I've said before, we still don't have all the facts. And it's possible that your dad could have been telling the truth, at least part of the time. Like about your mother's inheritance."

A knot forming in her throat, Rachel nodded. Mick didn't know how much she wanted to believe that.

"So what now?" he asked. "Where do we go from here?"

"While the girls are at school, I'll take a closer look at these documents and try to find more information on the foundation online. Maybe more about the corporate endowment, which I discovered is managed by Mount Isabel Bank & Trust."

She stood and started stacking the piles of papers, giving the collection a quarter turn each time to keep them separated. Then, returning to stand behind her chair, she glanced down at the name she'd jotted in her notebook. "Then I'll also see if I can find out anything about that guy, Phil Fuller, who was mentioned in the confession. We don't even know who he is. Or was."

"But you won't be going out anywhere alone, will you?"

"Other than for school drop-off or pickup, no."

"Good. I just don't think it's safe."

She didn't point out that she'd be alone in her home once he'd left for the station and she'd taken the girls to school. He had to be as tired as she was not to have reached that conclusion.

"Tomorrow—I mean later today—we have to look at relocating you and the girls to a safer spot."

Instead of arguing about that now, when she was too

tired to even make her case, she nodded. "There are clean towels in the bathroom at the back. Good night."

"See you in the morning." He stood up from his chair and grabbed his backpack.

Rachel shut off the dining room light, leaving him with only the lamp in the corner of the living room to guide him to the facilities or her to the stairs. As they passed each other on their opposite journeys, their fingertips brushed, causing a tremor to climb from her wrist to her shoulder.

She crossed her arms to resist the ridiculous temptation to reach up to him, allow him to fold her into his arms and provide comfort along with the safety he'd promised. But she already knew how that could end, and however delightful, they were both exhausted. She couldn't think about that, anyway, when so many questions still crowded in her mind, their answers elusive.

Making the smart move, she continued to the staircase, but stopped at the landing.

"Mick," she called in a soft voice just as he switched on the overhead light in the kitchen. He stuck his head out through the doorway. "Thanks for staying."

He nodded and then moved out of sight. She climbed the stairs, her head and heart as heavy as her footsteps on each tread. With Mick out here as extra security, she had at least a small chance of getting some sleep.

Chapter 20

Rachel pulled her minivan into the pickup line with ten minutes to spare. Though she should have set an alarm to remind herself to leave sooner, she at least hadn't gotten so caught up in her online research that she'd forgotten the time. The searches had definitely distracted from her dictation work, where she'd made it through only a single day of recordings. If she wasn't careful, in addition to everything else they were facing, she would be the second Hoffman out of a job.

She put the van in Park but left it idling, the interior not fully warm after the short drive. Grabbing her phone, she tapped out a text to Mick. She'd missed him this morning. Even eight hours later, she didn't know what to make of the strange emptiness that had filled her when she'd descended the stairs and found the couch unoccupied, the stack of blankets and sheets carefully folded and resting on one end. Her timing had never been great, but she couldn't have picked a worse time to have become attached to him.

Found a few answers but a lot more questions.

She waited for the blinking dots that would show he was responding, but only the "Delivered" line appeared beneath her message bubble. At least some people were working during office hours today.

The school's obnoxious trio of chimes sounded just like it did every day, and the chaos of racing children began with the usual small army of skilled adults doing their best to hold all that enthusiasm in check. After a half-dozen big yellow buses pulled from the lot with their precious cargo inside, the walkers and the parent-pickup kids were released from their holding corral inside the gymnasium.

The children spread out along an invisible barrier that ran the distance of the front walk, waiting for a school official who could match them with the parents or guardians authorized to drive them off school grounds.

From this distance, she couldn't see the twins, but that wasn't unusual. Even with the matching pink coats they'd begged for, she sometimes had a difficult time picking them out until the crowd thinned.

Like all the other drivers, she inched forward as educators on bus duty brought the children out of the line, one by one, and helped them into other vans and SUVs anywhere along that curb. They even helped buckle them in since parents weren't allowed to climb out of their vehicles during the pickup process.

Rachel still hadn't placed the girls once she was close enough to have a fairly good view of the whole line. Her leg, suspended where her foot was stationed on the brake pedal, trembled. She was overreacting, she told herself, as she shoved back a wave of dizziness and reached down to still her shaking thigh. The twins were out there somewhere.

Only they weren't.

Her heart was beating its way out of her chest when

she reached the front spot. She could barely keep her foot on the brake.

A sturdy paraprofessional she only knew as "Mrs. B." stepped to the van and then took a good look around. She was smiling when she gestured for Rachel to open her passenger window.

"Good afternoon, Miss Hoffman. I don't see the girls. Did they accidentally take the bus this afternoon? I apologize if there was a miscommunication. That does happen occasionally."

"Miss Hoffman?" the woman repeated.

Clearly, she expected an answer, but Rachel couldn't breathe, let alone speak.

"They never ride the bus," she finally managed, her hands tight on the steering wheel.

The movements of all the people around outside the car were suddenly jerky, their voices too loud. Her brother had ended up under investigation. Was this what happened to her and her girls when she'd failed to heed warnings to stop digging for the truth?

"Well, let's see what we can find out from the office," Mrs. B. said.

Though the woman's voice remained calm, her wide eyes gave her away. She took a few steps back, lifted the walkie-talkie to her ear and mumbled something into it.

With a smile pasted on her face, Mrs. B. held up a finger, asking for Rachel to wait. She couldn't wait, but she couldn't move, either, as her heartbeat pounded in her ears.

"They're checking," she assured Rachel through the open window.

Behind the van, other parents took turns driving up, waiting for their children to be buckled in and pulling around her and out of the parking lot. They were oblivious to the tragedy unfolding in front of them.

The para didn't help with any of the other children or parents. As the other educators hurried from student to student and occasionally sent curious looks her way, Mrs. B. stared down at her walkie-talkie, cradled between her gloved hands, as though willing a voice to speak through it. But nothing happened. It was as though the whole school staff had gone radio silent.

Unable to control herself any longer, Rachel shouted through the window. "What aren't you telling me? Are my girls...*missing*?"

Mrs. B. held up her index finger again and looked nervously over her shoulder.

Rachel grabbed her phone and typed in 911. But just as she started to tap the button that would initiate the call, she caught movement out of her side vision. The phone slid from her hand as the middle-age pixie of a principal, Mrs. Sumpter, rushed toward her minivan, her coat flapping behind her. The situation was so bad that they'd sent out the principal herself?

"Miss Hoffman," she said when she stopped by the window. "I'm so sorry—"

"Where are my girls?"

The woman raised both hands to ask her to stop, a motion she probably used for school convocations, but it wouldn't work on her.

"What have you done with them? Who did you release them to?" She pretended not to notice the adults sneaking peeks at her or the few remaining children watching her with scared eyes and gaping mouths.

"Miss Hoffman," Mrs. Sumpter said again, her hands gripping the edge of the van's open window like claws.

Rachel shook off her fog, and people, cars and even trees began to return to focus. She must have suddenly appeared reachable, as the administrator's stern expression softened.

"There, now," she said with a nod. "Your girls are safe. They're in my office, coloring pictures and eating sugar-free lollipops. I hope you don't mind."

"Lollipops? Mind? What are Carly and Carissa even doing in there?"

"That's what we're trying to figure out. So why don't you pull off into one of the visitor spots up there and come into the building." She gestured the same instructions with a wide curve of her arm. "Just hit the buzzer and show your photo ID to the camera, like always, and Mrs. Zielinski will let you inside."

Somehow Rachel was able to pull into a spot and park without causing a fender bender with one of the other cars. She grabbed her purse, tucked her phone in her pocket and hurried to the door. The principal's assistant hit the buzzer before she could even put her driver's license in front of the camera.

Already standing at the entrance to the main office, Mrs. Sumpter guided her into the room with a nameplate on the door. There, like the woman had told her, the twins were set up at a small table in the corner, a stack of coloring sheets and a tub of crayons centered between them. They weren't wearing their coats as though they'd been there a while. Those were piled in a visitor's chair across from the principal's desk.

"Hi, Mommy," Carissa called out when she looked up from her colorful sheet.

Carly pulled a red lollipop from her lips and held it out

to show Rachel. "Hi, Mom. Mrs. Sumpter gave us suckers. We told her it would be okay with you."

"It's fine." Then she couldn't help herself. She rushed at them and leaned down so she could wrap her arms around both at once over the top of the table.

The girls grunted and tried to wiggle free. Rachel had to force her arms to relax so she could release them.

"Mom," Carly said, stretching the word out until it became two syllables.

Her sister, usually more up for public displays of affection, frowned at her and crossed her arms. She'd embarrassed her girls? Well, too bad.

Rachel was still staring down at them and willing her racing pulse to slow when Mrs. Sumpter cleared her throat. She took an automatic step back from her daughters' artist station. Now that Rachel had stopped yelling at her, the principal offered her a compassionate smile. She probably thought she'd handled situations like this one before, but she was wrong

"Now, why don't we let the girls finish their masterpieces in here while we step into the copy room next door for a chat. Mrs. Z. will keep an eye on them for a few minutes." She lifted a file folder off her desk and moved to her office's side door.

"I don't know," she began, but at the other woman's firm nod, she followed her into a narrow hall and then another room in the office suite, no more than fifteen feet away.

Once they were inside the room, with two fancy copy machines on one side, a wall of staff mailboxes on the other, and two school chairs oddly placed in the middle, the principal closed the door.

"Let's sit."

Mrs. Sumpter indicated the two chairs. Rachel did as

she was told, taking the seat facing the front window, while the administrator took the one with a clear sight of the door, a narrow window offering a peek at the hall.

"Now, I'm guessing that something went wrong with our protocols today, and we want to make sense of it so that it isn't repeated," the principal said.

"I don't know what you're talking about."

"You clearly had reason to suspect that your daughters might have been abducted."

"Well, they just weren't out there like they were supposed to be, and—I don't know what I thought."

"Miss Hoffman, our goal is always to keep our students safe. We can only do that if we have all relevant information." The woman waited as though she expected Rachel to fill in a blank. "Like, for example, if there's a problem we should know about regarding your daughters' noncustodial parent. There was nothing about that in the girls' records. We checked."

She tapped the folder she'd rested on her lap.

"Noncustodial?" She shook her head, none of this making sense. "There's no problem with him. He's not involved in the twins' lives—or mine—in any way."

Mrs. Sumpter nodded, her carefully blank expression suggesting that she didn't believe her.

"Then has there been a falling-out with any members of your family? A reason for your reaction?"

She didn't say *overreaction*, but it was implied.

"Instead of tiptoeing around it, could you please just say whatever it is you're trying to?"

"Thirty minutes before the end of the school day, our office received a call, requesting for a change in today's pickup. I don't have to tell you that this is highly irregular since those requests are expected each morning."

"Who called?" she managed though it felt as if someone was choking her from behind.

The woman's eyes narrowed before she continued. "As I was saying, we received this call, letting us know that there was a family emergency and an alternate person would be picking up the girls. Even then, he said he would be about ten minutes late, so he asked if we could keep your daughters until he arrived. If it were much longer, I would have been forced to leave them in the after-school care room and charge—"

The principal stopped and glanced over her shoulder to the parking lot as though she still expected this tardy driver to arrive. All the cars were gone now, except for those of a few straggling staff members, parked in the angled spots.

"Mrs. Sumpter. *Please*. Who called?"

Rachel pressed her elbows tight to her sides to stop the tremor that started at her center and forced its way out. She didn't know what the administrator saw in her expression, but it caused the woman's eyes to widen.

"Your brother, Mr. Hoffman, of course."

At Rachel's gasp, Mrs. Sumpter flipped open the file and produced one of the same green emergency cards that Rachel had to complete in duplicate at the start of each school year. She pointed to the lines where parents and guardians could list up to three names of other responsible adults to whom the school could release their children. This year, Rachel listed just one name: Riley. Since her father's death, she had no one else.

"I don't understand." The principal pointed to Riley's name. "I've heard some rumors that your brother might be having personal problems. This is a small town, after all. But if you wanted us to remove him from your trusted-adults list, you needed to—"

"Mrs. Sumpter, my brother is absolutely still a trusted adult in my children's lives. One of only a few." She let those words sink in before continuing. "But right now, Riley's also inpatient at Forward Path Rehabilitation Center. He only occasionally has access to a phone."

The principal blinked several times, her lips forming the word *what*, but she produced no sound. "That doesn't make any sense. Was it a prank?" She shook her head and continued. "They couldn't have made it out of this building with those sweet girls without showing proper ID and putting their names in the sign-out book, but why would they even try…?"

"That I don't know, but I will try to figure that out," Rachel said. "All I can tell you is whomever your staff member spoke to, it wasn't my brother."

Pressing her lips together, the principal nodded.

"And for the time being, my children are to be released to no one—not even the name on my emergency list—except me."

Chapter 21

Rachel held both girls' hands as they crossed the one-way drive to the parking area, though there were no cars approaching them. She hoped that they couldn't feel the vibration since she still couldn't stop shaking. Though she sensed that the women in the front office were still watching her and the girls through the window, she forced herself not to look back. Whether or not they believed her story, they would be extra vigilant now in protecting the twins' safety.

Something she'd failed to do.

Had she really thought she could shield her daughters when she still had no idea who was targeting her family? To make a bad situation worse, she realized now that whoever had pretended to be Riley on the phone was just toying with her. Letting her know he held the whole deck of cards, while she carried an empty box.

"Why did you tell the school you would be late, Mom?" Carissa asked as Rachel slid open the van's side door. "Mrs. Z. and Mrs. Sumpter get mad when parents come late. I heard them say so."

"But you weren't late, were you, Mom?" Carly asked.

She helped the girls into their seats and secured their seat belts, at least protecting them in that one obvious way. "There was just a mix-up."

Her daughters had probably overheard more than a few choice words from the women who got stuck caring for the children of irresponsible parents. But it was easier to let the girls believe she was one of those than to admit she'd allowed players in a game she didn't fully understand to use them as pawns.

She hadn't given the principal a complete picture of what had just taken place, either. How could she when she still wasn't sure? She'd provided Tyler Lawton's name when Mrs. Sumpter asked about him again, but Rachel had clarified that the man wasn't on the twins' birth certificates. Some theories were hard to abandon, and she would give the woman hers.

As Rachel pulled into traffic, Carissa waved to her in the rearview mirror. "Can Mr. Mick come to dinner again tonight?"

Carissa's eyes widened, and she clamped her hands over her mouth. "Oops, I'm not supposed to tell the secret."

"It's not a secret with just us, but neither of you shared it at school, did you?"

"No, Mom," Carly assured her.

She twisted her mirror so she could catch both of them shaking their heads.

"It was hard, too, since Mallory was talking about all the fires." Carissa deposited the proper amount of distaste on the name of their fellow first-grader who'd worked hard to be a nemesis to both of them since the first day of school. "She said someone started all them on purpose. And Mr. Mick would have told her she was dumb."

Rachel cleared her throat to cover her chuckle. "I don't think he would have said that, but how about we let the police deal with those things."

She could have followed that advice herself.

"Do you think someone will put our house on fire, too?" Carly wanted to know.

"Of course not," she said, surprised to be able to get any words out at all. "Why would you think that?"

Rachel hated that her children's monster in the closet was less a product of their imaginations now and more a true possibility. If anyone in town was more in the line of matches than her family was, she couldn't produce a name. Even Mick couldn't guarantee that the trucks of Station 1 wouldn't be paying their tinderbox of a house a visit sometime soon.

She shivered at the thought of it and then straightened her shoulders as the answer to an earlier question cemented in her thoughts. "Maybe we can have dinner with Mr. Mick, after all. He even asked us if we want to spend a few days in a hotel. Like camping."

"Camping?" Carissa bounced, her legs kicking the back of Rachel's seat.

"I love camping," Carly agreed.

Rachel grinned at the road ahead of them, glad to at least give the girls something they could look forward to, while finding a way to keep them safe.

"Can we go swimming at the hotel?" Carly asked.

"Yay! Swimming!"

As she pictured the hotel pool with steamy windows where just about anyone could have been watching them from outside, Rachel shivered. "Sorry, girls. I don't think that one will work out this time. You've both outgrown your swimsuits, and there's just nowhere to buy them right now."

Unless they visited any store where spring break clothes were on the center aisle. Sometimes a little mom lie was an absolute necessity.

She challenged her daughters' chorus of *aw*s with some other suggestions. "We can watch TV in bed after homework and even *eat* pizza on top of the covers if you girls agree to be careful."

Swimming pools forgotten, the twins bounced in their seats, excited to get home to pack the matching lime-green overnight bags with their names on the sides.

"Will there be two beds in the hotel room?" Carly asked.

"Probably. And you two get to share one."

"Will Mr. Mick sleep in yours?"

Rachel brushed a hand through her hair as memories from the day before flooded her thoughts, warm and heart-endangering. How could it have been just yesterday when she'd still been no more than curious about the Bilton Foundation, and Stan hadn't been a suspected criminal?

"No, he'll have his own bed." Maybe his own room, if they could find adjoining ones.

Rachel had never exposed her daughters to strange men at the house, always careful to keep her dating rare and private. And though Mick wasn't a stranger to them, she had to figure out a way to deal with that rule now, when the stakes were so high.

She had yet to let him know that she'd changed her mind about relocating the girls with him. Later, she would tell him about the incident in the pickup line, but for now, she would just admit that he was right.

As though that huge admission had somehow inspired him to answer her text from earlier, her phone buzzed then in her coat pocket. He had great timing. And so many other qualities and talents she didn't dare think about if she had to spend a few nights in the same hotel room with him, even if she chose to sleep in the bathtub for her own good.

Coming to a stop at the only remaining traffic light between the school and their house, she unzipped her pocket. She sneaked a peek at the back seat. Good thing the girls were staring out the side windows at the people walking up and down Main Street instead of paying attention to her. She didn't want to give them any ammunition for when they were sixteen, and she insisted that they should lock their cell phones in the trunk to avoid the temptation to text.

"What took you so long?" she said under her breath as she fumbled beneath the heavy cloth to pull out her phone. With so much to tell him, she would need to pace herself.

She held the phone in her right hand and peeked down at it. The text, though, wasn't from Mick. An unfamiliar number appeared on the screen, and the words inside the bubble made her breath hitch. Gooseflesh covered her arms. Her whole body shook.

"There is no refuge from confession but suicide; and suicide is confession."—Daniel Webster (1782-1852)

Mick didn't bother putting down his coat before rushing into the hall and locking the door of his office. Already, he'd been forced to wait forty-five minutes after receiving Rachel's series of texts before having the opportunity to go to her. If he had to wait any longer, his tight chest would burst.

Captain Al Park, the oldest among the three captains at fifty-four and the leader on Rotation 2, entered from the apparatus bay before he could make his escape.

"What's the rush, Chief? Trying to make sure you don't give more than a minute of overtime on your cushy nine-to-five job?"

"Something like that." He shifted his feet when the

other man seemed to linger for more details. "I've got a meeting."

"Ooh, a meeting."

He said it as though Mick had just told him he was off to a clandestine hotel date. Which, in a matter of speaking, he was. At least as soon as he could get Rachel and the girls packed up and out of that house. He slid into his coat since he seemed to be stuck there.

"You do fast work, Prentiss, moving in on all those local gals. Maybe you'd even have luck with the new festival director, Delaney Malone. She's become a celebrity since she seems to turn down every guy who asks her out."

"Sorry. Haven't met her," Mick said in a clipped tone that he hoped would end the conversation.

He only had interest in one woman in Mount Isabel, anyway, the one who'd sent him that undecipherable text earlier.

They know I know. Incident at school. Girls OK, but need to relocate. Tonight.

Another message had given him an address and a time to meet her, but even in it, she couldn't have been stingier with details.

"Maybe you should stop trying to live vicariously through the rest of the crew's social lives," Mick said, likely too late, given the captain's curious expression.

"Gotta do something to battle the old-divorced-guy boredom," Al said after a long pause. "Even my pup, Brute, has got a better social life than I do, getting to hang out with his sitter every few days. Want to see a picture?"

"Next time," Mick said, though he hoped the man would drop his cell into the toilet between now and his next shift when he would show off more photos of the teacup poodle with its hypermasculine name. "I've got that appointment. See you, Park."

"Sure thing, Chief." He gave an exaggerated wink but let him pass by.

Mick knew he should tell the captain to knock off the personal questions, but even after a week at the station, only a few of the crew were fully relaxed around him. He appreciated them, but Park was almost too nice sometimes.

"Glad to have a slow shift after some of the others lately," Al said from behind him.

Mick glanced back as he opened the door for the apparatus bay. "It's been light."

"Last call was a 'smells and bells,'" he said, using firefighter slang for a situation involving the possible odor of gas. "Little anxious about tonight. We old-timers just get *feelings* about these things."

"I hope your intuition is off, and you and the rest of the crew have a long, boring shift."

Still, Mick could relate to the captain's discomfort. He'd been walking around for days expecting the other shoe to drop, and now it felt like every piece of footwear in town was falling from the sky. He continued past the bays and out the door without being interrupted since it was nearly dinnertime. Once outside, he had to force himself not to run to his truck. His heart pounded as though he had.

As he drove, a dozen scenarios played out in his head. What could have happened at the school? How could they know what she'd learned about her father? And even if someone had discovered that, what did it matter? Her dad was the only one implicated in any of the documents they'd found. Were they worried that she'd found the undoctored originals?

Back at the apartment, he threw some clothes in a bag and then poured them out again and folded them so he could fit in a few days' worth of street clothes. After putting his shaving kit on top, he glanced out the open blinds of the apartment's back window. It was still daylight. The time she'd given him probably included a healthy cushion after sunset. He'd never hated daylight savings time more.

He spent the next ninety minutes pacing, grumbling and waiting until he could finally go to her. She'd admitted she needed his help, or at least he'd inferred from that dearth of texted characters. But would she finally trust him enough to let him do whatever was necessary to keep her and the girls safe? And, still not knowing who or how many people they were up against, could he really protect them if he tried?

Chapter 22

Mick had tried to be patient through hotel bed jumping, pizza with more mess than they could have predicted and an extra thirty minutes of kid TV before they could tuck in the girls. But as he sat at the table near the window, waiting for Rachel to do one last check to see if their fellow guests were asleep, he couldn't keep his crossed leg from jiggling. He'd waited long enough. He had to know.

When she finally crossed the room to him, she dragged the second chair over until they were close enough to whisper. Close enough that he could have touched her, too, but she was still so keyed up that he didn't dare.

"What happened?" he whispered as soon as she'd lowered into the chair.

"I thought he'd taken the girls," she said in a low voice.

"What? *He?*" Mick pounded her with questions before he could stop himself and shot a look at the two sweet lumps in the bed, just to make sure they were still there. When he turned back, Rachel was watching him, her hands gripped in front of her.

"Please. Tell me."

Using detached, clinical words, she gave him an overview about the incident at the school, skipping over the terror she must have felt in those endless moments before learning that the girls were safe. He broke out in a cold sweat. His chest ached with his inability to shield them from any of this. Like the victims back in Chicago, he'd failed them.

"It was just a game to them," she said. "They used my daughters as a way to show how easy it would be to hurt me. They know my weakness."

With her arms crossed, she brushed her hands over her sweater from shoulders to elbows again and again. He shivered as well, though the room was toasty warm.

"Could they have actually abducted the twins?"

"I don't think they could have pulled that off. At least not there." Rachel shook her head, her expression pinched. "The school's safety protocols probably would have held. Even if the guy could pretend to be Riley on the phone, what would he do when he had to show his face and driver's license to the camera to be buzzed inside? After that, he still would have to go to the front office to sign out the girls, who would have said they didn't know him."

"Someone in the office might have recognized that he wasn't your brother, too," he said, nodding. "But what about if he—"

Mick stopped himself from saying that the guy could have shot his way into the building, but her brows lifted as though the same thought had crossed her mind. After a few seconds, she shook her head again.

"I don't think he—or they—would do anything so… public. Most of everything they've done, at least to us, has been threatening but not obvious to everyone else. Until today. Even then, the principal jumped to the conclusion that it probably involved their father."

"Could it be…?"

She lifted her chin. "Absolutely not. You have to give

a damn in order to go to that kind of effort. Tyler never cared about anything but himself."

"Makes sense." But it didn't lessen his suspicion of her old boyfriend. They couldn't rule anyone out yet, and the pool of possible suspects had become an ocean.

"They wanted to get under my skin. And they did. They even sent me one of their little quotes to make sure I got the message."

"Where? To your email address? Not Riley's?"

"To my phone."

She pulled her cell from her purse, opened her texts and let him read it. His shoulders jerked as the words stared back at him on the screen, the most damning of all the messages. It couldn't have been clearer that they were talking about the reason her father took his own life. Mick read it again, managing not to shiver visibly, but he was glad he wasn't standing since there was no way his legs would have held him.

"Webster said that 'suicide is confession.' So, this is what you meant when you texted that they knew that you knew."

"Maybe I should have written 'what I had discovered'." She tilted her head as though considering and then continued. "All those warnings, all the quotes like today's and even the cars though I still don't know how they're connected were about convincing Riley and me not to poke our noses into the past. But if they were too late, they wanted to scare us into silence.

"We can't let them succeed." She shook her head hard.

"But you also don't want to put yourself or the girls in more danger."

"I'm here, aren't I? I took us out of the house, even stopping by way of Stacy's place, so I could be sure I wasn't followed. And I'll continue to be careful."

"You won't go off and search for anything without me?"

"Of course not."

"Does this mean you're ready to take this to the police?" He pointed to the messenger bag that rested in the corner, next to their duffels. "Maybe to Police Chief Larry Gilman? He seems like an okay guy."

"Not yet. We still don't know if anyone at the police department is hiding something. Or at Station 1. Someone has information. We have to figure out who and what's in it for them to hide it. And we need to know who is connected to Bilton, besides Stan."

Mick watched her for several seconds longer, close to him physically though her thoughts seemed so far away. She had to be dissecting every memory from her childhood, trying to separate truth from lies. He stared at her gripped hands, longing to touch her, comfort her and ease the pain of a loss that no one could ever make right.

"There'd be no shame in just walking away," he said. "You and Riley could take the girls and go somewhere else. Somewhere safe."

He had to force himself not to suggest that she should include him in that relocation plan. One big happy family where he was still the unwanted guest, trying to squeeze in. She probably didn't want him for more than a temporary distraction, and even if she did, the timing couldn't have been worse. "You could let Mount Isabel rot in its own filth."

"No shame in it, huh?"

When she looked over at him again, she wore a sad smile. But she planted her slipper-clad feet on the floor and lifted her chin. "You know I can't walk away, don't you?"

He hated it, but he did know. Her motivation for searching might have changed, but she was no less determined to find answers than she'd been that first night he'd met her. She'd longed to right a wrong then, and her innate sense of justice wouldn't let her turn her back on the questions, even when the answers hurt.

"I have to do this for Riley. For my girls." She took a deep breath. "If I did nothing, I'd be no better than... Stan."

As Rachel's voice broke on the last word, Mick couldn't hold back any longer. He wrapped both her hands in the circle of his, and when that wasn't enough, he leaned closer and pulled her to him. At first, she held her body soldier straight in his arms, determined not to need him, but he held on, his grip loose as he let her decide. She softened against him in tiny increments, first arms, then shoulders, then neck. He could hardly breathe as she lowered her head near his collarbone, allowing him to comfort her over a hurt he could never heal.

"Even if we find out that your father did all the things written on those papers, and I'm praying we won't, you have to know you're not like him. Not like him," he whispered against her temple and then touched that spot he'd warmed with his lips. When she didn't push him away, he kissed her brow bone. Then the apple of her cheek. It took him three more stops to reach his sweet destination. But just as he covered her lips with his own, she smiled against his mouth and then eased back. His hands still gripped her elbows since he couldn't let go.

"You don't know that. There's still so much you don't know about me."

He dipped his head and stared into her eyes. "I know enough."

"There were good things about him," she whispered,

and then jerked her head back. "I don't know why I said that. Maybe, like you, I'm still hoping to find proof that he's innocent of at least some of the crimes. Is that silly?"

Mick shook his head, the complexity of parent-child relationships never lost on him. He waited for her to describe her internal battle further, but she only slumped back in the chair.

"Not silly at all. There had to be many good things in your dad," he said. "Because they're in you. And the girls. Your brother, too, I'm guessing."

He blinked as something she'd said earlier replayed in his head. Louder. Its message more distinct. "Before, you said these guys wanted to scare you into silence. Is it possible you and Riley aren't the only people they wanted to frighten?"

Rachel started shaking her head, but Mick's idea had already taken root in his mind.

"Now hear me out. We both know your father might not have been completely innocent." He pointed to the bag. "All those papers at least show he was involved. But can't two things be true at once? Even if your dad wanted to confess, could he have kept quiet to protect you and your brother? Could someone have threatened your safety to keep him from going to the police?"

"Maybe. That's assuming he wanted to confess."

"There's a confession right there in that bag."

She leaned forward in the chair and crossed her arms. "Which you said might have been coerced. Even then, he never gave it to the police."

"He could have wanted to tell his version of the story. But there might have been a reason he didn't. Or *two* of them."

Rachel dragged her front teeth over her bottom lip as

she stared at her hands. She clearly wanted to believe he could be right but was afraid to hope.

"Do you really think he deserves the benefit of the doubt?"

"Of course I do." He leaned forward and rested his hands on her forearms, bracing himself for the possibility that she would pull away from him again. That she would reject the reassurance he longed to offer her as much as she needed to accept it. "Don't we all deserve that?"

Rachel shifted her shoulders.

"Finding the answers isn't for your dad," he said. "It's for you. Your life. And your brother's. Your history."

"We'll never be the same." She let her head drop forward.

"Maybe not. You'll probably always see your father a little differently. More human. I'm an outsider, who can't possibly know for sure, but I have to believe he loved you, too. In his own flawed way. Maybe he wasn't so different from the rest of us."

At that, she looked up at him, her lips lifting slightly. "You don't have a packet filled with your own confessions that I should know about, do you?"

He smiled back at her. "Fresh out. But I'm not perfect, either."

"Pretty darn close to it."

He was still trying to make sense of her words when she leaned forward and touched her lips to his. Then she moved closer and wrapped her arms around his neck and sank into him, as close to a surrender as he'd ever seen from her. Ever hoped to. He could feel her heartbeat, her anguish, her grit, all wrapped up in a woman who'd drawn him out of the past and dared him to hope for the future.

This wasn't the time for him to admit the truth in his

heart, but he could no longer deny it, at least to himself. He was in love with her. Despite a situation that put them at odds and placed her and her daughters in the crosshairs, he wanted to be with her.

He stood and took two steps back from her, preparing for a quick trip to brush his teeth and a long night on the sleeping bag he'd thought to throw in his truck. No way would he get any rest when he could hear her breathing in the bed next to his spot on the floor. When his makeshift sleep area would remind him of a pile of quilts and those hours with her in his arms.

When he returned, Rachel was already under the covers, lying on her side facing her sleeping twins. She'd pulled the blankets and coverlet over her but had left the low-lit lamp next to her turned on so he could make his way back. As he stopped at his sleeping bag, unrolled in the aisle in front of the beds and the dresser, Rachel raised a hand to get his attention. Lifting a brow, he waved back, but she lifted up, twisted and patted the mattress behind her.

His gaze flitted to the tiny brunettes in the other bed and then back to her. He lifted a brow in an unspoken question. With a frown, she pulled the blanket up to her chin and then patted the spot behind her a second time. On top of the covers.

"Sure?" he mouthed, and then gestured to the girls.

She settled into her pillow and closed her eyes.

Mick dragged the sleeping bag off the floor and up on the bed. Why he'd bothered hesitating, he didn't know, when he would have joined her anyway. Once he'd settled next to her on top of the covers, using the sleeping bag as a blanket, she reached out and turned off the light.

"Good night," she whispered.

She surprised him by rolling to face him in the dark.

She reached out to touch his face, hitting his nose before her fingertips settled on his mouth. Then she replaced her hand with her lips. With excruciating gentleness and only once.

When he leaned in, his body responding to hers as it had every time he'd been this close to her, she rolled away from him, her chuckle low and deep. "Sorry. I won't be able to stop. But give me your hand." She lifted hers next to him.

Grinning into the darkness, he reached up and entwined his fingers with hers. Always a gentleman, he was happy to help a lady out, so he waited for her to place his hand wherever she needed his touch most. She pulled it with her as she turned away from him and settled into her pillow, spooned against him and with his arm around her.

He snuggled against her, moving his head to her pillow and burying his face in her hair. It felt like the most intimate thing he'd ever done without making love. He was still smiling as he closed his eyes. The situation was far from perfect, but there was nowhere on earth he wanted to be more.

Chapter 23

Rachel pushed open the door to her father's house late the next morning and flinched at the squeak of the hinges. She shouldn't have been so jumpy. After not so much as checking on the house the whole time Riley had been hospitalized—her cozy garage visit two days before didn't count—she would be lucky if she didn't find something scarier than a noise living inside. Like a whole family of mice.

She yanked off the gloves that stuck to her clammy hands and tossed them on the kitchen counter. After a quick look over her shoulder, she crossed back to the door and bolted it. *Jumpy* didn't begin to cover the cold sweat under her coat collar or the way her knees had turned into noodles. She'd already dreaded coming here where she would be cocooned with her memories, but today she might find more proof that some of her fond recollections were based on lies.

Mick was right, too. She shouldn't have gone on this field trip alone, even if she'd tried to convince him that the threats she'd received had no real teeth. It didn't feel right to go behind his back, either, after he'd slept so sweetly last night pressed up to her. Even if she hadn't loved him before, which she had to admit she did, she would have taken the leap right then. But would he ever understand what she was doing there now?

After catching sight of a Mount Isabel police cruiser in the parking lot at drop-off time, she'd realized that yesterday's incident was more than another warning. She had to call it what it was: an escalation. A sign of urgency. She was running out of time. That left her with no choice but to try to find information that could expose others and possibly shield her father's memory before those involved in these crimes could hurt anyone else. Even if she had to do it without Mick's help.

She was there now, anyway, so she had to stop second-guessing. If only she could shake the uneasy sense of being watched as well. She was being ridiculous. The blinds were closed. Only a few cars had even passed her on the drive from town and none since she'd turned on her father's rural road. No one knew she was there. She needed to search the place quickly and get back to the hotel with whatever she found. Then she would figure out how to tell Mick she'd gone without him.

When her phone buzzed in her coat, she nearly climbed out of her skin. Her hand trembled as she clawed in her pocket for it.

"It's not from them." She repeated the words like a mantra, willing it to be so as her heart tapped out a message in Morse code.

At the sight of Mick's name above the most recent text, she forced her shoulders that had lifted nearly to her ears to relax. She let herself breathe normally again. Of course, he would have texted to check in with her. They were supposed to be working together. She didn't know what that said about her. Or at least didn't want to hear it.

She looked back to the phone in her palm and clicked to open the text.

How did drop-off go? Anything different?

Ignoring the fluttering in her belly, Rachel typed a quick response.

Other than the chat about the guy sleeping on the floor, no big changes.

That the lie came so easily shouldn't have surprised her. The teenage rebel inside her had become an adult, but she'd never changed. She braced herself for Mick to ask where she was right now or to mention his stealthy sleeping-bag-relocation plan from earlier that morning, but he did neither of those things. At least she didn't have to hate herself for lying to him again or wonder why he put his trust in her. She hadn't earned it.

Hurrying from the eat-in kitchen to the living room, she tried to focus on something else. That didn't ease her disquiet, either. It was like seeing the place for the first time. She was a visitor to a stranger's home.

"Where would you have hidden the documents, Dad?"

Her throat squeezed as she used the term for the first time in two days, an ache settling deep in her chest. She still wasn't certain how many of the statements made about him in the papers they'd located were true, and she could admit now that she'd come to find evidence to clear his name, but it was more than that. He was her father, and she would love him, even if the original documents proved Stan's guilt.

Still, she couldn't shake the sense that some proof of

her father's involvement might have been all around her. First, in the land that she and Riley now owned. Then in the walls of the house built to her father's specifications with the dark-paneled walls, the bay window that invited in the afternoon light and the built-in cabinets with bookshelves that stretched to the ceiling.

She turned a slow circle in the space, taking in the same sturdy wood and leather furniture that had survived from her own years of watching Saturday morning cartoons to the nights when Stan had read books to her children in his recliner, one tucked under each arm.

Pushing aside the lump that formed in her throat, she tried to look at each piece through a financial lens. If he had been as wealthy as the Bilton oil would have made him, then why had he lived an ordinary life as a fire chief? Sure, they'd had a few extravagances—the basketball court, her ring, the fancy garage to store a decrepit truck—but that didn't begin to account for all the wealth that had probably been pumped out of that land. Where were the sports cars, the fancy watches, the sculptures and paintings?

"He didn't care about things like that."

Where was the rest of the money? Though Mick had asked about it, Rachel wasn't sure she wanted to know. Some of it could be seen in buildings and projects all over Mount Isabel, but blood money didn't become pure just because it was donated to a good cause.

Something else Mick had said flitted through her thoughts again, making her restless as she stalked to the back of the house. Everyone deserved the benefit of the doubt, even her father. Did she as well after lying to Mick today?

Because she wasn't ready to consider that, she hurried

upstairs and into her father's office that had once served as the twins' nursery, with a pair of windows to let in the morning light. She pushed aside those sweet memories as well and dug in the center drawer of Stan's desk for the filing cabinet key.

"Why did he even lock this?" She pushed aside the overstocked files with manuals for old TVs and VCRs that had long ago ended up in the landfill. Riley had probably already looked through those papers while searching in the same cabinet.

During her next stop in Stan's room, she found empty drawers, where her brother had disposed of their father's socks and underwear and donated his nicer clothes. He might have located the files he'd put in the messenger bag during that difficult task that he'd shielded her from as well.

As she closed the final drawer, she scanned the closet and the bedside table, trying to see from a different perspective all the places her brother had already searched. But as she moved around a few sweaters Riley had left at the top of the closet, another location popped into her mind. Its existence was a foggy memory—she couldn't have been more than four at the time—but she shivered as it swam in and out of focus.

"Did Riley even know about it?"

She rushed back to the office to the set of cabinets and bookshelves that matched those in the living room downstairs, already knowing the answer. If her brother was aware of the space, he'd never learned about it from her. It was a secret, like the one they'd shared with the twins about Mick visiting their house. Only she'd kept it for more than twenty years.

The muscles in her neck tightening with the ridiculous

notion that she'd be caught like the last time, she closed the office door and then moved to the far end of the bookshelves, past rows of her dad's beloved mysteries, westerns and biographies. Then she crouched in front of a cabinet where she'd promised her furious father she would never play inside again.

Even now, her whole body shook as she opened the door. The inside looked ordinary enough, just shelves like those above the cabinets but with little space between them so everything on them had to lay flat. That didn't make sense. Even as a preschooler, like the day he'd caught her, she and her fashion dolls couldn't have fit in a space that small. Were her memories faulty, or had the cabinet changed?

She pulled out the firefighting magazines and old copies of *Time*, stacked in surprisingly tidy rows on the top shelf and more carefully arranged books in the open space below. Even when that part of the cabinet was empty, it didn't look right.

On her hands and knees, Rachel leaned her head near the floor and used her phone as a flashlight to examine it closer. The light showed a small gap between the back of the cabinet and its bottom when the rest of it appeared to be well made. She tried to remove the shelf, but it was stuck, so she used one of the hardcover books to pound on the wood until it came loose. When she yanked it out, an extra back panel pulled free with it.

Her breath caught as it opened. She leaned closer and directed the phone flashlight inside. Beyond the cabinet, in a section of wall created by the office's L-shape, was a tiny room, about four feet long and three feet wide, accessible only from inside the cabinet. Just big enough for a preschooler to squeeze inside with her toys. Or for a grown man to hide a lifetime of secrets.

There were two file boxes in it now. Rachel pulled out the first, sat crisscross on the floor and opened it. Unlike the mishmash of papers in Stan's filing cabinet, these files were carefully labeled and alphabetized as though her father had gotten his papers in order, expecting someone to read them after he died. He'd been right about that.

She flipped through the files with titles like "Land Contract" and "Petroleum Quality Reports." But when she came to the letter *R*, her breath caught. The file said simply "Rachel and Riley."

She jerked the folder from the box and opened it flat in her lap. A letter was right on top, handwritten on lined paper in a familiar, messy script.

Dear Rachel and Riley,
If you're reading this, I have passed from this world. From these records, you'll see that I deserved everything I got. I'm sorry. A better man would have figured out how to confess and keep both of you safe. I wasn't that man.

You'll be hearing a lot of things about me. Some will be true. Some won't. But I didn't report the things I knew, so that makes me just as guilty.

I don't expect you to ever forgive me, but please know that I loved you both, your mother and those two sweet little girls more than anything money can buy. That's the truth.
Dad

By the time she'd finished reading, the words had blurred on the page. A tear escaped the corner of her eye and dripped onto the paper, smearing the ink. As she scrambled up from the floor to grab a tissue, her nostrils filled with a strange scent. Like something was burning.

Her chest tightened, and her heart pounded, as the lights in the room flickered. Suddenly, the room was cloudier than it had been a few moments before. How had she been so caught up in those documents that she hadn't noticed? The ceiling light blinked again and then went dark.

Just as her mind started to wrap around the possibility, the smoke alarm in the hall blared. *Fire*. After a lifetime of practice and instruction from the men in her family, she dropped low to the floor and pulled her sweater up to cover her nose and mouth. Though she told herself she couldn't panic, as she reached around for her phone and found her back pocket empty, a cry escaped her. She closed her eyes, shoving back her hair, and then forced them to open again. She refused to die here.

On her hands and knees, Rachel made her way back to the cabinet and reached inside. A gush of relief filled her as her hand closed over her phone. She tapped to awaken it, rested it on the floor and dialed for help.

"Nine-one-one, what is your emergency?" the dispatcher said once the call connected.

"My father's—I mean my brother's—house is on fire. I am inside."

"And who am I speaking to?"

"My name is Rachel Hoffman."

The all-call tone went off just as Mick stepped out into the apparatus bay to monitor the morning inspections.

Captain Louie Nash moved to the center of the room. "McMillan, Ellison, Lucas. Engine 1 will be command."

As the whole crew went into action, staffing Engine 1, Ladder Truck 1, Tanker 1 and Squad 1, Mick raced to the locker room and suited up himself. All hands would be needed on this call.

With his face mask already in place, he slid into a seat across from Felicia and accepted the headset she offered to him. By the time he'd slid his arms into his SCBA, tested the line and buckled in, they were already on the road.

"Did you hear the address?" she said into her microphone.

"I did, but—"

"It's the chief's place. I mean the former chief," she clarified.

Mick gasped into the mask and then cleared his throat to cover it. He couldn't manage the question that burned on his tongue. The one his gut told him he already had the answer to.

Cody Ellison, one of the newer crew members on Rotation 3, spoke up instead. "But I thought that Hoffman—"

"He's not there," Felicia said. "Rachel called it in. She might be trapped inside."

Mick blinked several times, the faces inside the rig blurring.

Felicia waved a hand at him, low near the leg of her turnout pants. When she had his attention, she pointed to him and then made the okay symbol, asking if he was all right.

He nodded and then took a few more breaths to make it less of a lie. At least she hadn't said it in the microphone with the captain and driver/pump operator right up front and listening. The last thing he wanted to do was to arrive on scene and be unable to help. But he could barely hold himself still. Rachel might have been still inside that house, and all he could do was sit inside this rig, begging it to go faster, so they could reach her before smoke became too much for her or the flames trapped her inside.

When the rig arrived at the house and, as command, Nash surveyed the scene to orchestrate the attack, Mick had to force himself to not do something ridiculous like run into the house without a plan.

Felicia caught hold of his shoulder as they unloaded the first hose and the rig pulled away, stretching it along the driveway. She said something that sounded like, "She's going to be all right, Chief," but with the mask, plus the deafening sound of the diesel engine and the pump, he couldn't be sure.

He didn't even care that someone had figured out he was with Rachel. Or at least his heart was. He only prayed that Felicia was right.

Chapter 24

A loud thud brought Rachel's head up from the floor where it was becoming easier to stay. Whether it was help arriving or the ceiling beams starting to fall, she couldn't tell. Around her, sizzling sounds like frying bacon filtered from all the outlets, and even with the collar of her crewneck sweater over her face, her nose and throat burned. Her eyes were on fire. She had to work just to draw in air.

Then came a shattering of glass. She lifted her heavy head again and turned toward the windows on the opposite side of the room. Daylight outlined the shape of a firefighter in a helmet, mask and full turnout gear. The thing in his hand must have been an ax.

"Mick?" she called out, her voice sounding strange. But it couldn't have been him. As chief, he didn't have to climb ladders, at least not regularly, and after she'd put herself in this situation, he had no reason to volunteer.

"Rachel?" a muffled voice called out.

Its owner climbed in through the office window and dropped to the floor, where Rachel had let the dispatcher know she was trapped after a test of the hot doorknob told her it wasn't safe to go into the hall.

"Over here," she said and then dissolved into a coughing fit. She tried to shift to a crawling position, but her limbs were heavy, uncooperative.

The firefighter said something else she couldn't make out but then crawled along the wall, brushing hands over the carpet in broad sweeps. In the space of the broken window, another first responder appeared, backlit by daylight.

As the first one reached her, Rachel peeked over her sweater collar. It wasn't Mick.

"Ma'am, we're going to get you out."

Though still garbled, she understood the voice this time, and it turned out to be a feminine one. Felicia. The firefighter shifted her onto her side and started pulling her toward the window. Rachel flailed her arms to make the woman stop.

"I have to…get…boxes—" She couldn't help breaking into another round of coughs.

"Sorry, ma'am. There isn't time."

"No! I have to—"

Ignoring her pleas, the firefighter dragged her toward daylight. Near the window, she hoisted Rachel off the floor and put her through the opening headfirst. Mick was on the ladder, set against the frame.

She jerked again as the first firefighter tried to shift her into Mick's arms.

"Stop fighting," he call out in a muffled voice. He shifted her around so that she was in front of him on the ladder, facing the house, and leaned his body heavily on hers, his thigh pressing into the back of her leg. "You'll make us both fall."

She continued to fight, her chest tight with desperation. "But we have to get the boxes… I found—"

"We have to get you out. That's all."

"No!"

He pressed tighter into her back until she finally slumped forward. Then he started descending again. She had no choice but to move with him. Felicia followed right behind them, an ax still in her gloved hand.

Once on solid ground, Mick wrapped his gear-covered arm around her shoulder and half guided, half dragged her over to the squad truck. Another crew member wrapped a Mylar blanket around her shoulders and covered her nose and mouth with an oxygen mask, securing it with straps. Mick and Felicia seemed to have vanished.

The first responder turned out to be veteran firefighter and certified paramedic Brice McMillan, his words at first seeming garbled to her though he wasn't wearing a mask.

"We're going to take good care of you, Rachel," he said in a calming voice while directing her to sit on the skirt of the truck. "Let's get your vitals and let me check for injuries before the ambulance arrives."

"I'm fine," she tried to say through the oxygen mask.

"Even so." Brice tucked in the ear tips of his stethoscope. "We won't let anything happen to Chief Hoffman's daughter."

A sob escaped her before the man could even bring the chest piece close to her. Several hundred feet away, flames shot out the roof of her childhood home that had served as both prison and sanctuary to her. Firefighters trained massive sprays of water on both sides of the house, the hoses dousing her memories and the truth. They were only focused on the exterior now, as though trying to contain the blaze and prevent it from spreading to the garage. They appeared to have conceded what was called an interior attack.

Her chest heaved under the weight of it all, her already sore eyes burning even more as tears blurred the scene all around her.

Mick suddenly reappeared in front of her, his helmet and mask probably back on the fire truck, his dark hair soaked, and worry etched in his features. Though Brice had stepped away, giving them space, he lowered his voice.

"You okay?" He paused and took two long breaths before continuing. "You'll have to go to the hospital to get checked out."

"Brice already said that."

He blinked over her curt comment but kept talking. "I'll get word to your friend. It's Stacy, isn't it? Then we'll call the school so that she can pick up the girls. Just give me the number and—"

"I'll take care of it," she said in the same tight tone as before.

This time his gaze narrowed, and he took a step forward and lifted a hand as though to touch her shoulder. She flinched and pulled the blanket tighter around her. The hurt that flashed in his eyes cut straight through her, but she braced herself against softening to it. Nothing he could do would make this right.

"Look, I know you're upset, but—"

She pulled the mask off though Brice had told her to leave it on. "Then why wouldn't you…listen…to me?"

Breaking off into a coughing fit, she shot a look at those around them. The first responders on the scene were all pretending not to notice them. She tried again in a lower tone but spoke through gritted teeth. "Why didn't you?"

"What were you even doing in there? You promised." He searched her eyes, his own wild, frightened. "Didn't you realize—"

"That I had to find the files…before it was too late?" She paused to cough some more. "I…found them, but we'll never know what was…in them. They're gone."

"What did you expect me to do? Risk your life? And Felicia's? And mine?"

"Now I don't have—"

"Did you *look* at that place?"

His jaw flexing, he pointed his gloved hand at the house, where the second story had already folded into the first, leaving only a shell of the exterior. Even from this reasonable distance, the heat from it spread over her face.

"It's gone. A total loss," he said. "And you could have gone with it. You could have…*died*."

She shook her head, hearing his words but not wanting to accept them. Around them other firefighters continued to battle the flames. And more sirens could be heard in the distance, coming to join the fight. As the fire had also taken place in daylight, it had begun to draw a crowd as well. Cars were even arriving from town, drawn by the sirens and the smoke.

After putting the mask back on for a few breaths, she tried again. "You don't understand. The boxes could have—"

"Rachel, stop!" He shot a look around and lowered his voice, but everyone was already watching them. "You have to stop digging. Even if it could have proven that your dad isn't guilty of some of the crimes, you nearly died trying to find that proof. Nothing in the box was worth that."

"We could have gotten the boxes out," She insisted again with a sigh.

He stepped closer and spoke only for her. "There were multiple ignition points in that fire and near both exits. Someone didn't want you to get out alive."

She swallowed and then stared again at the house as a huge column of water poured over it. Had she really come that close to losing her life just to find those answers?

After another round of coughs, she cleared her throat. "Thank you…and Felicia…for saving my life."

Mick shook his head, not ready to hear it, and leaned close again. "Is your life so worthless to you? Do you want your girls to end up like—"

Her? Mick stopped, his eyes going wide, but she got the message. He was accusing her of trying to leave her daughters as orphans. And he couldn't have said anything crueler.

"Well, I'm glad you got to play the hero again. I know you're still trying to make up for the losses back in Chicago. But this situation wasn't the same. Whoever wanted to get to me also wanted those records destroyed. They're still out there, and there's no way to prove they're guilty. I'll never forgive you."

As soon as the words escaped from her mouth, she regretted them, and not just because his head jerked back as though she'd stabbed him in the gut and left him to bleed out. Had she tried to injure him since he'd hurt her?

"Look, I'm sorry. We're both upset. So let's…" She didn't know what she would have said next, but she didn't get the chance as he held both hands up in surrender and backed away from her.

"You were waiting for me to do something to justify pushing me away. To prove you don't deserve anything good. Well, I'm glad I could oblige before it was too late."

"Mick, wait."

But he didn't. His shoulders were straight as he marched to the rig and away from her, the back of his turnout coat, with "Mount Isabel FD" at the top and "M. Prentiss" at the bottom, reflective yellow stripes between them, growing smaller with each step.

She wanted to run after him, to tell him…what? That

she wanted him, needed him? But she couldn't. She was furious with him, too. For what? Saving her life? It wasn't as simple as that, either. And even if she could go after him in front of all those people, her lungs hurt so much that she wouldn't have made it across the driveway.

More sirens announced the arrival of the ambulance. After it parked, more EMTs descended on her, rechecking all the levels that Brice had already noted and then insisting that she climb onto the stretcher for a trip to the hospital.

But as they pulled away from the house she'd grown up in, she was convinced that she'd lost far more than two boxes of records that day.

In his office late that afternoon, Mick clicked through a series of photos on his computer monitor that crew members had shared with him. Crowd photos of interested residents, some more curious than others. They all looked the same, just a bunch of bundled farmers and some underdressed city workers with shoes too pristine for the mud-streaked snow.

Some of them hadn't even bothered to get out of their cars. They'd just parked along the road and waited to view the action. He hit the arrow for the next picture, grateful to have something to distract him from the scene he'd made with Rachel or from wishing he could've gone to the hospital with her.

They'd had it out in front of the whole crew—heck, the entire town, given the crowd size and the proficiency of the rumor mill. They might as well have taken out an ad in the *Informer* to announce they were together. Only they weren't. And wouldn't be.

"What did she expect me to do? Leave her in a burning

building?" He glanced at the door to see if he'd been overheard, blew out a breath and lowered his chin. Should he have tried to bring out the boxes with her? Should he and Felicia have taken critical seconds to transfer those things out a second-story window? He shook his head, knowing that if he were given the same set of circumstances, he would have made an identical decision ten times out of ten.

"People, property and environment," he whispered the statement he'd first learned in his Firefighter Level I training all those years ago. Those priorities had never changed, other than today the "People" part had taken on a whole new significance. He hadn't just wanted to rescue any victim. He'd needed to save *her*. From the fire. From herself. Whatever it took.

A knock on the door allowed him to avoid further dissecting the events that had led up to that scene. She'd lied to him, not once but twice in the past eighteen hours, and he'd still ridden in on his white stallion to save her. What was he supposed to do with that truth?

After a second, Felicia pushed open the door and leaned her head through the opening. "Can I talk to you for a minute, Chief?"

He waved her inside. This would be awkward, but he needed to get it over with.

Leaving the door partway open, Felicia took one of the guest seats, crossed her left ankle over her right knee and folded her arms. "So today was…interesting."

"You did a good job out there, Lucas."

"You, too, Chief. But that's not what I came here to talk about."

"Didn't figure."

She shifted in her seat, chewed the corner of her lip and then leaned forward. "You know a lot of us love the whole

Hoffman family. Mourned Stan's loss. Hated the events that led to Riley's firing. And resented you for showing up to fill the void they left."

"Well, you're the first to say it out loud, but thanks for that."

"From what I've seen, you're a good man. I've known Rachel for a long time, too. Since she was a teenager, battling it out with her dad." Then she gave him a wide smile. "It doesn't surprise me that she'd fall for a guy like you. You're a lot like him, you know."

Tightened his arms to his sides, the last part giving him chills. He didn't want to be like Rachel's father. That Felicia had suggested it made him want to pull rank and send her off for more training. "I'm not. I mean, *we're* not… you know…together."

"Yeah, I saw how not together you were. Inside the house and outside." Again, she smiled. "But you wish you were. You also wanted to be the one to bring her out. Thought I was going to have to arm wrestle you to get to go in first, and as uncooperative as she was, we needed you to bring her down the ladder."

"Good thing you didn't have to challenge me, either. Your reputation as a scrappy champion precedes you."

She chewed the corner of her lip as though considering whether to say more. "Don't give up on her, Chief. She's had more than her share of dark days for someone so young. I don't know what's going on with her family right now, but she needs someone. I'm thinking that you might, too."

Felicia held her hands wide and grinned. "And you don't work together, so you're not even breaking any regulations."

With the reminder of the list of personal rules he and

Rachel had set and then broken, Mick shifted in his seat and then pushed back from his desk and started to stand. "Not that it matters now."

"You mean the boxes Rachel begged us to bring out? You made the right call. We both did. There was no time to get anything else out. Just precious human cargo. People first, right?"

"Always."

He would have tried to stand again and let her know that their awkward meeting was over, but Felicia pointed to the monitor behind him. "Checking out the curious neighbors?"

Mick swiveled in his chair to face the computer. "Just seeing if anyone sticks out."

"Isn't that Kenny Davison? I didn't know he lived around there."

"Several people came out from town," he said, but he would have to pay closer attention since the village manager was one of them. "Some saw the smoke. Others have been following us on the scanners."

"Guess we've been as exciting as a Red Wings game lately."

He studied the screen again. Davison couldn't have looked more out of place in his suit, tie and overcoat when standing next to local farmers in duck coats and muck boots. But it was the young man next to him in the photo, fitting in perfectly among the others, who caught Mick's eye. Where had he seen him before?

Was it the grocery store? The city offices? The hotel? He'd been so busy helping Rachel since he'd arrived that he still hadn't had a chance to check out many places in town. But he'd seen the kid in the photo somewhere. Closing his eyes, he tried to picture the location, and then his eyes popped open, his pulse racing. And he knew.

Slowly, he turned back to Felicia, who was already standing.

"Looks like you have another meeting."

Captain Nash stood in the open doorway, a file folder in his hand. "You got a minute, Chief?"

Mick straightened in his chair as the firefighter left, and the officer replaced her. They were about to discuss the humiliating scene he'd made on the call, and as command, Nash had every right to bring it up. Even a responsibility to do so.

"Look, Captain, I'm really sorry about—"

Louie waved off his apology. "I just wanted to let you know about some paperwork that the investigator located at the scene. You know, the MIPD is opening an attempted murder investigation, don't you?"

"I suspected they would."

Still, hearing that fact spoken aloud made it so much worse. Mick sneaked a shallow breath, wishing he could stop blinking. They'd been able to recover some of the papers? Would it be enough to prove whatever Rachel thought she could with those boxes she'd found? And would she be able to forgive him for forcing her to leave them behind?

Louie wouldn't have noticed Mick's oversize reaction, anyway, as he sat staring down at the folder in his hands. But he didn't open it or rest it on the chief's desk.

"After the upstairs came down, I didn't think anything in the house would have been recoverable, let alone paperwork." He shook his head, still not believing it. "Did he find something from the boxes in the office?"

Louie shook his head, chuckling. "No, not in the house.

Stan's place was so full of books that it burned like a paper company."

"Then what are you…?"

"Someone dropped this at the scene. The investigator found it, not near the house but where the crowd was standing."

The captain rested the folder on the desk between them and opened the file. Inside was an inkjet photo of a sheet stored inside a clear evidence bag. The note itself had been folded so many times that it had square marks all over it.

Mick's breath caught as he took a closer look. The word *TORCH* had been handwritten at the top of the page in what looked like pencil. A kid's handwriting. The sheet itself was a formal document with one-inch margins, a readable font, numbered sections and bulleted details. But as he read the list, his fingertips went cold.

Someone had left a step-by-step, how-to guide for setting buildings on fire.

Chapter 25

Mick forced himself to wait until Louie made another copy of the letter for him and headed back to the kitchen to help with dinner before he rushed over to his filing cabinet. The two-inch binder was right where he'd left it, with cadet program applications and photos of all those hopeful candidates inside.

He lunged for the book and carried it back to his desk, perching on the edge of his seat and coming up on his toes. His legs refused to stay still. Once he'd opened the cover, he couldn't turn the pages fast enough. Was it possible that the answer to the questions about the rash of fires had been in Riley Hoffman's office—now his—all along?

"What was his name? Kevin? Curtis?" He flipped the pages harder as the answer didn't instantly appear. The name didn't matter, anyway, because he knew the kid's face.

Maybe all of these fires had started as some game, some "TORCH" for people who thought it would be fun to destroy other people's property. That was dangerous enough. But today was different. This morning someone, maybe a participant in that game, had tried to murder the woman he loved. Had tried to burn her alive. And there was no way he would be getting away with it.

"He's here. He has to be here," he said, though a weight settled in his chest over the possibility that he could have been wrong. That he was just grasping at straws.

Still, he continued to rip at the applications that weren't even alphabetized. Just punctured with a three-hole punch and threaded onto the rings, probably as the packets arrived during the monthlong application period, each marked with the date it was received. As that thought settled, Mick flipped the whole book to its back cover to look at the earliest applications submitted. After working backward through two letters of recommendation and the transcript, he stopped on the first page from the earliest applicant.

And there he was. Cameron Lewis Phillips, the sheet said at the top. For several seconds, he could only stare at the photo clipped to it. He could have been any teen that Mick had passed on the streets since arriving in Mount Isabel. White. Ordinary. Only if Mick was right, he was also the kid who'd tried to kill Rachel.

To be sure it was the same boy, he turned back to his computer and moved the mouse to awaken the monitor. The photo that had been there earlier filled the screen. Mick zoomed in to get a better look, but from even at a distance, he could tell it was a match.

Mick couldn't help it. He lifted the photo and read the whole application, trying to glean details from the typed words. Though in this day of helicopter parents, he recognized that the boy might not have completed the application himself, his answers suggested that he had. The kid listed only computers and video games as interests, even referring to himself as a "computer wizard." His answers to the question about why he wanted to consider a career in firefighting weren't so different from those on any of the other applications, but Mick gave them a closer inspection.

"A 'hero' and 'big part of the community.'" Mick whispered and then reread every word. "He has big plans, all right."

But when he scanned to the bottom of the page where Cameron had added a little something extra to make his application stand out, Mick's blood went cold. The boy had added a quote.

"A coward turns away, but a brave man's choice is danger."
—Euripides (c. 485-406 BCE)

He grabbed his phone, searched for a number and tapped the link to dial it. His throat tightened as it rang.

"Mount Isabel Police Department, how may I help you?" the dispatcher said.

"I'm Fire Chief Mick Prentiss," he said, pausing to clear his throat. "I'd like to speak to Chief Gilman."

Mick's whole body and his head ached by the time he pulled his truck in front of his apartment two hours later, the sky not quite dark but well on its way. He should have known that the police wouldn't want to waste any time collecting the cadet program application to match with the crowd photos from the crime scene.

Now he wouldn't even get a chance to try to see Rachel at the hospital. Not that she would have agreed to talk to him, anyway. But he could have tried.

He'd used the electronic key to open the main building door when he heard footsteps behind him.

"Mick Prentiss?"

He stopped and turned his head to the side, trying to

stay calm. An officer had told him that Cameron Phillips was already under arrest before he'd even left the police station. Clearly, someone had missed something. Maybe an accomplice?

"Who's asking?" He waited, trying to come up with a weapon he could use, besides his bare hands.

"I just wanted to get a look at the guy who took my job."

Mick dampened his lips, then slowly turned around to face him. He'd seen the photos on Rachel's wall. The man standing in front of him, with wavy blond hair, light-blue eyes and the kind of pretty-boy looks that Mick never had, was definitely Riley Hoffman. If not for the photos, he never would have guessed they were related. He looked nothing like Rachel.

This wasn't the way he'd intended to meet her brother. But he hadn't expected him to ambush him at his apartment, either. Come to think of it, Rachel had done the same thing to him. Maybe the thrill of surprise ran in the family.

"Mr. Hoffman?"

"Riley will do."

Only it didn't feel right, given that Mick had just left the man's former office a few hours before. "I didn't know you'd been—"

"Released from rehab?" Riley finished for him. "Yeah, they tossed my butt earlier today. Four weeks max, and even that was after getting two extra weeks approved."

"If you're looking for your sister, I'm sorry to have to tell you—"

"That she's in the hospital? Yeah, I've heard. In fact, I've heard a lot of things." Riley paused to eye Mick until he shuffled his boots in the snow. "Like that I can't go home because, apparently, somebody burned down my house."

Mick was relieved that Rachel's brother hadn't gone into details about what else he'd learned. "I'm so sorry. That has to be a hell of a way to come home. Especially now when you're—"

Riley cleared his throat, crossing his arms and moving into a defensive pose that reminded Mick of his sister. They were related, all right.

"Don't worry about me. I'm fine," Riley said.

The younger man must have recognized that he'd spoken too quickly, too defensively. He glanced over his shoulder to the street and then turned back again, his expression a calmer one.

"I did hear that police took a suspect into custody about an hour ago," Mick said.

"Now, that I hadn't heard."

"A seventeen-year-old named Cameron Phillips."

"No way! Cameron? I thought he'd finally given up." Riley blinked several times and tilted his head. "Wait. Did you say he was a suspect for the fire at *my house*?"

"Yeah. Sorry. How'd you know him? I saw his picture in the fire cadet program applications—"

"Again?"

Mick narrowed his gaze and waited for him to explain.

"He applied last year, too," he said and then shrugged. "When it didn't work out for him, he kept calling, wanting to know why he wasn't accepted. I guess it messed up his big plans. He lives on a hobby farm with executive parents who work near Lansing and aren't around much other than to buy him stuff."

"Like computers and video games?" Mick lowered his voice to ask the next part. "Didn't seem like a good psychological fit for the program?"

"Something like that."

Mick nodded, aware that information should have been confidential, except possibly between the two of them. "Hey, it's getting cold out here. I don't have any furniture, but come inside. I have tea, cocoa or coffee."

"I kind of had another idea," Riley said. "Since I don't really have anywhere to stay, and my car's in the garage—if there still is a garage—I wondered if you could give me a ride to the hospital. I need to see my sister and see if I can camp out at her house for a while."

"I can take you, but why me?"

At that, Riley chuckled. "From what I've heard, we're practically family. I do have to say you work fast, though. I wasn't gone that long. And from what I hear, you've been in town an even shorter amount of time. The twins are crazy about you. And my sister—"

"Sorry." Mick lifted a hand, signaling for him to stop. "This is just too awkward. In addition to that, your sister, uh, doesn't want to see me."

"Well, that's too bad because you're my ride. She'll just have to live with it." Riley gestured to Mick's truck, and they both started toward it. "Could we make a stop to pick up Carly and Carissa on the way? I'm dying to see my girls."

They were parked outside Stacy's house before Mick tried again.

"How do you know about…"

"I have my ways." Riley grinned at the windshield. "Seriously, I told you I got kicked out today. I needed a ride. Peter was off, so he helped me out."

"And filled you in."

He smiled again, not disagreeing, though he couldn't help wondering just how much his friend knew. Then, for the first time since he'd met Riley, the man's expression became serious.

"You're not just 'hanging out' with my sister, are you? Because she's been through a lot, and I don't think she could take—"

"No. Never." His vehemence surprised even him. "But like I said, we're not..."

"Good. I'd hate to have to kick your ass when I've only just met you."

"And since I'm your ride."

A few minutes later, the girls were buckled in the back seat of the quad cab, chatting about fires and how their mom was okay, as they drove toward Mount Isabel Regional Hospital.

"You two will figure it out," Riley said, breaking the silence in the front seat.

Mick nodded, his throat thick. "Either way, if you ever need to talk with someone about...you know...anything, I just wanted to let you know that my dad's an alcoholic, so..." He stopped and shrugged.

Riley kept staring at the windshield. "I've got a lot of work ahead of me. Doing my 'thirty in thirty,' attending an Alcoholics Anonymous meeting every day for a month. I was able to attend one at the center before I left today."

"You know, I think we're all going to be okay." Mick hoped by saying it, he could make it true.

"I hope so, man. I really hope so."

Chapter 26

Rachel leaned forward in her hospital bed as the certified nursing assistant propped a pillow behind her head and then checked the amount of saline in her IV. At the door, past the curtain that separated the double room, the veteran, take-no-prisoners staff member who'd written "Anne" on Rachel's patient board, called back to her.

"Looks like you have a handsome visitor out here," she said. "A very *late* visitor, who we hope won't stay long."

Rachel sat up straighter and swiped at her hair to push it back from her face, her heart racing. She didn't know why she bothered fussing. Mick had already seen her at her worst, and after the fit she'd thrown at the fire scene, she'd guessed he would never speak to her again. She still wasn't sure what she would say to him if he did.

But the man who rounded the curtain turned out to be her brother instead. She let out a yelp when she saw him. "Oh my gosh, Riley. How did you find out I was here? When did you get…out?"

Already, tears were threatening, so she took a few deep breaths, trying to hold them back. It was bad enough that he had to see her like this, but it would be worse when she told him that his house had been destroyed because of her.

"You didn't think they'd keep me there forever, did

you?" he said. "Those beds are in high demand, so they tossed me. I told you they were going to the last time we spoke."

"Oh, I forgot. I'm a terrible sister."

"You're a great sister, other than that you were hanging out at my house and ended up trying to roast marshmallows in the living room."

She lowered her head. "Riley, I'm so sorry."

"We can talk about it later. But for now, are you okay?" He pointed to the monitors. "What did the doctor say?"

"That you're going to have to keep me around for a while," she said with a grin.

"Well, that's tough news, but I guess I'll have to take it."

She held her hand out to him, but when the tube of her IV caught on the bed's plastic side rail, she offered him the other hand. Smiling, he stepped forward and took it. She lost the battle with her emotions as tears welled in her eyes.

"You look so—" She reached up to touch his face, but he stepped back and preened.

"Buff? Gorgeous? Ultra masculine?"

"Stop it." She brushed her damp cheek on the shoulder of that ridiculously oversized hospital gown. "You look… healthier."

"Now, that wouldn't take much. I was a broken shell." He cleared his throat and pushed back his shoulders, his eyes damp. "But I want to thank you for taking me there."

He clapped his hands as though to announce that the topic was closed and then pointed from her IV to the machine monitoring her heart rate, blood pressure and body temperature.

"Looks like I got out in the nick of time."

"They just kept me for observation because of the smoke inhalation." Then she lowered her head, the tears coming hot now. "I'm sorry. I shouldn't have kept looking. You told me not to do it. And now...the *house*."

"I know. Rachel, it was just a house. One we shouldn't even have—" He stopped and shook his head hard.

"But you warned me—"

He raised a hand to interrupt her. "The only thing that matters today though is that you're okay. I don't know what I would have done— You and the girls...you're all I have..."

At that, her brother moved to the window to look out at the dark sky. Her heart ached with the truth of it. It was the same for her though a voice inside told her she could have had someone else as well. She squashed it since it hurt too much to listen.

"I wasn't there to pick you up. How did you even get home? And here?"

"I had help."

As if he'd timed their entrance, Carly and Carissa bounded into the room, both holding out candy bars. They scrambled past her brother and right up on her bed, forcing her to shift her arm so one of them wouldn't dislodge her IV.

"Uncle Riley said you had a fire." Carissa said, already fumbling with her candy. "Can we eat them? Please?"

"Maybe in a little bit."

Carly glanced over from her snack, her gaze intense. "Did you get hurt, Mommy? Mr. Mick said you're okay. But please don't play with matches anymore."

Mr. Mick? She had to force herself not to ask as Riley had already turned back from the window and was watching her closely.

"I won't play with matches," she said, holding back a grin. "Promise."

Her breath hitched when Mick rounded the curtain as though he'd been chasing the girls.

He gave both adults apologetic looks. "Sorry. Kept them out of here for as long as I could."

"And bribed them with candy, I see." Riley pointed to the evidence. "Would have done the same thing myself."

Mick turned his head to look at her. "Hi."

"Hi." Their gazes held for a few heartbeats before Rachel lowered hers to her right hand and touched her finger to the tube taped on the back side. Her chest ached more than it had all day.

Rachel pointed back and forth between the men. "You two came here together? How do you even…?"

Riley answered for them both. "Technically, it was four of us."

She lifted her chin and gave Riley the mom look.

Mick took a step toward her. "Your brother and I had a talk after I got back from the police station."

"Police station? How long have I been in here?"

"A few hours." Mick stuffed his hands in his pockets. "They arrested a suspect for the fire at your father's house."

"You mean all of this could be over?"

"At least the part about the fires, I guess," Riley answered for Mick.

Her pulse increased on the monitor as details flooded her thoughts, too complicated and interwoven to be unraveled with a single arrest. "But we still have to figure out—"

"Yes, we'll have a lot to make sense of," Riley said, "but not today."

"He's right," Mick said. "You should get rest so you can come home tomorrow."

Her brother stepped over to the wardrobe, where the

nurse assistant had helped her store her clothes in a plastic bag. "But would it be okay if I get your keys so I can take the girls there? It seems like you might need childcare, and I need a place to stay. The garage gets a little cold."

Her gaze flicked to Mick's and away, but her attentive brother didn't miss it.

"Bet there's a story there."

Mick stared at his feet. Rachel's cheeks burned, probably giving more hints away.

"Yeah, take the keys. You're in charge."

While her brother fumbled in her purse, she gave him a cautious look. This wasn't a perfect time for him to take on extra responsibilities as someone so newly sober, but, for tonight, they had no choice.

"Well, let's take the girls out to the waiting room lounge so they can eat those candy bars." Riley pointed to Mick. "Could you take them out there? I'll meet you in a minute."

The twins popped off the bed and followed Mick into the hall. No one mentioned that they could have easily nibbled on them right in the hospital room. Riley stepped to the side of her hospital bed, rested his hands on the rail and leaned in close.

"Give the guy a chance, okay? You're so hard on everyone, except me."

"You don't understand. The stuff he made me leave in the fire might have helped prove—"

He shook his head until she stopped. "Mick already told me. But it doesn't matter now. We'll just have to figure out another way."

"There might not be…"

His lips lifting in a sad smile. "Remember when we were kids, and I said you were the dumbest girl I ever knew?"

She drew her brows together but nodded.

"If you let this guy go, you'll prove I was right."

Mick braced his hands on the sides of the hospital room's doorframe and then propelled himself inside. He wouldn't have the chance to say everything that was on his mind tonight, but since he might not get another opportunity to talk to her, he planned to have his say.

When Mick stepped around the curtain, Rachel stared back at him, her hands gripped together on top of the blanket. He pulled a chair closer to the bed and lowered into it.

"Thanks for bringing my brother and the girls here." She squeezed her hands tighter. "And thanks again for... *everything* earlier."

His throat filled, but he forced himself to smile. "It still pains you to say we saved your life, doesn't it?"

"It's just that...everything's so messed up in my head."

"I still don't think you recognize that you really could have...*died* today." Mick hated that his voice broke on the word. He needed to stay in control, no matter how much it hurt.

"I do get it." She gestured to the tube in her hand and then to the developing bruises on her arms, where he'd secured her to the ladder for her own safety.

"You could have left your whole family behind," he continued, straining to hold his composure. His voice sounded steady in his ears, though his mind raged. *You could have left me*, he wanted to shout, but he kept it inside where it festered and burned.

"I know. I know." She shook her head. "I just wish—"

"You've made it pretty clear what you wished."

"It's just that there was a letter in the box to Riley and me. My dad admitted that he was guilty of some of the crimes but said not all of the things we'd learn would be true. He also said he wished he could have confessed and protected us at the same time."

Mick didn't miss that she'd stopped calling Stan by his first name. That was something. "You see? Just like we thought, he was trying to protect you."

He didn't mention that he'd been the one to suggest it. "At least you got to see the letter and know it existed. You might have to let that be enough."

"I want to. I do. But I can't."

That was the crux of it. Mick accepted the truth that stood between them. He couldn't take back the decisions he made at the fire scene—no, *wouldn't*—and she couldn't forgive him for them.

"I want you to know that given the same set of circumstances, I would have made the same choices I did today." He lifted his shoulders and lowered them. "Other than that I wouldn't have participated in your rescue at all."

She'd been staring down at her hands, but at the admission, she looked up, her brows knitted together.

"Don't you get it? I'm in love with you."

She stared back at him with wide, shocked eyes. His own reaction was no less extreme, his chest aching as though he'd yanked the words right from his center and left all the torn flesh behind. This wasn't how he'd pictured telling her. Or how he'd hoped she would receive the message.

"And *because* I'm in love with you, I had no business trying to be the hero by participating in your rescue. Everyone knew it. I set a terrible example for my whole crew."

She swallowed visibly and opened her lips a few times as if she planned to respond. Then she closed her mouth and lowered her head. It was the first time since he'd met

Rachel Hoffman that he'd struck her into silence, and pain sliced through him that it had taken his confession of love to do it.

But it gave him an opportunity to say more, and he was already on a roll, so he took advantage of it. "You said I was trying to make up for the losses back in Chicago. Maybe you're right. Maybe I'll always be trying to repay my debt for that. But at least I'm making something good out of a horrible situation. What you're doing is just the opposite. You're trying to destroy the future to make up for the past.

"You don't think you deserve to be happy. But you do. Someday I hope you find someone you can really put your trust in. Without fear or strings or escape hatches."

With tears falling down her cheeks, she nodded. He hoped she would contradict him, would say everything that had happened that day didn't matter, and there was still a chance for them. Instead, she said nothing at all.

His heart heavy, Mick stood, but he had one more thing to say.

"You didn't have a choice over some of the bad things that have happened to you. Losing your mother and your father. Then the perfect father you thought you had. Even the jerk who abandoned you."

"This time, I want you to know you had a choice."

It took Rachel about thirty seconds to realize what a big mistake she'd made. The same thirty seconds required for Mick to stride out of the room and out of her life.

What had she done? She'd just pushed away the best thing that had happened to her since the birth of her daughters and the possibility of a future with someone who loved her, someone she loved, because of records that had gone up in smoke. Papers that could never bring her father back or make him the perfect person who'd lived only in her imagination, no matter how much mitigating proof they would have found in those boxes.

She tore at the tape on her IV and considered yanking it out and chasing him down the hall. But what would that prove? To him or her daughters?

You're trying to destroy the future to make up for the past. Mick's words taunted her, the truth in them as clear as the nursing assistant's red handwriting on that dry-erase board. He was right. But to whom was she still trying to prove herself? Her father was gone. Nothing she could do would change that. Riley wanted what was best for her, too, even if that meant entrusting his only remaining relatives to the man who had already taken his job.

And Mick loved her, enough to want her to be happy with someone else if she couldn't be with him. Given the choice, her heart longed for him. She knew it with the same certainty that she'd had, realizing that someone in Mount Isabel was keeping secrets.

She wanted him, and she hoped he still wanted her, despite the thuds of his footsteps that had carried him away. Somehow she had to make this right.

Chapter 27

Mick had just hung up his office phone the day before the beginning of spring when Peter Russo knocked on the door and pushed inside. Most of the other crew members had learned to give him space lately, or risk the consequences of his constantly sour mood, but they'd been friends for years, and Peter must have thought that gave him special privileges and immunity. He would have to talk to him about that when he finally felt human. That wasn't today.

"Hey, Chief. You just get off a call? You've been holed up in here all afternoon on the phone."

"It's been a busy one. Have a seat, Russo."

He studied the other man for a few seconds, a knot forming in his belly. Had he been listening outside the door? If he had, through how many calls?

Rather than sit in one of the guest chairs, Peter slumped back on the sofa, where Mick had found Rachel on the first day they'd met. Personally, he'd avoided sitting there all week. Since Cameron Phillips's arrest, and the kid's confession that he'd targeted the Hoffman family because of the cadet program rejection, he hadn't been as diligent in observing members of the crew. Maybe that had been a mistake.

"Any new discussions with the village council?"

"Some," he said vaguely, growing more suspicious.

"Have you talked to Riley Hoffman?"

Now Mick pursed his lips and narrowed his gaze. "Why are you asking all that?"

Peter threw his head back and laughed. "Because he told me what you did for him, boss. I think it's amazing."

Mick's shoulders, which had crept up during the interrogation, relaxed. Beyond that Peter had picked up Riley from rehab, he hadn't even been aware that those two were such good friends. "Does everyone know?"

"Probably by now," Peter said, wincing. "It was great of you to convince Mayor Bilski and the village council to bring Hoffman back as assistant chief."

"The plan still has to go before the full council, but after he lost everything but his garage in the fire, it'll be hard for them to say no." Especially now that the computer forensic investigator had proven the station's books were hacked.

It still bothered Mick that longtime Mayor Clay Bilksi had required a lot of persuading, and had insisted Riley's employment was contingent on his continued sobriety. But a mention of a possible lawsuit for wrongful dismissal had gotten the ball rolling.

Mick didn't share those details or that he'd volunteered to resign so Riley could have his old job back. Rachel's brother had nixed that idea himself, requesting a position with less responsibility while he worked his program and became stronger in his sobriety. Mick had to respect that even if it meant being in Mount Isabel a little longer and risking seeing Rachel every time he walked in the grocery store.

"Any other new developments in the arson cases?"

Mick narrowed his gaze at Peter again. The guy really

was milking him for information today. "Just what you read in the *Informer*."

"If we relied on the information coming from the local weekly with its exclusives from the Public Safety Office, we still wouldn't know multiple arrests have been made," Peter said. "From what I've heard, nearly a dozen kids have already been rounded up from that TORCH video game. Among them, they'd set all the suspicious fires lately, and the Phillips kid was the ringleader. A computer genius at that. There's even a chance he might have invented that game."

He kept a carefully blank expression. "Can neither confirm nor deny."

Peter's sources were good. Mick would have to remember that.

"You're no help. I've even heard the kid who left the gas can in the middle of the living room in that one house fire turned himself in after your quote in the paper," Peter said. "And that his confession helped police build their case against Phillips for attempted murder."

Mick chuckled and shook his head. "Sounds like if the *Informer* is looking for a new reporter, you might be the man for the job. If you want to quit fighting fires, anyway."

"Does that mean my information's accurate?"

Spot-on, but there was no way Peter would hear that from Mick. "Again, I can neither confirm nor deny. I like keeping my job. So, are you about done with your fact-finding mission?"

"I am. Sorry, boss. I had to try. It's the most interesting story that's happened around Mount Isabel in decades."

On that, his friend would be dead wrong, but Mick wasn't volunteering that either.

"Well, we've got training this afternoon, and I thought

you were working on your EMT Basic certification online work, so—"

"So, I'll be getting out of your hair." Peter stepped into the hall and then stuck his head back inside. "Oh, one more thing, Chief."

Mick rolled his eyes. "What's that?"

"Rachel Hoffman and her girls are waiting for you in the day room." He grinned as he added, "They've been waiting there a while."

Mick was still grumbling when he made it to the front of the station though he probably could have competed for a medal with the time he took getting there. He found Rachel and the twins sitting in the recliners in the day room, some cartoon kids' show on the seventy-two-inch TV screen.

"He's here," Carissa called out as she leaped up from her chair and held out a rectangular box of chocolates.

"Hi, Mr. Mick." Carly popped up like her sister had, only she had a cellophane-wrapped bouquet of daisies in her hands.

Rachel was slower than the other two, but she carefully stood and held out a pizza box, the scent already filling the room. "Hi. What took you so long?"

"I was waylaid." He frowned at Peter, who grinned back, unrepentant.

Mick turned back to his three guests and held his hands wide. "What is all this?"

He glanced to his left and right and then looked all the way behind him to the kitchen. Sure enough, every crew member on the shift had taken a few minutes from other assignments or gym time to get to watch this show, and that included Scott Ingram, who was back on dinner duty cooking up something else that smelled amazing. Why did they have to be slow on calls today?

"It's just that you make it tough for someone trying to organize a grand gesture."

"Grand gesture?" He took in the candy, the flowers, the pizza, his gaze narrowing as his thoughts took on a life of their own. Was Rachel—? Could this mean—?

"You have sort of single-handedly created a new position for my brother."

Mick nodded and looked at the floor. He would have tried to say that he'd only done it for Riley, but it would be hard to lie in front of all these people. Part of it was for her. Maybe most of it.

"He deserves the benefit of the doubt," he said, though he no longer had any questions about Riley's innocence. "And a second chance."

"Don't we all?"

Her grin reminded him when he'd said the same thing about her father.

"Though our gesture will never compete with something like that, the girls and I would like to ask you a question."

Mick folded his hands in front of him and shifted his weight from one foot to the other. "Okay. So ask."

"We would like to know if you would go on a first date with us," Rachel said with a grin.

"Yes, will you, Mr. Mick?" Carissa called out, bouncing on her toes.

"Will you?" Carly chimed.

He lowered his hands to his sides, his chest feeling full. "Just a first date?"

Rachel set the pizza on the table next to one of the recliners, crossed her arms and gave him a warning look.

"Now, don't get ahead of yourself, but if you're nice, and the girls approve, there could possibly be a second. And a third."

"Well, thank you for your kind invitation. But I'll have to think about it." He'd never seen three prettier or sadder faces. There was no way he could hold back that grin. "Are you kidding? I accept."

Rachel swiped at her forehead with the back of her sleeve. "Glad to hear it because this next part wouldn't have worked if you'd said no."

She took about five steps forward until she had to look up at him. "I know this is supposed to come at the end of a date, but let's not get lost on technicalities."

Then she did the thing he'd been dying for her to do from the moment he'd seen her in the station. She lifted up on her toes, rested her hands on his shoulders and touched her lips to his. Mick didn't give her a chance to step back. He wrapped his arms around her waist and pulled her to him, kissing her the way she deserved to be kissed. And would be regularly, if she gave him the chance.

Only at the sounds of applause and wolf whistles did Mick pull back slightly, feeling dazed. Rachel stared back at him with wide eyes and a big smile. The girls had gathered on both sides of them, turning the whole thing into a group hug for four.

"Maybe he won't be such a grouch now," Scott called out from the kitchen.

"Hey, what's all this PDA nonsense in the station?"

At the familiar voice, Mick turned to find Riley standing in the kitchen, clapping along with the others.

"This is where I come in," Riley said. "How about the crew takes the twins on a tour of the station while those two head outside for a minute? Looks like they could use it to cool off."

"Another tour?" Carly said, her shoulders curving forward.

"Fair point. How about someone lets you sit in Engine 1?"

With squeals, they headed off in the direction of the apparatus bay, with Peter and Riley trailing behind them.

Someone pressed Mick's coat into his hands, Rachel slipped into hers, and soon they were standing outside in the parking lot next to his truck.

He leaned his back against the tailgate. "Now you're sure you can do this? Us?"

She gave him an incredulous look. "I did just ask you out in front of the whole crew *and* my daughters. Especially my daughters."

He nodded. She would never do anything to hurt them. "But you said—"

"I said a lot of things that day. Most of them wrong."

"Where'd you mess up the worst?"

"When I thought I could walk away from you and not leave a part of my heart behind." Though she'd been staring at the ground, she looked up and met his gaze. "I love you. I trust you, too. No escape hatches."

"That's good, since I fell in love with you the day I found you napping on my couch."

"It was really comfortable," she said with a grin.

He leaned in to press his lips to hers again, his touch gentle but purposeful.

But when she pulled back, she squinted at him. "Are you sure you wouldn't rather just walk away from the Hoffmans entirely? There are still so many questions about our father. About Bilton. Riley and I have decided not to turn the records over to the police yet. We will, eventually. Just not quite yet."

"I get it. A mystery that's been buried for forty years can stay that way a little longer."

"And I probably won't be able to let it go entirely."

He smiled at her admission. "Never thought for a minute that you would."

"We still don't know about the whole threatening quotes thing."

"Cameron Phillips told police all about that idea. He did it to scare Riley and then you. Says he's big into quotation websites. Your brother's email wasn't hard to find. Neither was your cell phone number."

"And the thing at the school?"

"Yeah, that one took some creativity," Mick said. "The police investigator told me that Phillips was really proud of that one. Loved that he terrorized all those people at the same time."

Mick still believed there was more to that story, but since the police were accepting it, they would have to for now, as well.

Rachel shook her head, pursing her lips. "But there were *two* different cars. Did he say he drove both of them?"

"Says he dumped the white SUV after we saw him in it."

She held her hands wide. "The kid's going to take credit for everything that happened, whether it was his plan or not. And he's not going to turn on anyone who was instructing him, either."

"He kind of has to. It would ruin his street cred if he admitted he was just someone else's puppet. This way he gets all the glory."

"And, hopefully, all the prison time," she said.

"Oh, that'll happen. The prosecutor's trying him as an adult. All the other local gamers who were playing TORCH, where Phillips suggested that they turn their favorite pyromaniacal fantasies into real fires, have chosen to testify against him to save their own skins."

She frowned at that. "Guess they're learning young how to get by in this world."

"Can we get back to the kissing?" Mick shivered. "I don't know about you, but I'm getting cold."

At his reminder about the temperature, Rachel shuddered, too. Then she lifted up again and touched her lips to his as she'd done inside.

"Now you're sure you can do this? Us?" She grinned as she repeated the words he'd spoken moments before.

"I think I am. I just kissed you in front of my whole crew." He grinned down at her. "And in front of your daughters."

He dipped his head and gave her another long, tantalizing kiss that left both of them without any need for their coats.

When he pulled back, she reached up to touch the whiskers on his cheek before her fingers trailed over his sensitive lips.

"And you still want to take this fire engine ride with us?" she asked.

Mick kissed her once more and then smiled against her lips. "As long as when we're in the rig, you let me drive."

Epilogue

The recipient of his call answered on the first ring, just as he'd been directed. At least someone had the good sense to follow orders.

"Is the kid sticking to his story?"

"Sounds like he is."

"You don't *know*?" He ground his molars again. That the dentist had said they were flat now didn't surprise him at all.

"He is. I know. He wants to be a celebrity."

"That's all we need." But he could breathe easier, knowing that no one would be sniffing around in his world. He'd been at this too long to let a pissant psychopath mess up his plans.

"You don't think he kept it all in the house, do you?"

"If he did, it's ash and sludge now."

"But you don't think so, do you?"

He made a noncommittal sound in his throat. It was always best to keep others guessing. Otherwise, they started thinking they could make decisions for themselves. Like the pyromaniac, who'd gone rogue and burned down the Hoffmans' house. Because he didn't get in some cadet program, no less. That well-placed directions list at the crime scene had drowned the boy's matches, and the kid's own hubris would prevent him from naming names. Perfect solution for someone that they no longer found useful.

"Do you think his son and daughter know anything?"

He made the same sound, but on that he was certain. The only question was what they planned to do with what they'd found.

"Just make sure the kid sticks to his story."

He clicked off the call without saying goodbye and tossed the phone on the table. Because the Phillips kid had brought so much attention to the Hoffmans by setting fire to the house, they couldn't go after them now.

But they couldn't be protected forever, either. They'd be vulnerable again soon enough. Like lambs left in a field, defenseless. And when that happened, he'd be waiting.

* * * * *

Get up to 4 Free Books!

We'll send you 2 free books from each series you try PLUS a free Mystery Gift.

FREE Value Over **$25**

Both the **Harlequin Intrigue®** and **Harlequin® Romantic Suspense** series feature compelling novels filled with heart-racing action-packed romance that will keep you on the edge of your seat.

YES! Please send me 2 FREE novels from the Harlequin Intrigue or Harlequin Romantic Suspense series and my FREE gift (gift is worth about $10 retail). After receiving them, if I don't wish to receive any more books, I can return the shipping statement marked "cancel." If I don't cancel, I will receive 6 brand-new Harlequin Intrigue Larger-Print books every month and be billed just $7.19 each in the U.S. or $7.99 each in Canada, or 4 brand-new Harlequin Romantic Suspense books every month and be billed just $6.39 each in the U.S. or $7.19 each in Canada, a savings of 20% off the cover price. It's quite a bargain! Shipping and handling is just 50¢ per book in the U.S. and $1.25 per book in Canada.* I understand that accepting the 2 free books and gift places me under no obligation to buy anything. I can always return a shipment and cancel at any time by calling the number below. The free books and gift are mine to keep no matter what I decide.

Choose one:
- ☐ **Harlequin Intrigue Larger-Print** (199/399 BPA G36Y)
- ☐ **Harlequin Romantic Suspense** (240/340 BPA G36Y)
- ☐ **Or Try Both!** (199/399 & 240/340 BPA G36Z)

Name (please print)

Address _____ Apt. #

City _____ State/Province _____ Zip/Postal Code

Email: Please check this box ☐ if you would like to receive newsletters and promotional emails from Harlequin Enterprises ULC and its affiliates. You can unsubscribe anytime.

Mail to the Harlequin Reader Service:
IN U.S.A.: P.O. Box 1341, Buffalo, NY 14240-8531
IN CANADA: P.O. Box 603, Fort Erie, Ontario L2A 5X3

Want to explore our other series or interested in ebooks? Visit www.ReaderService.com or call 1-800-873-8635.

---

*Terms and prices subject to change without notice. Prices do not include sales taxes, which will be charged (if applicable) based on your state or country of residence. Canadian residents will be charged applicable taxes. Offer not valid in Quebec. This offer is limited to one order per household. Books received may not be as shown. Not valid for current subscribers to the Harlequin Intrigue or Harlequin Romantic Suspense series. All orders subject to approval. Credit or debit balances in a customer's account(s) may be offset by any other outstanding balance owed by or to the customer. Please allow 4 to 6 weeks for delivery. Offer available while quantities last.

Your Privacy—Your information is being collected by Harlequin Enterprises ULC, operating as Harlequin Reader Service. For a complete summary of the information we collect, how we use this information and to whom it is disclosed, please visit our privacy notice located at https://corporate.harlequin.com/privacy-notice. Notice to California Residents – Under California law, you have specific rights to control and access your data. For more information on these rights and how to exercise them, visit https://corporate.harlequin.com/california-privacy. For additional information for residents of other U.S. states that provide their residents with certain rights with respect to personal data, visit https://corporate.harlequin.com/other-state-residents-privacy-rights/.